The State of Nirvana

Awakenings

Book 1

K.P. Boudreaux

First paperback edition November 2024
Book design by K.P. Boudreaux
Original cover created by KPB using Canva
ISBN 978-1-7366326-7-3 (paperback)
ISBN 978-1-7366326-6-6 (eBook)
www.kpboudreaux.com

To the family and friends who have walked with me on

this incredible journey.

Table of Contents

Chapter 1
Friday, January 4, 2075

I've hit that point in life where every day seems the same. Oh, there may be different things on my schedule. But I wake up, go through my morning routine, check off the boxes of the day's to-dos, then have dinner with the same people who offer the same laughs and the same smiles, all the while celebrating the day's fabricated reason to party. It's all the same. I then come home, cycle with my partner, and go to sleep, only to wake up and do it all over again. The venues may change, but, in the end, I still stand in my nightly circle, telling the same boring stories of my day, my month, my life, and numbing my mind with drugs to kill the pain of my secret. I need to feel passion, not the physical type, but the emotional desire that gets you out of bed every morning with a jump in your step as you anticipate what the day may bring. Unfortunately, this thirst can only be quenched by real change; the status quo doesn't cut it anymore. My New Year's resolution for 2075 is to seek this change. I will find life's passion and embrace it.

"Kip, hello, anybody home? Stop living in your head! We've got to get to our seats," Blu said. "You're not going to lose credits again, are you?"

"No, nothing like that. I was just thinking about my New Year's resolutions," Kip answered. "Which way?"

"We go left and up. And promise me you're going to be enthusiastic today. We only have two more days together. Let's end on a positive note."

"Two men trying to kill each other in a ring. What's not to be psyched about?" Kip touched her lower back. She reflexively pushed his hand away. "I'll try to be happy for you as they bash each other's brains in," Kip said.

"Good. Don't do anything to embarrass me. Remember, you can't afford any more demerits." She scanned the bleachers in front of her. "There's Pinc and TF." She waved.

They climbed the concrete stairs, passing row after row of stone bleacher seats until she stopped on a stair with the numbers "1200–1210" marked in red paint.

She gave him a casual peck on the cheek. "This is my row. Try to have fun and don't forget to stand and clap. I'm serious, you need to earn some credits. You could be sitting with me if you did."

"I know and I will. Enjoy the bloodbath."

"Stop it, they could be listening." Her eyes threw the daggers that her voice couldn't express.

"I'm sorry, I was kidding. I'll behave." He waved to Pinc, whose bright hair stood out against the drab colors of the crowd. She was nice and pretty, maybe a future partner choice.

She returned the gesture with a half-hearted wave. TF stood beside her, his hands rigid by his side, eyes forward, no effort made. No matter. He'd see them all later at the dispensary where'd they'd get their weekly ration of alcohol or the State-sponsored "Meds," a lab-created intoxicant that kept the citizenry high, happy, and compliant.

Kip continued his walk up, stopping on the stair with "1050–1060" painted on it. The second-to-last row in the stadium. After squeezing by a few tired-looking men, he settled into seat 5 next to a tall woman with an athletic build, curled black hair, and light-blue eyes. She offered a forced smile.

"Afternoon," Kip said.

"Good afternoon. Welcome to the seats with rarified air."

He laughed. "We are pretty high. I'm thinking I might need to raise my social score if only to avoid the heart attack from all these stairs." He shrugged. "By the way, I'm Kip." He offered her a fist.

She reciprocated, closing her fist and bumping his. "I'm Sky. And I think this area is officially known as the nosebleed seats for the barely viable derelicts." She bundled into her jacket, the morning chill still in the air.

"Hey, at least we're in the stadium. How many didn't even make it in?" he replied.

"A silver lining; I like that. You're right. It could always be worse," she replied. As she finished, music started playing.

"And so, it begins," Sky added. She rose to her feet and placed her hand over her heart.

Kip did the same. He drew his tall, muscular frame to its full height and pulled his shoulder-length brown hair back in case the cameras wanted to evaluate him. He scanned through the giant video screens placed strategically around the stadium. If he was going to be noticed, he needed to be locked in watching the gore.

Words started to scroll across the screen, and the crowd recited the pledge. Kip joined in, almost screaming so those that listen could hear. "We pledge our allegiance to Nirvana and its Citizens. We cherish our leaders and will assist in their duty to uphold the law by reporting any violations, no matter how small. We will toil together as one to provide a better life for all Citizens, rich and poor, free from hunger, free from poverty and free from disease. We do this as equals for the good of our community."

As the pledge ended, a man dressed in all white came into the screen's view. A voice resonated through the stadium. "Our righteous leader, Citizen One, will now join you as an equal."

Citizen One stepped to the podium in his private box, located just above the stadium pit and filled with the city's elite. He wore a vested white silky shirt with an open collar and pressed gray pants. His dark hair was manicured to perfection, not a strand out of place, creating the perfect frame for his striking green eyes. Standing next to their esteemed leader was a mountain of a man, his notorious bodyguard, Rage. A pardoned champion of the games, he was a head taller than everyone else. His black eyes and scarred face gave a glimpse of the monster inside. They say that wherever he goes, death is sure to follow.

"Fellow Citizens," Citizen One started, "welcome to the twenty-fifth anniversary of Nirvana's founding and the new year of 2075!"

Applause burst from the crowd. Kip clapped until his hands hurt, knowing the watchers were out in force. He felt a buzz on his wrist. "+1 credit" flashed on the screen of his watch.

Citizen One raised his hand, stopping the extended applause. "Thank you! Thank you! It's a very exciting time for all of us. We have a few big days of festivities prepared, including the Cleansing and Changing celebration." Applause erupted again; he allowed it to go on for a few seconds before raising his hand. "I know we're all eager to get on with the next three years of our lives. But before we say goodbye to our old partners, our old friends, and our old lives, let's appreciate all that Nirvana has given us by asking not what we need, but what can we do to be better Citizens in the next Triennial. If we all strive to obey the law, to follow the direction of those in authority, and live our lives with less waste, our collective social score will be higher than ever before. And more important than that, our city will thrive being the cleanest, safest, and most livable it's ever been."

Applause exploded again, reverberating through the stadium. Kip clapped like he meant it, stomping his foot for additional effect. A second "+1 credit" buzzed his watch.

Citizen One raised both arms above his head as if victorious in a battle, hands waving for silence. He moved forward to the podium again. "To kick off this perfect time, in this perfect city, we bring you today a very special event for the Cleansing." He paused for the recognition then held up his hand, all fingers extended. "Five—count them—five blood matches, including our main event where Trex, Nirvana's champion, takes on The Savage, a half-human from the Wasteland. I can tell you to watch out; we lost quite a few men catching this predator."

The crowd frenzied into whoops and whistles, a few screams sounding like old Native American war cries were thrown in. The civility of the Citizen sheep was lost as they transformed into a mob of blood-thirsty thugs.

Kip played along, clapping and screaming, hoping his thoughts didn't betray him. To him, the games were barbaric, nothing but bread and circus for an unempathetic, superficial mob. They did not, as a "+1 credit" buzzed in.

Citizen One held up his hands for quiet. "Let me conclude by saying, have fun these next few days, but don't forget to go to Confessional on Sunday. And lastly," he held his words for a second, then screamed, "*Long . . . live . . . Nirvana!*"

Once more, the crowd exploded and Citizen One stood with his arms raised. Sky reached toward Kip with her fist closed, and he raised his in response. She obliged with more than just a bump, forcefully slamming her fist into his in a symbolic cheer for the start to the games. She held her stare, ending with a shy smile.

He met her eyes and his pulse quickened. "It's time for some blood!" he said for effect.

"Time for some blood! Oh yeah!" she urged in return.

The video slowly faded from the leader to focus on the center of the stadium, which held a circular pit of dirt and muck. A platoon of guards stood just inside the fence at standard intervals. They were armed with the Nirvana-built laser weapons that could kill, maim, or stun. From Kip's vantage, the gladiators now entering were small and difficult to see. The scene on the screen was much closer to the combat, even offering instant replay, in case one missed the gory details live.

An equally groomed and nondescript announcer took to the podium. With flawless features and immaculate clothing, he closed to speak into the microphone. "Welcome to the Cleansing! A day we symbolically shed the troubles of our past and allow our purer selves to move forward." He led the crowd in a forced round of clapping that slowly faded out. "To celebrate this special event, we have five terrific Free-or-Die blood matches. And as a reminder, this is a winner-take-all format where those under

13

conviction will receive a pardon after Punishment; and for the loser . . . death!" He waited for the crowd's applause. "For our first bout, we have two criminals reformed by their hard time spent at Elysian Fields Reform Center. . . ." His words trailed off with excitement.

The first combatant came through a sliding metal gate separating the thick barbed wire surrounding the pit. The intimidating man wore black faded pants, boots, and what appeared to be a leather vest. His head was shaved, and he had a long reddish beard off his chin.

The second man followed just behind. Shorter and stouter in build, he entered the ring practicing a martial-arts-style kata, much to the crowd's pleasure. His white outfit gleamed in the midday sun.

The crowd's roar greeted the combatants.

"From the Eastern District of the Flats, he's a two-time winner here in the pit—that's commuted life sentences for three murders—it's the butcher of Tinder Alley . . . Kong!" the announcer screamed.

The crowd's response was deafening as the man with the red beard paraded around the circular pit, waving and strutting.

As the roars dropped, the announcer continued. "From the Southern District of the Flats, convicted for the slaughter of two guards while at reeducation for rape; it's the Asian Assassin . . . Aiko!"

14

The crowd gave a less enthusiastic cheer with some boos scattered in. Aiko gave a single wave, then refocused on his kata.

Each man went to the armaments wall at the end of the pit and selected their weapon of choice. Kong chose a brutish club, while Aiko selected a long-handled axe with a polished blade that gleamed in the sun. Both men returned to the center of the circle, Kong still playing to the crowd.

As they went through the ceremonial steps, Kip wondered how many people in the crowd sat like him, pretending to be something they are not, pretending to be one of the animals who takes pleasure in another man's injury or, worse, death. When the two men finally started fighting, he watched as enthusiastically as he could; trying to feign interest as the bloodbath proceeded. He followed as Aiko slowly and surely cut away at Kong, bit by bit, until the bearded man couldn't stand. With his opponent on one knee, Aiko attacked with a huge swing of his long blade, cleaving the man's head clean off. The crowd went crazy. Kip jumped to his feet and bounced up and down, screaming with the rest of the mindless horde that surrounded him. Sky did the same. If she suspected his reaction was anything but genuine, she didn't show it. A "+1 credit" buzzed on his watch.

"Did you see that? What a move," Sky gushed.

"Are you kidding me?" Kip pretended to slash down like Aiko had. "I couldn't turn away."

Sky inched closer to him, her body practically leaning on his.

Kip endured three more of the gruesome events, each more horrifying than the last, each more accepted by the animalistic crowd, and for each his enthusiasm more fabricated. Thankfully, he knew it was almost over.

Between the matches during the gruesome cleanup period, the crowd was fed a liberal dose of what it takes to be a good Citizen. Infomercials ran on the giant screens with Citizen testimonials showing positive reinforcement of better rewards for supporting a cause or turning a fellow Citizen in. Occasionally, an attractive news reporter with revealing clothing would provide updates on the Wilderness Campaign, a decades-long war being fought past the Outer Boundary of Nirvana in a place called the Wastelands against the half-human savages named the Omasus. Kip watched these with interest, noting that this may be the only thing the government was efficient at: keeping the savages at bay.

With four matches complete, areas of dark stained dirt were now scattered throughout the pit, reminding the spectators of the game's brutal nature. The pit keepers had just finished smoothing over a particularly wet and gouged area where the last contestant had lost an arm.

The pit gate opened one last time. The first person through was a brown-skinned man, with long, straight black hair and a face that could have been chiseled from stone. His broad shoulders were bare, and his upper body rippled with long, thin muscles. An unusual band of tattoos colored his biceps.

"From the wilds beyond the Outer Boundary, a savage never before encountered," bellowed the announcer. "A half-human Omasu, who murdered a dozen soldiers bringing critical medicine to his tribe. It's The Savage from the Wasteland . . . Rock!"

A chorus of boos flooded the stadium as people flashed either a thumbs-down or middle-finger salute to the challenger. Rock strode in deliberately, his head held high in a proud indifference to the noise from the crowd.

The stadium fell silent as a rousing anthem started playing. The announcer's voice started low, building to a crescendo. "And hailing from the mean streets of the River District, a legend of the ring who needs no introduction. He's been pardoned for murder through victory, winning an astounding ten blood matches. He's every man's nightmare and every woman's dream, the Punisher of Pubtown, Nirvana's own son . . . *Trex!*"

The crowd erupted once more, louder and more aggressive in their calls; it was borderline pandemonium. As the roar peaked, a giant of a man walked through the gate. Close to seven feet tall, his gargantuan frame was fitted in spiked leather pants with a matching shirt, culminating in spiked shoulder pads. To add to his intimidating appearance, his face was painted white with black skull-like features on a shaven head. He roared a primal scream meant for the fans as he raised his fist to salute them. He then lowered his hand and pointed a single finger at his opponent, followed by a throat-slashing gesture. The crowd ate up Trex's antics, responding with cries of fury, screams of joy, and sobs from those taken by desire.

Rock had already gone to the Armament Wall and selected a double-pointed spear with a metallic daggerlike tip on each end. He walked slowly and confidently to the center of the ring, observing as Trex made his way to the wall.

Trex studied the weapons, started to select, then stopped and put his hand to his ear, prompting the crowd for help. They were more than happy to oblige. The chant, "Mace! Mace! Mace!" rose in unison. Trex eagerly grabbed the metal handle and swung the deadly spiked ball for all to see. The crowd howled for the murderous showman.

Trex strolled to the edge of the ring, mace over his shoulder, staring at his would-be victim. Rock, standing proud, his black, penetrating eyes fixed on his opponent, showed no signs of fear.

The two men moved to the middle of the ring, each holding their weapon with eyes locked on the other. Trex growled something inaudible and spit to the ground. Rock stood motionless and unfazed. The roar of the crowd grew in intensity, their bloodlust still unsatiated. And just as the tension was about to explode, the announcer, in his impeccable clothes, grasped the microphone. "Citizens of Nirvana, prepare yourselves for one simple phrase: to the death!" The Citizens responded with competing chants of "Trex!" and "To the death!"

Kip kept his act going, "Trex! Trex! Trex!" he shouted.

A bell clanged and a clock on the screens started counting down from fifteen. Trex lifted his mace. Rock readied, body coiled, crouching with his spear pointed forward. In unison, the crowd started counting. "Six, five, four, three, two, one!"

"Fight!" The order issued from the loudspeaker simultaneously flashed on the screens. The mob roared their approval.

Rock took a step away from Trex, holding up his free hand. "I have no quarrel with you. I do not want to fight!" he exclaimed as the crowd fell eerily quiet.

"Good," Trex shouted as he shot forward with catlike quickness, unusual for a man his size. He swung the mace at Rock's head. The spiked ball was a blur as it whizzed over the diving savage, who rolled to his feet, weapon now ready.

Trex chased, attacking once more. The Savage spun, spear extended, swiping at the giant man's legs. The tip caught on Trex's thigh. A red liquid soaked through a rip in his leather. "*First Blood*" flashed on the screens.

Trex made a boisterous laugh at the cut. He dipped his fingers into the blood, then drew lines under his eyes. This was a game to him.

Trex reengaged, moving forward while avoiding the pointed jabs made by Rock. When just over an arm's length away, Trex swung down with the mace, the ball just missing the shoulder, but clipping the arm of The Savage. Swung with such power, the mace ball embedded into the ground. The glancing blow ripped skin and knocked Rock down, forcing his hand off the spear. Seizing on his advantage, Trex stepped forward and threw an uppercut that caught Rock flush, lifted him off his feet, and pummeled him yards away. The crowd exploded as Trex circled the fallen man. Trex raised his arms, a maestro leading his orchestra of rabid crazies.

"Trex! Trex! Trex!" they answered in unison.

Rock fumbled with his spear, finally raising it with a bloody arm, waving it at his opponent. Trex wasted no more time celebrating. He pulled the mace free and attacked again, hammering the metal ball down once more, trying for the coup de grâce. Rock attempted to block the incoming blow with the middle of the spear's handle. The deadly ball missed Rock's head, but sliced through the spear like paper, splitting the weapon in half and burying the mace's head once more in the dirt. Now holding two short spears, Rock countered. Moving quick, he jabbed each tip into the front thighs of the giant, who missed with a wild swing with his fist. Rock dodged and rolled behind his opponent, giving two quick stabs into Trex's lower back near the kidneys, then two more behind each knee. Each blow was precise and lethal to Trex's mobility in their own way. The giant man was being disabled, one stab at a time.

Trex pulled at the mace, trying to dislodge it. As it came free, Rock lunged, plunging his spear tip deep into Trex's abdomen. The giant's blood spurt from the wound when Rock withdrew the lethal point. Trex wobbled, catching himself on unsteady legs. But this wound was too much, and Nirvana's own killer eventually fell to his back. With mace still in hand, he writhed, trying to get up, a pool of blood building.

Rock approached with caution, careful of a possum play. The crowd hushed in a murmuring silence. With a half spear in each hand, Rock stood over his fallen opponent, blood oozing from his wounded arm. He raised his spear, and with snakelike speed, he plunged the dagger tip toward his opponent's head. A collective gasp came from the crowd.

After a hushed moment, Trex rolled his head away. The spear was sunk deep in the dirt, perilously close to the giant's face. Rock moved from the injured man to face the nearest camera. He spoke clearly. "I will not kill a man in cold blood for the mob's entertainment. Even if he is a killer." He took one step away, toward the gate, single spear in hand.

Denied their terminal ending, the crowd started hissing at The Savage.

Behind him, Trex rolled to his knees, then labored to his feet. He grabbed the mace and took a wild swing at Rock while hissing, "To the death." The brutal image of his contorted face was crystal clear on the giant screens.

The Savage easily dodged Trex's wild blow and the giant man stumbled forward. With ruthless efficiency, Rock plunged his spear's tip under the chin and up into Trex's head. A fleeting glimpse of surprise laced Trex's eyes before they dimmed and went vacant. He dropped like a tree cut fresh in the forest, an audible thud echoing through the stadium speakers. A disbelieving silence fell over the crowd until a lone voice from the crowd called, "The Savage killed Trex."

For some unexplored reason, Kip found this result strangely satisfying. He never relished in any man's injury or death, but watching the Nirvana hero's demise in the ring to the hated Savage seemed almost karmic. He hesitated for a moment, giving a fleeting consideration to the social risk of nonconforming. Then, in a moment of uncaring rebellion, he slammed his hands together, again and again. A single person clapping in the silent stadium. He then started chanting, "Rock! Rock! Rock!" Sky stared at him like he was a crazy man.

One by one, the crowd joined in, continuing to rise in volume until it peaked, "Rock!" The stadium shook with the chant. Kip felt his watch buzz, he saw a "+5 credits" pop up. He flashed it to Sky, who beamed her approval.

"In a shocking match, Rock is the winner!" the announcer called. "And will receive a full pardon after Punishment! If he chooses, he will fight in the future as a free man!"

The crowd erupted once more and clapped and cheered until the announcer held up his hand for silence. "And now for the Punishment. Five lucky Citizens will be invited down to lead the all-important final step of the Cleansing to help Rock atone for his crimes and send him into private Citizenship as a free man."

Kip slid back, trying to be invisible in the crowd, wanting nothing to do with the Punishment. The face of the first selected Citizen shown on the screen. A petite woman with golden hair started jumping up and down, not able to contain her enthusiasm. The people around her were happily reaching out to congratulate her, trying to touch her with their approval. The selection continued three more times, with each Citizen more ecstatic than the last. Before the last selection, the noise in the stadium dropped in anticipation. All eyes were focused on the ample screens posted around the stadium. This person of honor would deliver the last and liberating blow to the savage, symbolically sending him into free society.

The image flashed up. Kip stared in disgust as he saw his face on the screen. Sky leapt into his arms and gave him a hug.

"You did it, you're the last Citizen! Thank Citizen One! This is unbelievable, you did it!" she screamed in his ear. People around him were patting him on the back, grabbing his shirt. His watch was buzzing with message after message from friends and associates. He even saw one from Blu containing just a heart.

He'd return the messages later; first things first. He started down the aisle to the stairs. Sky grabbed his arm, turning him. "Will you meet me at the Changing? I'll be in the group room in Midtown's Southern District. It'll be worth your while. I promise."

He nodded, the thought of a more intimate encounter enticing. "Of course. I'll find you."

He continued down the stairs, pausing at row 75 to search for Blu. She was already racing down the aisle toward him, dodging the Citizens in the row.

She wrapped her arms around him. "You did it, you earned a spot in the Punishment!" She hugged him tight. "You know what this means for your score," she whispered.

"I've got to go."

"Go. I'll meet you after at the Dispensary. Time to celebrate!" She pecked his cheek.

He let her go and headed down the stairs in a jog. He was the last of the five to arrive at the ring. An armed guard escorted him through the gate into the packed dirt arena. An uncomfortable feeling sat in his chest; he didn't want to be there.

The guards had strung Rock's hands to posts high above his head, his muscled bare chest fully exposed. They lined the five chosen Citizens in front of him. Citizen One watched from his box just outside the ring. A guard handed a weapon to the first Citizen. The medieval device had a long, thin handle with five whiplike rawhide cords coming from the handle's tip. On the end of each cord, an oval weight was attached with razor blades running its length.

"And now, the Punishment to cleanse Rock of his crimes, ushering him into free society," the announcer proclaimed.

The petite woman stepped forward. With a step and a hop, she swung with everything she had and whipped Rock. A loud slap came, followed by streaks of oozing blood from the wounds opened on his chest. She gave a giddy laugh as she handed the weapon back.

This same cruel process was repeated three more times and created a crisscross of slices in the man's brown skin. Blood streamed down his chest.

During all four of the swings, Rock never flinched nor cried out. He stood, staring ahead into nothing, never revealing his thoughts or emotions.

"And now, the final Punishment, completing the Games and sending this savage to freedom!" The announcer's voice ended in a crescendo of enthusiasm.

Kip was handed the whip. He took a single step toward Rock. He studied the man's black eyes. He thought of the savage's attempt to avoid the bloodshed, his intentional miss of Trex's head, and then the words he spoke into the camera. Rock shifted; he met Kip's gaze, holding it.

Kip saw not just the fear and pain of the moment, but enlightenment and compassion. This was no savage, no half-human killer, but a man just like him with the same fears and aspirations. A man being brutalized by the society Kip represented and hated. A man who had been forced to kill or be killed.

A moment of clarity struck; he knew what he had to do. He started to swing but stopped. He dropped the whip. He faced Citizen One's booth and spoke with a clear conscience. "I will not torture a man for your entertainment." He glanced at The Savage, whose eyes were now locked on him and gave a small nod.

A chorus of boos rained down from the crowd. He didn't care. His watched buzzed; he checked it. "–50 credits."

A murmuring rose from the crowd. Kip glanced up to see Rage jump down from Citizen One's box. His towering frame walking deliberately toward him. With one hand, he pushed Kip away, almost knocking him over. Then he picked up the whip. He gave Kip a menacing stare, then took a massive swing at The Savage. The blow hit with a crack, the bladed cords mercilessly finding flesh. With blood pouring from the crisscross of cuts, Rock's face transformed from stone to a look of seething hatred. The Savage's black eyes bore into his attacker.

Rage didn't care. He bundled the whip and shoved it into Kip's chest. Kip had no choice but to take it as the announcer screamed over the frenzied crowd, "Long live Nirvana!"

Chapter 2
Saturday, January 5, 2075

Kip and Blu strolled down the zoo's walk. The events of yesterday's games were weighing on him, but he was determined to enjoy his last day with Blu as a partner. A lion roared from the adjacent pen. "That's Leo. I can tell by his voice. It's deeper than Sinbad's," he said.

"You know him by sound?" Blu asked.

"I'm here every day, and frankly, it's one of the benefits of working here. I get to care for the lions. They're my favorite exhibit." He held his watch next to a small black machine mounted on the brick wall. The door next to him unlocked and popped open. They stepped through the portal and into an immaculate office space. The outer area of the spacious room was taken by private workspaces, each office with a sizeable glass wall facing into a common area. The interior space was organized with sleek glass desks holding holographic screens. In front of each screen sat an ergonomic chair strategically placed for the comfort of its daily users.

"Let me grab the universal key," Kip said. "We'll go anywhere you want."

"Does Tik know you're doing this? You can't afford any more demerits," Blu responded, her voice icy.

"As a matter of fact, he does," Kip said with a grin, trying to lighten the moment. "I told him it was our last day together, and that you wanted to spend it here. He was all too happy to oblige." Kip moved toward the far desk. "I think there may be something more to it than just being nice. He doesn't do a whole lot for others without getting something out of it. In fact, he may be pursuing you tonight at the Changing Celebration."

"God, I hope not. I mean, he's nice enough. But he smells like animals." Blu covered her mouth, trying to suppress her laugh.

Kip chuckled with her. It was good to hear her laugh, a rare occurrence as of late. "You'd tell me if I did, right?" He reached into a drawer and grabbed a small black fob.

Blu nodded. "Definitely."

"Thank you for that." He stepped to the far door that led into the zoo compound. "Alright, let's go. One first-class zoo tour coming up." He offered Blu his hand as a courtesy through the door.

"Thank you, but it's okay. I got it," she said.

They walked mostly in silence, dodging the crowds through the bear pens, then the amphibian center. Every so often Kip would offer a select piece of information that only an insider would know. Blu would ask a question now and then, but for the most part she kept both her physical and emotional distance.

Once out of the amphibian center, he stopped at the corner of a fortified wall with an engraved granite block anchoring it. By design, the cement barrier created the demarcation to the primate center.

He squatted next to the granite block. "It's hard to read, but this was the anchor stone to the main wall that formed the original zoo here."

"Really?"

"Yeah. It's well over one hundred years old, from before the Nirvana uprisings, even before the great pandemic."

Blu stepped closer to see the writing better.

Kip continued. "Little known fact, after the war, the first zoo was completely destroyed. The animals were slaughtered for food, some escaped, the others . . . who knows?"

"How'd you get all these animals then?" Blu asked.

"Long story, but during the uprisings, the world's exotic animal population was pretty much wiped out. After the Peace Conciliation, the city leaders decided to preserve the plant and animal diversity of the planet. They implemented the plan to build this world-class facility." Kip gave a sweeping hand gesture. "Some animals were gifted, some were local, but most were grown through cloning with some gene manipulation. You could argue they're not the original species, but better than nothing."

"I'd never have known if you hadn't told me. I mean, they appear just like what you see in school or on those nature hologram videos," Blu replied.

"Good, that's exactly what we're going for." He started walking. Blu followed. "This zoo is the centerpiece for the city and its leaders. It's always given the most resources, way overstaffed, and runs like clockwork. Thanks mostly to yours truly." He laughed as he finished. "I'm kidding, of course," he added when Blu didn't join him.

Avoiding another awkward moment, he glanced over to see his new coworker Jen in the enclosure next to them, trying to give a chimpanzee a pill. The gentle creature kept twisting her head away every time Jen tried to stick the pill in its mouth, only to turn back and smile. She did finally manage to get it in, only to have the creature spit it out. The game continued. It was clear Jen's frustration was growing.

"Come with me," Kip said. He walked over to Jen and Blu followed.

"Hi Jen. This is my partner, Blu."

Jen gave a short wave. "Nice to meet you, Blu."

"Old partner," Blu said as she waved back.

Kip ignored Blu's correction and continued. "Saw ol' Bessy here, giving you a hard time. Let me teach you a trick."

"That would be great. She's teasing me."

"See that apple? Cut a slice, and put the pill in it. Bessy loves apples. She'll do anything for them."

Jen did as Kip suggested. The creature eagerly took the apple slice from her, then scurried off while gobbling it down.

At that moment, a fleshy man with thinning hair approached, his stride stern. "What are you doing?" he said to Jen.

"I was just giving Bessy her medicine."

"Did I say give her an apple with the pill?"

"I'm sorry, sir. It's just that—"

Kip interrupted. "That's my fault, Tik. Bessy was in a playful mood and wouldn't take her meds. I told Jen to use the apple. I thought she would get behind schedule, and I know you like things punctual."

"I do, but that's no excuse. I'll deal with you later." He focused on Jen. "You do what I tell you, when I tell you, no deviations. There's a reason for every rule we follow."

"Yes sir, Tik, I'm sorry."

"Okay, I'm not going to demerit you this time," Tik said. "But don't break my rules again. Always remember slow and steady wins the race. Now go clean the monkey cages."

Jen slumped her head and trudged away.

"I'm sorry, Tik, it's just that I've seen you do that before when Bessy's acting that way."

33

Tik's face went red. "Teaching a new worker to break my orders and take short cuts is dangerous. I'm tired of you doing your own thing!"

Blu stepped forward. "Hi Tik, it's me, Blu. I haven't seen you in a while. How are you feeling?"

Tik took a deep breath. "Hi Blu. I'm fine, kidneys have stabilized. Thank you for asking. And I'm sorry you had to see this. Especially on your last day together."

"I understand, Tik, more than you know. I've been with him for three years. But listen, I also know that he respects you more than anyone else here. He raves about your management skills to our friends all the time. He'd never challenge your authority on purpose. Never!" She reached out and rested her hand on Tik's forearm.

Tik started to blush. "Thank you for saying that. I try to keep things organized here. And I guess I could see past it this one time, for you Blu." He pointed his finger at Kip. "But you do this again, and you'll not only get demerited, I'll cut your basic income as well. You'll be living in a container in the Flats. You got me?"

"I'm sorry, Tik, it won't happen again."

"Okay, well, I must be getting along. Blu, will I see you tonight at the Changing?" Tik seemed to be sucking in his fleshy gut as he asked.

"I should be there, probably in Midtown's Southern District Bondage Room," Blu answered.

"Okay." Tik hesitated. "I'll try to find you. Anyway, good seeing you again," he added before strutting away.

"The Bondage Room? You hate that place," Kip said.

"I know! I won't be anywhere near it. That's why I sent him there."

"That's funny." Kip started walking toward the big cat enclosures. "And thank you; that was nice of you to cover for me. You even touched him. . . ."

"Consider it a parting gift," Blu said.

Kip appreciated Blu's effort this late in their partnership. Usually by this time, partners were ready to say goodbye, which was often reflected in both harsh words and actions. Blu was tepidly trying to keep the doors to friendship open, being indicative of the person with a penchant for social climbing that she was. Kip would always look back fondly on their time together, but was also ready to move on.

Kip continued. "He's an ass and an idiot. If he wasn't friends with Citizen Seven, he'd never be in that role. It kills me somebody so stupid is my boss." As he finished, his watched buzzed. "–1 credit" popped up in red letters. "Great, they were listening. You better tell them I said that at Confessional on Sunday. They have the recording; no reason for both of us getting in trouble."

"Don't worry, I will." She paused, meeting his eyes. "You know Tik is right about you. You have trouble following the rules. And frankly, I don't understand why. For three years I've watched the most intelligent and athletic man I've ever met sabotage himself time and again. Like the pit the other day. Just take the swing! Rock wouldn't have died, he be scarred. And you'd be one hundred credits richer and the hero of Nirvana. But now, a few more demerits and you'll lose your housing and have to live outside the city walls. For what, that savage's feelings? Why? Everybody wanted you to do it."

Kip stopped in front of the lion's enclosure. Three majestic big cats lounged behind the glass in their savannah-like home. The largest male with a huge mane stood up and strolled over, almost as if he recognized his keeper. Kip squatted to eye level, fingers on the glass, whispering to the beast.

After a moment, he stood. "I couldn't do it because it felt wrong. I don't trust everything our Citizen leaders say. And when I remembered Rock's actions, his words, then looked in his eyes, something within me said he was innocent, a victim in the process. I can't explain it, but it's like I had an inner voice that was guiding me. I made a snap decision." He turned his head away, not wanting to see Blu's reaction. "Believe me, it would have been a lot easier to just swing, but I couldn't live with myself without knowing he was guilty for sure."

"I'll never understand you."

He took her hand. "Look, I'm sorry for any grief I may have caused you. I never meant to, and I do care."

Blu allowed her hand to slip away from Kip's. "No, just like with Jen, you never mean to, it just happens."

He found Leo, who was now lying by the glass, his huge eyes watching them.

"Just curious—why did you want to come here today, of all places?" Kip asked.

Blu thought for a moment. "I like it. It's clean, it's orderly, the animals are well fed and cared for. I don't know, I just feel comfortable and safe here I guess. I thought it'd be a nice place to spend our last day together in the controlled comfort of the animals."

"I'm not positive old Leo would agree with you on the comfort thing."

"What do you mean?"

"Look at him. He's not evolved to live behind glass. He's a hunter; he should be roaming the savannah stalking a kill."

"Those days are passed. If he went back to the wild, he'd die. It's safer for him to stay in his cage."

Kip studied the lion's yellow eyes. They were subdued, almost domesticated, the inner beast slowly dying. "Is it?"

Chapter 3

"Fifty credits! I can't believe you didn't take the swing!" TF exclaimed as he swaggered down the sidewalk with Pinc on his arm.

"I couldn't," Kip answered, following just behind them, Blu at his side. "I'm telling you, that man isn't the savage the government says he is. I saw it in his eyes."

"You're telling me you could read that man's life story from his eyes in the ten seconds you had? You're a freaking idiot!" TF said, swiveling to see Kip's reaction.

"I don't know, Kip. Maybe you were mistaken," Pinc interjected. "They say he did some pretty bad things, like killing a dozen of our best soldiers in the Wasteland, and you saw him in the ring. He took out Trex and barely broke a sweat."

"To change the subject, there's the building," Blu said, checking her makeup in a hand mirror. Across the street was a large white warehouse-type structure. A crowd of people were lining up outside, waiting to get in. "I just hope your decision doesn't impact me at the Changing. I mean, if people knew—I might just go home alone."

"Just do what you did to me three years ago and you'll have your choice of a dozen partners." He made an awkward step toward Blu. "Well, I guess this is it." Kip leaned down to kiss Blu on the cheek, wishing they could've been more connected and trying to keep the awkward moment positive. She did not reciprocate. "Good luck tonight. I hope you find someone nice," he said, hoping his tone reflected his sincerity.

A few feet away, TF kissed Pinc's cheek, and started whispering intimately, both oblivious to Kip's goodbye. Kip noted that they appeared to have ended their three-year partnership on a less businesslike note.

"Are you even getting in?" Blu asked him.

"I think so. My score is just high enough."

"Then good luck to you as well," Blu said. "It's been . . . an interesting three years."

"It has. Hopefully we don't become strangers. Let me know if you need anything in the future." Kip reached for the door and opened it for her. TF then Pinc followed her through.

"Maybe I'll see you in there?" Kip said to Pinc as she passed.

"Oh, okay." Pinc fidgeted with her hands. "I'll try to find you."

TF just kept walking. Blu followed TF, pulling Pinc along with her, leaving Kip behind. They entered a short line of people. Men and women were dressed to perfection, all wearing varying degrees of makeup to better accentuate their key features in hopes of attracting a better partner.

Kip considered the process in which he found himself. For the last three years, he had committed to Blu. Tonight, their partnership dissolved, and he would search for a potential new mate. It was just as well. True to form, their relationship had run its course. What started as hot and heavy had suffocated into cold and withered. Three years is about the most anyone can expect to be together and stay passionate lovers. The spark always dies— always. So tonight, he'd spend an evening of lustful cycling with potential partners, seeing if there was a mutual physical attraction that could be the basis for the next three-year commitment, until that, of course, withered as well.

He once learned in history class that years ago, people socialized for months and then used that compatibility as a test for a long-term relationship, possibly even raising children together. It was a process doomed for failure as the number of divorces rose and occurred earlier and earlier in marriages. He shook his head at the crazy barbarians of old.

They arrived at a security checkpoint. An officer held a scanner to Kip's watch. His personal information popped up on the guard's screen, including his social score. It read "1,001." "Cutting it pretty close, Mister One Thousand and One." She waved Kip through.

They came to a voluptuous woman, who had more clothes off than on, her ample breasts fully exposed. As they passed her, she handed each person a small plastic shot glass with a single

41

red pill inside. She offered one to Kip. "Here is your HAP." Catching his eye, she added, "You're a tall one. Why don't you find me later? I'll be playing in the Toy Room."

Kip accepted the pill, a government-issued drug cocktail designed for this exact occasion, something they called HAP. A combination of aphrodisiac, performance enhancer, and antibiotic. It had the effect of lowering inhibition, improving stamina, and magnifying the various sensations the body would be experiencing while protecting against unwanted viruses and bacteria. It was truly a magical elixir. He smiled at the woman, popped the pill in his mouth, and swallowed.

He entered the dressing room where a congregation of people were in various stages of undress. When done disrobing, they all wore a unique-to-them, loose-fitting thong that barely covered their front genitals. He walked with the crowd, exiting into the main hallway. Heading toward the rooms where the festival had already begun, he saw Pinc and Blu enter the Single Hetero Room, where men and woman met for a one-on-one private experience. He peeked through its door to see a large group milling about like any house party, socializing for that special connection that would lead to something more. Withdrawing, he passed a similar room for those interested in the same gender, then continued by a few fetish rooms, including bondage and toys. He paused at the Toy Room and considered making a later fallback visit to his welcoming friend, but for now he would try to find Sky.

He found the Group Room from the erotic picture above its entrance.

He entered, somewhat skeptical she'd be waiting for him. Standing at the entrance, he scanned the semi-naked crowd, searching for her lean figure. The imagery of bodies entwined, the aroma of sweaty cycling, and the audible moans filling the air all stirred something primal inside. His heartbeat quickened, his senses sharpened—he needed a release soon. The HAP was working its magic.

He paced to one end of the room, trying to avoid eye contact. Several women already engaged with both male and female partners in various positions waved him over. Whether their intent was solely desire or something less basic, he'd couldn't be sure. He was about to give in to a sensual blonde who had cycled an exhausted man lying still next to her, eyes closed, sweat streaming down his muscled chest. She spread her legs in invitation to Kip, a possible glimpse into his three-year future. Giving in to his desires, he started toward her when he heard his name. "Kip!"

He spun to see Sky push her suitor away. The man reached toward her, saying something, the agony of frustration etched in his face. Sky stepped back to the spurned gentleman.

Stroking his flesh, she allowed him to finish with an involuntary twitch. She kissed his cheek, then shifted back to Kip.

She approached aggressively, naked body glistening, full breasts highlighting her athletic abs and small hips. She slid her fingers into his hand, pulling gently toward the sitting area, biting her lower lip in what could only be anticipation.

"Have you cycled yet?" she whispered in his ear.

"No, I was waiting for you . . . I didn't mean to interrupt."

"You didn't interrupt anything; he was a fallback. After the pit, I didn't know if you were coming."

"I just made the cutoff." His fingertips touched her silky skin, an erotic tingle springing from the contact. "Good thing my social score didn't get any lower."

She ran her fingernail down his bare chest. "Well, you're in. Now let's get you started."

She reached down and touched him, caressing his body. He closed his eyes, the desire consuming him. All was forgotten as pleasure rolled through his frame, radiating out to the tip of every finger and toe, building in waves, amplifying with each gentle caress until the exploding crescendo came. His cycle peaked with multiple jerks. Sky kept going harder and faster until he pushed her hand away, not able to take anymore. She stood, eyes finding his, ensuring he watched as she massaged his warm release over her breasts. Taking his hand, she lowered herself to the couch and opened her thighs. "Let's take our time." She pulled him down, guiding him to her desired destination.

Lost in the moment, Kip explored her body gently as she softly moaned. He continued this slow pleasure, tongue dancing over her body until she gripped his head, arched her back and quivered the completion of her cycle. Her frame relaxed as he moved up, playfully kissing her perfect skin along the way.

The next hours were a haze of hedonistic ecstasy where inhibitions melted away, leaving only two voyagers discovering the limits of both mind and body. In a room filled with people, they were on an island, all alone.

Kip was near the edge of exhaustion, a final cycle coming. Sky rode him, grinding long strokes into his pelvic bone, her motion quickening the closer she got to her own cycle. With one last thrust, they peaked together, locked in a deep embrace, two souls joined as one.

Finished, Sky collapsed into his chest while Kip watched the kaleidoscope of colors behind his closed lids, gasping hard and savoring every breath.

When Sky recovered, she raised her head, reading his face. He was already watching her, gazing into her blue eyes, wondering what lay behind them. And then he felt it, there in the touch of her hands, the smell of her perfumed body, and the sweet taste of her scented skin. Happiness welled within him as he welcomed it, something missing in his life that he'd always desired—a human connection. That emotional bond where you care more about another than you do yourself. Where you love and willingly protect emotionally and physically. Where you gladly navigate the unexpected, together, to see what life brings. He pulled her in, kissed her lips with a passion that was foreign to him. In three years of partnering with Blu, he had only dutifully kissed her cheek, never really moving emotionally beyond the self-gratification achieved during a one-night stand.

Sky seemed confused by the gesture at first, but soon relaxed into the moment. She cupped his face with her hands, holding him close. He could feel her heart pounding. For the first time in his life, he coupled with another, wanting to not just share that moment but to explore life—together.

After a long, blissful kiss, she pulled away. "What was that for?" she whispered.

"I don't know. I've never kissed anyone like that before. It just felt right." His eyes broke from hers. "It's probably just the HAP."

She placed a finger under his chin and raised his face, so their eyes met again. "It did feel right, like it was meant to be." She leaned in, kissing his lips again, recapturing that perfect, blissful instant in time. A few moments later, she pulled away with a flick of her tongue and gently said, "You never switched partners. Do you want to cycle with someone else? Just to be sure?"

"I've never been with just one person at the Changing." He studied her, seeing concern creep into her eyes. "No, nobody else, you're all I want." As he spoke, he ran his fingers through her hair, moving a strand off her delicate face.

She started kissing his chest, moving her way down. Kip stopped her, pulling her into him, fighting the urge to continue things at the Changing.

Sky rested her head on him. "You okay?"

"Yeah, except you wore me out."

"I told you I'd make it worth your while to find me." She nestled in, her lips kissing his neck, her fingers finding his hand, prolonging their physical contact. It was a sensation Kip enjoyed but wasn't used to.

He ran his finger down her skin. "Well, you did that and then some."

"Does this mean we're partnering for the next Triennial?" she asked.

"If you'll have me. My social score is not that great. I could be a limitation to you."

She beamed, her nail playfully brushing his nose. "There's something different about you . . . about us. So yes, I'll take the chance."

"Should we go?" he asked.

"Unless you want another ride." She gave a seductive smile.

"How about one at my place, then we can fall asleep."

She hopped up, eagerly tugging at his hand, helping him to stand. "Come on, let's get dressed."

He rose, his exhausted body a mix of aches and pleasure. They walked hand in hand to the dressing room, separating only to shower and retrieve their clothes.

As Kip zipped his shirt, a naked Pinc walked out of the shower, her shoulders slumped, the haze of disappointment across her face.

"Everything okay?" he asked.

She shrugged. "Yeah, I guess. I got two offers, but their scores were not as high as TF's."

"It'll be fine; score is not everything, and sometimes people surprise you. If not, it's only three years."

"I'm sorry, I should have found you. Did you meet someone?" Pinc's eyes darted away, clearly uncomfortable with the question or maybe the coming answer.

"I did. I'm excited about her. If she's half the person I met tonight, this Triennial will be fun and exhausting." He paused. "How about Blu?"

"Yeah, she did. Although, it was weird. She accepted the first guy who offered after only thirty minutes or so. I think she's been gone a while."

"He must've had a high social score. Good, I'm happy for her." He reached out, touching Pinc's upper arm, "I hope we can stay in contact as friends." As he finished, Sky walked up.

"I hope so too," Pinc said. She gave a half-hearted smile and walked away.

Kip watched as she left.

"Who was that?" Sky asked. "Did you want to cycle with her before we go?"

"She's just an old friend. And I thought we're going one more time at my house."

"We are if you think you can handle me."

"I'm up for that challenge." He took her hand and started walking. As they passed the exit, they raised their clasped hands together, signifying their new partnership to the watchers. The ID scanners picked them up. Kip's face flashed first on the electronic board, as did his social score. It read "1,006."

"Yes! I'm up five points!" Kip exclaimed.

Sky's image flashed up next to his. Her score read "1,403."

"Wow, good for you, that's a great score," he said

"It is. I don't like to brag, but I saved a busload of children from a fiery crash this morning." She laughed at her own joke before becoming serious. "And don't you worry, we'll find a way to get your score up."

Chapter 4

Still on his HAP high, Kip walked with his arm around Sky. The chill mist, which crept in nightly, had begun to blanket the city. They strolled through the darkened streets with little concern, the occasional buzz of a security drone a reassurance they were protected from the would-be criminals that once frequented these Midtown streets.

Almost fifteen years ago, while transitioning to an independent state, the Citizen leaders adopted an intrusive surveillance of the city that utilized satellites, aerial and land-based drones, robotic security assets, and a cyber-judicial system that delivered immediate justice. It was this same system that forced every Citizen to have an ocular implant, a procedure that was now performed at Emancipation. The tiny device wirelessly tapped the optic nerve and cerebral cortex and monitored a Citizen's sight, voice, and thoughts for a short period of time. If a Citizen committed a crime, the security download revealed what they saw, thought, and said, thereby helping Citizen leaders determine the crime and deliver immediate justice. They even had a catchy name for it, the AST, standing for Action, Speech and Thought System. The AST provided the desired effect; crime went from being an extreme problem to almost nonexistent overnight. Unfortunately, as is usually the case with governments, the program crept into other areas of concern for those in power and was soon utilized to monitor all speech and most thought. Hence the watchers were always there. The only saving grace to complete government monitoring was the data intensity of the program. There was no way the watchers could collect and store every thought, every sight, or every word for every person and analyze them. The people and systems couldn't handle it. So those in power did three things. First, they started monitoring the real-time AST randomly, so no one individual would ever know if they were being watched. They also created a secret list of keywords to monitor, and when those words were spoken or thought, officials were alerted. Words such as *rape* and *murder* were known to be triggers. Lastly, they made the implants erasable such that every five hours, new data overwrote the old data of a Citizen's life. There was no interest or use in keeping the records of the inane like a bath or a walk in the woods.

The AST system had been the main problem for Kip. He'd say or do things usually at the wrong place and time and be cited by the Security Force, the managers of the AST. As with every Citizen, for every good deed or job performed, he earned credits to his social score, the measure developed by the government to determine the suitability of any one individual to be in society. This included doing, saying, and thinking anything in support of the Citizen leadership, a rare occurrence for him. For every violation, like his actions at the Pit, he would get demerits to his social score. This seemed to be the norm lately. Citizen One had the highest score in the city, a mind-blowing 10,543. Kip had a paltry 1,006. The threshold for a Citizen's continuation in the Midtown city proper and access to most of its functionality, like the Changing Festival, was 1,000. If Kip dropped below that level, Tik was right, he'd lose his Elite status and the benefits that came with it, including his job, basic income, food, premium medical, and housing. He'd be sent outside the walled city into the Heights or the Flats until he earned Elite status again, a task that was difficult to do without a job and limited other ways to earn social score credits.

They turned the corner of Pruitt Street, named after the first Citizen One, and walked up Kip's sidewalk to his front door. On the stoop sat his refrigeration box. He opened it to find it filled with his daily allotment of Green, the algae-based protein farmed and distributed by the city. Each person received their exact ideal caloric intake delivered to their door every day. The government's program ensured no one went hungry and all were treated equally. Kip was indifferent to the stuff, often finding himself supplementing his allotment with fresh produce bought at the farmer's market—when he could afford the exorbitant pricing. Ever since aerial spraying, the fiasco that was the misguided fix to global warming, the earth had cooled significantly, and carbon dioxide had plummeted, meaning the growing season shortened and plant food was limited. This made growing land-sourced algae that thrived in a colder, low-carbon environment a necessity as food for the masses, and basic fruit, a luxury.

Kip grabbed his food and opened his front door. He motioned around the single room that doubled as both his living room and kitchen. "This is my place in all its glory. Make yourself at home."

"It's nice and bigger than I thought it would be. My place is smaller, albeit I like my area a little better." She paused. "Um, I have to use the bathroom. Where would I find that?"

"Right through that door next to the bedroom." Kip pointed. "And don't flush. I have to go as well. After my shower this morning, I'm almost through my daily water allotment."

"No problem, happens at my place all the time," Sky answered.

As she excused herself, Kip flipped on the Holovision and put the Green in his small refrigerator. He was bent down when he heard the words, "Citizen Alert."

He closed the fridge door and stood up to watch. A young spokeswoman with brown librarian glasses in a low-cut top sat behind a desk, her face expressionless. "Tonight, we're reporting that The Savage from the Wasteland, known as Rock, has escaped City Hospital and is on the run. Let's join Citizen Four, head of Truth and Information, for an official comment." They cut to another holographic clip with Citizen Four standing, appearing spotless in his official uniform.

"Fellow Citizens, we have an emergency that we must face together. The savage, Rock, has escaped his care facility. As you saw in the pit, he is an extremely dangerous and violent person." Citizen Four paused for dramatic effect. "Everyone should go home immediately, and no one should attempt to capture him. If you see him or have any news on his whereabouts, please notify your local security drone. Nirvana's Security Force will be in touch immediately thereafter. Let's all be safe and follow the law here." They cut back to the spokeswoman.

"Finally on this story, there is a mandatory curfew for eleven o'clock tonight for all parts of the city. Everyone should return home as soon as possible and no one is legally allowed to be outside after eleven p.m." As her words finished, they flashed a three-dimensional picture of the fugitive, rotating it around to show an all-sides view including his unique bicep tattoo.

Kip felt the buzz of his watch, a notice of the curfew flashing in red letters.

Sky entered the room, catching the last glimpse of the picture. "I just got buzzed on the curfew." She pressed a button to rewind the video feed and froze it on the image of Rock. She stared at the hologram for another second. "Is that the guy from the pit? What's his name, Rock? What's happening?"

55

"Guess he escaped from the hospital. He's on the loose in the city."

"Escaped? I thought he was a free man."

"That's a relative term. My bet is the Citizen leaders tried to hold him so he can fight again. And he chose not to."

"Well, that's a little crazy, but they'll get him. The drones catch everyone."

"It won't be that easy. He's a wildling from the Wasteland, so unless they had the foresight to chip him, he's not like us. The only way they find him is if they get line of sight. Plus, it's the Changing Festival with lots of people out. My bet is he knows how to stay hidden," Kip said.

"That's right, no chip and bad timing for the Security Force." She stepped to him with a playful gleam in her eye and started removing her own shirt. "You know, all this talk about bad guys is making me want to get punished. You'll have to cuff me, Security Officer Kip. It's the only way I'll squeal."

With the last vestiges of HAP still in his system, Kip was happy to oblige one more time. He grabbed her hand and moved toward the bedroom. "This way to interrogation."

Chapter 5
Sunday, January 6, 2075

Kip woke to a scratching noise at the bedroom window. He lay there for a moment in a sleepy fog, ensuring he hadn't been dreaming. Focusing his senses, he heard the rhythmic breathing of Sky sleeping comfortably next to him. But there was something else. He heard it again, like someone quietly tapping at the frame from the outside. He slipped out of bed and tiptoed toward the living room, all the while listening, hoping it was just his imagination running wild. A louder thump came. It wasn't a dream; someone was out there. His thoughts focused on Sky's safety. He grabbed a kitchen knife. Moving fast, he hit the emergency button in his kitchen alerting the local security drone, then stepped to the front door, slid it open, and stepped outside.

He moved silently, going toward the back of the house, hidden from the street in front. As he reached the rear corner, he peeked around, searching for the intruder. All he saw was a flash of black hair and dark skin, then came a paralyzing blow to the gut, following by a hammering shot to his chin that sent him down, stars in his eyes and a shooting pain in his skull. He rolled to his knees and tried to regain his breath, shaking his head to clear his cobwebs. His assailant took off, jumping the rear fence and dashing through a neighbor's property. The man stumbled on a random bin, creating a racket. A light in the neighbor's house turned on.

Kip tried to follow. He grabbed his knife off the ground and started after him. Jumping the fence, he dashed through the neighbor's area, avoiding the mess his assailant left behind. He sprinted across the side street, into a narrow alley and then down the city walkway before skidding to a stop. He scanned the chill night. Everything was dead quiet, a result of the lockdown curfew and a compliant citizenry. With the exception of small night-lights inside the houses, the area was black. Due to lack of crime and for energy-saving reasons, the city had long ago mandated all streetlights switch off at eleven o'clock, which now offered his assailant cover for his escape.

The man had vanished. Kip stood for a long moment, waiting and listening. When the security drone buzzed the area, he started walking back toward his home, watching for any sign of the intruder. As he reached his street, the drone finally found him.

"Citizen, stop and identify yourself," the drone ordered in its robotic voice.

"I'm JU450625, I live right here at 4905 Pruitt Street."

The drone flew closer. A yellow beam of light shot from its frame and scanned Kip's face and body. "Identification confirmed. Please wait for Security Force members. You are in violation of curfew and in possession of a weapon."

"What? No, I'm not. Somebody tried to break into my house. I notified you."

The drone didn't acknowledge his statement. It only answered, "Citizen, please wait, Security Force is twenty seconds away."

Kip heard the low hum of the approaching electric vehicle and saw the flash of its red lights as it rounded the corner.

An officer in full battle gear emerged from the passenger seat, and a security droid exited the driver's seat, situating itself a few feet away from Kip, a laser weapon directed at him.

The officer pointed to Kip. "I'm Security Force Officer Ko. How about you drop the knife and we talk."

Kip complied, tossing the weapon down. "Yeah, I don't want any trouble."

The officer bent over and picked it up.

Sky exited the house and started toward the group. "Kip, are you okay?"

The officer held up his hand to her. "Please stop there."

Sky froze.

The officer asked her, "Do you have any information about this situation?"

"I don't. I don't even know what the situation is. I woke up alone and saw the lights flashing."

"Then I'm going to ask you to return inside. We'll handle this."

"But he's my new partner."

"We'll get him back to you good as new. But for right now, you're in violation of curfew. We need you inside."

"Sky, I'm alright, go in," Kip added.

Sky gave a helpless frown, then went inside and closed the door.

"Thank you for your assistance with her, Citizen," the officer said.

The drone flew low in front of the officer. It played the video of its encounter with Kip. The officer and the security droid watched without a word. When finished, the officer spoke to the drone. "Have there been any other Citizens outside in the last thirty minutes?"

The drone took a moment scanning its data, then answered, "No," in its robotic voice.

Ko said, "We've got the information. You can return to patrol."

The drone didn't reply, only buzzed up and away.

Officer Ko spoke to Kip, "What do you call yourself, JU450625?"

"Kip."

"Okay, Kip, here's the deal. You're in violation of curfew, you're carrying an unauthorized weapon, and you say you were attacked but there's been no other Citizen in the area for the last thirty minutes." He paused, stepping closer to Kip, studying his face. "You've got the start of a bruise on your chin."

"That's right, because I was assaulted. Scan my implant. It'll show on the video."

"That's what we're going to do next." The officer reached to his belt, removing a silver circular device with a screen. He pointed it at Kip.

Kip watched as his face and social information came up, confirming his identity. A video then started playing in reverse from the perspective of Kip's eyes, following all of Kip's movements and experiences. Officer Ko stopped it when Kip got out of bed, then played the video to watch as the events unfolded. The officer flinched when the two blows were delivered. He watched until the chase into the alley when Kip decided to return home.

"This confirms your story. Do you know the guy?"

Kip hesitated. "I—I don't know."

"Citizen, what are you not telling me?"

"That it could have been the guy who fought in the Cleansing. Rock was his name. I saw that he escaped." He paused. "But I can't be sure. I only saw what you saw in the video. The black hair coming at me."

"Alright, I'm going to have to bring this forward for judicial review," the officer said.

"Judicial review—why? I didn't do anything."

The security droid stepped forward. A panel opened in its shoulder, revealing a hidden video screen. The picture cleared. A serious-looking man with gray hair, wire glasses, and a purple judicial robe came into view. Kip recognized him at once: Citizen Eight, the head of the entire Judicial Branch. He couldn't help but wonder why such a senior judge would handle his minor case at this time of night.

The judge was reading something out of the screen's shot. After a few seconds, he finally faced the camera. "Good evening, I'm Citizen Eight, Chief Judge in the Judicial Branch. I have your file and I've read it." He paused, coming closer to the screen. "So, somebody tried to break in, you grabbed a knife and went outside to confront him, got your ass kicked, then chased him at grave peril to yourself with said knife. Does that about sum it up?"

Kip didn't like where this was going.

Security Officer Ko spoke up. "Citizen JU450625 has been cooperative and truthful in all parts of the investigation."

"That's good to hear. And I understand that you have video confirming that somebody did try to break in, and you've seen the confrontation. But that also nobody was picked up by the security drone."

"That's right, I think it was Rock from the Cleansing. That would make sense—he's not chipped," Kip interjected.

"Why do you think I'm here?" The judge's tone was terse. "I'm the senior judge for all of Nirvana. You don't think I have better things to do than chase petty criminals? I'm leading the task force to apprehend that savage. Now, do you know this criminal, Rock? Do you know where he could be hiding or going?"

"Only from the Cleansing." Kip said, his anxiety rising. "I was the fifth Citizen chosen for the Punishment. But I never spoke with him."

The judge's eyes narrowed on the screen. "Nor did you punish him. Why not? Was he coming to you for help again tonight?"

"No, he wasn't. He doesn't know who I am, nor where I live. In fact, I only learned he had escaped a little while ago. You can ask my partner; I've never met the man."

"And why didn't you punish him?"

Kip hesitated. "I don't know how to answer that question, besides it just didn't feel right. But I wasn't trying to help him, I just didn't want anybody else hurt."

"That's what Punishment is, Citizen, reciprocal atonement for a crime. Five lashes with the cutter are an easy payment compared to the lives he took." Citizen Eight looked down to write something. "I'm inclined to believe it was just coincidence that Rock found you tonight. His attack and your knife both tell me you weren't trying to help him escape justice.

But I can't ignore the fact you left the safety of your house trying to do the Security Force's job, in violation of the curfew and with a dangerous weapon. All violations of law. How do your respond to these charges?"

"I don't deny them. I did all of that." Kip said with confidence, knowing he did the right thing. "But in my defense, I called for Security Force first. They took ten minutes to get here. In that time, when I was waiting, I had to . . . no, I'm obligated to defend my partner. I did it the best way I knew how. Take the fight to him and away from her. If I'm guilty, so be it. But she's safe, and no one got hurt."

"Nobody got hurt by sheer luck!" The tension in Citizen Eight's voice rose. "You could've been killed, her taken hostage. For goodness' sake, you can't imagine the permutations that could have occurred with that savage, all because your ego wanted to play hero. You should've stayed inside your house and waited for the Security Force to arrive." He stared into the camera. "I find you guilty of all charges, and fine you fifty social score credits and one hundred bank credits." He removed his glasses, his tone softening. "But given your honesty with the Security Force and me, I'm going to credit you back thirty social score credits as a reward for good behavior."

"You can't do that. I'll lose my house, maybe my job!" Kip shot back, his anger bubbling up.

"I can do that, and I just did." The screen went blank.

Officer Ko offered Kip his knife back. "Bring this directly into the house and nowhere else. And thank you for your help tonight." He slid into the passenger side of the car, then watched Kip. The security droid followed his lead, robotically moving into the driver's side.

Kip stood for a moment trying to calm himself down, feeling neutered by the system. It was a losing battle. He trudged to the door. As he entered his house, he heard the security car hum away.

Sky was there, impatiently waiting. She threw her arms around his neck. "What happened? Are you okay?"

Still boiling, Kip seethed, "Some freaking judge just fined me twenty social credits! I'm going to lose this house."

"Why?" she asked.

"Because he's an idiot!" he said. "I hope he gets what's coming to him."

"Kip, what do you mean?" Sky asked.

Kip hesitated, then followed with, "Karma, you know, you reap what you sow."

She touched him on the chest in a soothing gesture. "Calm down and tell me what happened. Think about the words you use—they could be listening. And know that it'll all work out. There's nothing we can't solve together."

Chapter 6

Kip roused from sleep, sore and exhausted, last night's events still heavy on his mind. He rolled over, the thought of Sky being there lifting his spirit. Only, she was gone, and the bedroom door was closed. He grabbed his black watch off the nightstand and checked his social score. A "986" shown in red lettering with the text "Score Alert Message." He clicked on it, reading; *Citizen Below 1000 SS—Elite Status Removed.* His heart sank. He next checked his bank credits. A "–100" electronic debit was taken at 1:03 this morning. The Hall of Justice wasted no time in moving. He had some things to figure out.

He slid out of bed, the morning chill hitting him as the government-timed heating system hadn't kicked on yet. After dressing in a loose shirt and pants, he started thinking about his housing options. Maybe he could negotiate a temporary stay and perform some community service to get his social score up. As he approached the door, the delightful aroma of food cooking wafted into the room and he felt a reprieve from his worries: Sky was still there.

He entered the kitchen to find her standing over the single-burner electric stove he used, stirring something in a pan. Even with her makeup from last night gone, she appeared radiant.

She beamed a smile, her blue eyes sparkling. "Good morning, sunshine."

"Good morning. What smells so great?"

"Just stir-frying some Green. I used what spices you had. Which, by the way, is something we need to talk about." She switched off the stove and removed the pan. She then wrapped her arms around him, kissing him on the lips. "We're partnered now. You need something more than Nirvana's allotted spice rack. This won't do."

He leaned in, kissing her lips again, liking it much better than the cheek. "Wow, that's really nice. I can't believe I haven't embraced kissing like this before," he said.

"Same here. Guess we haven't had the right person to embrace it with. But we do now."

Kip peeked into the pan, then back to her. "Do you know how long it's been since somebody cooked my breakfast?"

She laughed. "About as long as it's been since I cooked somebody's breakfast. And you haven't tried the Green, so I wouldn't celebrate quite yet."

"It's the gesture that matters, so thank you for that." He leaned in, giving an intimate hug, to which she reciprocated enthusiastically. As Kip held her, he soaked up their connection, savoring the touch of her skin, the smell of her hair, the beat of her heart. He hadn't been this happy for a long time.

"Time for breakfast," she whispered, slipping away from his arms.

They sat at the small kitchen table. Sky poured some koffee she had made using the instant powder and hot water. Koffee wasn't real coffee, it was rare to taste the real stuff anymore since the vast majority of bean crops had failed due to the cold. So now they drank a lab-created flavored drink with caffeine added to simulate the real thing. Kip had tried real coffee once; the substitute was pedestrian in comparison.

He sipped his drink, then tried his liberal helping of Green. "That's good. You're too modest of a cook."

"I've had many a failure in getting this good, and I suspect I'll have a few more." Sky took a small bite, then continued. "What's the game plan after last night?"

"Well, they've already dinged my social score. I'm no longer Elite status. And they've taken the fine. I'm one hundred credits poorer."

"I suspected as much; they don't waste any time." Sky nibbled her Green. "It'll be really hard if you have to return to the Flats every night."

"I know. I've been considering that. I'm thinking one step at a time. First, I'll do Confessional this morning to see if that helps. Then I'll go to work and confirm nothing has changed with my job. Tik—my boss—should be in today."

"That sounds good so far. And then?"

"And then I have to figure out if I can delay the housing change and if I can raise my social score. I don't know, like volunteer at a Senior Resort. I heard they need help."

"You usually have forty-eight hours to get to your new housing, so you need to move fast." She took another small bite. "And I'd be careful about working at those Senior Resorts. I hear they're an infestation of disease with a healthy dose of abuse."

"I've heard the same horror stories. But I'll do it if it means keeping my status."

"You also need to allocate some time to check out your new housing. They'll assign you one shortly and I hear some are pretty sketchy." She took another bite. "Although, your score is high, especially in comparison to most in the Heights, so hopefully that's working for you."

"I can't believe this is happening. What are the chances that Rock finds me and tries to break in?"

"Doesn't matter. It is happening, and we'll deal with it. Worse case, you spend a couple of weeks in your new place until we get your score up."

"I'm sorry. I hope you don't regret partnering with me."

"Don't be silly," Sky said. She reached out, taking his hand. "I meant what I said—there's something different about you." As she finished, a chime sounded on Kip's watch.

"I'll have to finish this in a few. That's my three-minute warning for Confessional," Kip said, releasing her hand.

"Go. I have mine in thirty minutes. We'll talk about it later."

Kip moved to the living room, sitting up close to the Holovision. At precisely eight thirty, the screen flipped on, and the hologram of a man's face came up, the top of his judicial robes just evident. He was an older gentleman by Kip's standard, maybe around forty years old, still a few years away from being sent to the Senior Resorts.

"Good morning, Citizen JU450625, let's start with your own confessions."

"Good morning, Citizen, I've two things to confess and am hoping for forgiveness from the State."

"Proceed," the hologram said.

Kip summarized the events at the Cleansing where he didn't punish Rock, then through the events of last night with the Security Force. At the end, he concluded with, "I take responsibility for my actions and apologize for any damages I've caused." He finished with, "I'm asking the Citizens of Nirvana for forgiveness and the elimination of my fine. I don't want to lose my housing."

"I've read you were exemplary with the truth last night. That is a credit to you, Citizen. However, a third offense has been reported against you. Citizen MU270426 has confessed she was with you when you disparaged your boss. A penalty of one social score credit was enforced. Is this the case?"

71

Kip thought about the time spent with Blu at the zoo. She was right to disclose. "I'm sorry, it is. I forgot about that. Blu, my old partner, was with me. I'm glad she confessed; I was angry at the time and wrong."

"Are there any confessions you have about your fellow Citizens?"

"Not really, I guess maybe one. My new partner AU392726 did leave the house for a minute last night during the events." Kip knew he had to report Sky. They'd have the records from the Security Officer last night, but thought it best to minimize the severity of her actions. "She was concerned for me. I think she technically broke curfew. But she returned immediately when asked by the Security Force."

He tapped something off camera. "Yes, we have that in the system. Thank you for reporting her. Is there anything else?"

"Not that I recall."

"Given your actions and considering your stated remorse, I'm going to let the penalties imposed stand. They seem fair in comparison to your potential impacts, and I hope will serve as a future deterrent. A reminder for you of what happens when you disregard the laws of Nirvana. I also wish you the best in reestablishing your Elite status in the future." The judge scanned some paperwork. "Lastly, I want to emphasize your obligation as a Citizen of Nirvana to confess any action, speech, or thoughts deemed unacceptable no matter how small. We do this for the good of our community."

Kip just sat, staring at the man in the hologram.

"Do you have anything to say?" the man asked.

Kip thought about asking if there was anything he could say or do to change his judgment, but knew they would be futile words. "No sir, I accept your assessment and will be a better Citizen in the future."

"Long live Nirvana." The hologram terminated.

Kip's watch buzzed. He read the message out loud. "*New Address: 333 River Street, Suite C, Pubtown, Nirvana.*" He clenched his fists. "You've got to be kidding me. Pubtown is the pits, it's in the Flats. I didn't get assigned to the Heights."

Sky came over and put her arm around him. "It's okay, we'll make it work. It's not forever." She put her finger to her lips, thinking. Then said, "I wonder if I could transfer some of my social score credits to you."

He kissed her. "You're so sweet to offer, but you can't. They outlawed that a few years ago. Each Citizen stands on their own, no support from community, friends, or coworkers."

Chapter 7

Kip walked into his work offices and was surprised by the new face sitting at the far desk. A man about twenty years old had a large picture book opened to a zebra.

The man's focus was broken by Kip's approach. "Hi, this is a zebra. Do you want to see it?"

Physical deformities were rarely encountered in Nirvana's civil society due to the laboratory process used for embryonic selection. Being more difficult to identify, intellectual limitations slipped through more often and, once identified, were fully managed by the State. Kip knew this man was cognitively challenged, but was unsure as to what level.

Kip stepped over to him. "That is a zebra, and they run fast. Do you like zebras?"

"I do, but I like the bears the best. Grizzly bears are my favorite. They can beat a zebra."

"You're right about that. What's your name?"

"Tom."

"It's nice to meet you, Tom. My name is Kip and I work with bears and zebras. What are you doing here?"

"He's here to work," Tik said as he walked into the room. He made no attempt to hide his disgust.

"What's happening, Tik?"

"You're happening!" Tik snapped back. "I was told to get rid of you, and the people in power sent us Tom to replace you." Tik stepped closer, speaking under his breath. "He's a functioning moron, but somehow connected to Citizen Five. So, they're shoving him down our throats." He shook his head. "Can you imagine being put in a role just for who you know and not based on capability? It's not right."

A quick thought flashed in Kip's mind about the irony of that statement, but he quickly squelched it in case the watchers were listening to his thoughts. "Get rid of me, why? Not because of last night."

Tik met his stare. "I don't know why. I got notified directly by my boss's boss to terminate you as soon as possible. I managed to buy you some time, but the inevitable is around the corner. So, plan on it."

"This doesn't make sense. I was demerited some credits last night, but it was all a misunderstanding and I'm just below Elite status. It's not like I'm criminal level." He shook his head. "How much time do I have?"

Tik ran his fingers through his wispy hair. "A handful of days, max. Unofficially, I go in for a procedure soon. I told them I need you here to train the new guy. No one else is qualified and there are a lot of animals at risk."

"A procedure—are you okay? It's not the kidneys again, is it?"

Tik whispered, "Not here. Come in my office." He tried waving at Tom to get his attention. "Hey Tom, you keep studying the animals. I'll be right back."

"Okay, Mr. Tik," Tom answered without breaking his focus on the book.

They entered Tik's office. He walked around his desk and switched on some music, raising the volume. He then grabbed a small electronic writing board with a stylus.

Tik stepped close to Kip and wrote, *If the watchers hear any substantial background noise, they won't scan your thoughts. They can't differentiate the background noise from thoughts. It's the reason why thought scans are not reliable and done infrequently. Remember this tip.*

Kip raised his eyebrows, surprised to hear the reading of thoughts was done less often than advertised by the State. They seemed to demerit him all too often for minor thought offenses.

Tik erased the board, then continued writing. *I know we haven't always seen eye to eye, but I've always trusted you to do the right thing.*

Kip again nodded.

Tik had already erased the writing. He continued. *My kidneys are dying, the government won't grow me a new one in the lab, too expensive and I'm not useful enough to save.*

This time Kip shook his head, mouthing the word, "No."

Tik continued writing. *Yes, so I'm going on a vacation to get a new kidney from the black market. I've got twelve hours before the surgery, and I need a few days of bed rest.*

There were so many things Kip wanted to say, including *Don't do it!* but he couldn't figure out how.

Tik anticipated as much, waving his hand for silence. He wrote, *I may not see you again. I don't know what's going on, but be careful. What's happening to you smells of corruption, maybe payback for the Punishment.*

Kip met his eyes, the spark of understanding flicking on in his mind.

Tik wrote one more line. *Watch your back and be careful who you trust.* He erased the board, then stepped away, flipping off the music. He stepped back to Kip, a serious frown on his face. "Kip, I'm sorry. You're being terminated. I'm taking a vacation through next Saturday, so you'll have to train Tom while I'm gone. Plan on Sunday being your last day. I'm sorry, but that's the way it is. I'm happy to provide a reference if you're diligent this last week. Citizen Qu will be popping in to ensure everything is okay."

"Thanks for everything, Tik. It's not the way I wanted it to end, but I appreciate all you've done." Kip glanced at his watch. "I need to go."

"Where are you off to?" Tik asked.

"Right now, I'm going to Pubtown. I need to go check out my new place."

"That's a rough neighborhood. Be careful out there." As he spoke, he wrote on his board, *Find Ann at a place called The Tavern. She'll keep you out of trouble.* He then erased it.

"Thanks . . . for everything," Kip added. "Best of luck to you and enjoy that vacation."

Chapter 8

Kip considered Tik's warning. Was somebody getting payback for his refusal to participate in the Punishment? The whole situation didn't make sense. His social score had dropped due to last night's incident with Security Force. Somebody with seniority would be monitoring that. And given the quality job he had, they'd want an Elite Citizen in the role. Even so, why would somebody so senior be worried about his employment so quickly? His social score change would have gotten to Tik eventually, it was part of their monthly review. And, when it dropped too low, it became a daily discussion. What was the rush?

He tried to push aside these troubling thoughts. He may never understand their motivations, but he knew the job would be history and he'd have to move on. He was thankful that Tik bought him a week to search for something that paid higher than the minimum income all Citizens received. Mulling over these suspicions, he left the zoo to visit his new home.

An old electric bus pulled up. Kip entered through its dented sliding door and took a seat two rows behind the driver. He scanned the passengers, who, for the most part, were general laborers servicing the residences and businesses of the Uptown

District, the centerpiece of Nirvana. The Perfect City, as the leaders called it, was built in the foothills of a mountain range split by the Cascade River, a fast-flowing waterway that originated in the Rocky Mountains.

Segmented into four distinct districts appropriately named Uptown, Midtown, the Heights and the Flats, the city at one time held a population of over one million residents. The First Pandemic of 2030 devastated its Citizens, as it did the world population. With scarce resources and much infighting for them, a series of uprisings occurred within the greater Nirvana region, which thinned the population to what it was today. These uprisings also sent a large portion of the populace into hiding in the Wilderness regions, otherwise known as the Outer Boundaries and the Wastelands. These ex-Citizens devolved into the savages that presently wage war on Nirvana, the societies that created the likes of Rock.

Kip watched in silence as the mansions and high rises of Uptown passed. Built on the peak of a hill, the Uptown District contained the posh area that catered to the Elite establishment of Nirvana. These were the political, industrial, and intellectual leaders with the highest social scores and held unswaying power over the larger populace. The area reflected this exclusiveness, with its high-end housing, luxury amenities, and unparalleled medical care. They also had their pick of the best food and clothing. Although everyone here got their designated portion of

Green, theirs was often donated to the service and help workers that supported the area.

The bus hummed down the road, passing the Great White Walls of Uptown. Built after the last uprising, it was the permanent separation between Uptown and Midtown, but also between the haves and the have-nots.

Still going downhill, the bus entered Midtown, the industrial engine for the State and Kip's home since Emancipation. All embryos are developed in a laboratory, these children are raised and educated by the State, being groomed into Citizenship. Each child is given an alphanumeric identification at birth. Kip's was JU450625. Raised in Nirvana-run group wards, the parentless children of Nirvana know only the State indoctrination for their education in both ethics and scholastics. At four years of age, in a rare chance for individualism, each child picks their own name. The process results in a lot of short names and common things. At fifteen years of age for boys, based on the young Citizen's unique capabilities and intelligence, their placement in societal structure is determined. Kip was assigned a good job and housing in Midtown. Someone like Tom, the zoo's newest employee, would be given something more menial for work and maybe a place in the Heights, which traditionally housed the working class.

A similar process is followed for girls, but usually done at fourteen years of age. At that time, in a sterilization process, all females donate their ovum to the State for future harvesting for the next generation of Citizens, thereby ensuring a diverse and strong population.

After initial placement, the Elite claim that your future is defined by you. They'd point to the one-off rags-to-riches story whereby a person elevated from poverty to Uptown by working hard and being a good Citizen, thus improving one's social score. As the bus passed Midtown's city center with its quaint, if not orderly market district, Kip shook his head at that thought. It seemed to him that the modified Orwellian quote "all men are equal but some more equal than others," applied. It was certainly not his experience to date, and now it was clear he was on a downward social trajectory, and fate wasn't helping. He smiled at that thought. At least fate had brought Sky. Fate is a fickle character.

Making numerous stops while watching the soul of Nirvana board then depart, he continued his ride to the heart of the Heights, where he transferred to an even older bus. The Heights was a transitional area located on cliff-like hills overlooking the Flats. Not wealthy, not poor, this modest area was the heart of the middle class, its residents typically honest and hardworking. With that said, it had pockets that reflected more of a Midtown ambiance and others that had that seedy vibe so often found in the Flats. Kip wondered why he didn't get housing here. It was certainly closer to his old job. Again, whether by chance or design, a question that didn't matter, proverbial water under the bridge.

As the bus traveled down, the transition to the Flats became evident. The terrain leveled, albeit still running somewhat down to where it met the river, giving the area its signature name. Kip had never ventured this far past the Heights. He stuck mostly to Midtown and Uptown with an occasional, if not rare, trip outside the city to hike. Kip noted the streets of the Flats were lined with a mix of row-type housing and rundown businesses, not unexpected as the area was known as a playground for those who wanted to enjoy the seedier pleasures of life. Whether the watchers didn't monitor the transgressions or, more likely, didn't care, no one here knew for sure. What was abundantly clear is that many of the establishments were running bootleg liquor, illegal flesh, and various drugs, both the natural and pharmaceutical types, and no one stopped it. There was the occasional Security Force presence, but their focus seemed to be more on violent crime and not the petty individual. In fact, more often than not, the Security Force was involved in the petty crime. Bribes and kickbacks for protection or willful ignorance were a mainstay to the local businesses that traded in the illicit activities.

The most infamous area within the Flats was a neighborhood called Pubtown. Named for its high density of liquor establishments, it was also known as the Babylon of Nirvana, where the only rule is survival. Having spawned the likes of Trex and a handful of other serial murderers, it was best for the patrons to keep to themselves with their heads low. And now, it was Kip's home. He raised his eyes, focusing on the neighborhood, fighting the depressing feelings this thought brought.

The bus stopped at the corner of Main and Lotus streets a few blocks from the riverfront. As Kip rose and started to exit, the bus driver spoke. "This is your stop? I don't think you belong here."

"It's my first trip in. My new address is a couple blocks from here."

"Sorry to hear that." He raised a hand, asking Kip to wait. "A couple of tips. Keep your valuables in your front pocket, and don't make eye contact. And remember, the bus runs every hour, twenty-four hours a day, if you need to get out."

"Thanks sir, and good luck to you," Kip replied.

"No, good luck to you. You'll need it."

Kip exited, standing for a moment to get his bearings. River Street paralleled the water, so he needed to continue down a few blocks. He started to walk, head held high, scanning the neighborhood. He saw people hurrying down the streets, their heads down. Those who loitered in front of the bars and other businesses held a wary glare, always watching for the predator or the prey.

Kip noted a group of young working women standing on the street corner, huddled against the cold. All were dressed in revealing outfits fit for their trade, the oldest profession still thriving. Strangely, two Security Officers stood near them. One started shouting directions while the other held the door, giving the working ladies access to a seedy hostel-type hotel. Kip filed that under things not to question.

He hadn't gone far when a man approached him awkwardly, seeming to intentionally collide with him. Kip's hands quickly went to his own pockets, catching the man trying a grab-and-run on his e-wallet. He pushed the man away, Kip's larger frame an asset.

The man laughed, backing up, giving a whistle. "I'll be seeing you later, Cupcake. Promise."

Kip hurried away, remembering the bus driver's warning. *Don't make eye contact.* With his head low, he continued down the street, a bad feeling in his gut. It wasn't fear that was nagging him, but more the uncertainty of what might be next.

He took a left on River Street, hiking a single block until he came to a rundown two-story house. The wooden building was a shadow of its original grandeur. Its white sideboards were now faded and its two-storied weathered front porches needed repair and a few coats of paint. He traversed the front stairs, gave a quick knock, then entered through a sturdy wooden door whose lock was clearly broken. Once in the worn hallway, he passed two doors labeled with "A" and "B." He went up the set of inside stairs to find the door with "C" on it. He knocked.

Footsteps clacked across a wooden floor, and then a woman's voice carried through the closed door. "What?"

"I'm here to see the house. I'm the new Citizen Occupant, JU450625."

The lock clicked, and the door opened. An elderly woman who'd seen hard days stood in front of him holding a mop. "I thought we had until tomorrow. I'm still cleaning up."

"I have another day at my other place, but I thought I'd come see what the house was like."

She creaked the door open all the way. "Well, here it is in all its glory." She motioned around the room.

The living space was smaller than his place now, with a single sitting room, bedroom, and kitchen combined. The worn and dirty bathroom off of this living area was closet-sized, with just enough room for him to squeeze in. The only upgrade he had was outdoor living space—a front porch overlooked both the riverfront and the street.

The old woman went back to work scrubbing a brown stain on the sagging wooden floor.

"What is that?" Kip asked.

"Do you really want to know?" she answered in her raspy voice.

"Yes, I do."

88

"It's blood. The old occupant died here two days ago." She stopped mopping to gage his expression.

Kip stepped away from the stain, wondering what the hell was going on. "What the . . . What happened?"

"Security didn't tell me if it was self-inflicted or murder, but it was violent," she answered. "That's all I know." She started mopping again. "By the way, I'm Trase. I live in A below."

"I'm Kip. Nice to meet you." He peeked out the front window. "Is this place safe?" he asked, the bad feeling in his gut growing.

"As safe as any place in Pubtown. But I find minding my own business and not asking questions makes it safer."

"When does the Green get delivered?"

"Ha!" she laughed out loud. "You're in Pubtown now, there is no house delivery. You pick up your allotment every morning—if it comes at all." She continued mopping.

"If it comes at all?" Kip didn't like the sound of that. "Where do I get it?"

"Closest place is down on the docks; delivery truck usually comes first thing. I get there early to get first choice."

"Thanks for the tip," he answered. "Is there anything I should know before I move in?"

Trase stopped her mopping, her haggard face softening. "It's a mean town with ugly people. So be careful who you trust, especially if they work for the State."

"Thanks. You're the second person to tell me that." He started to leave but stopped. "Last question—do you know a place called The Tavern?"

"Yes, it's off Lotus, a couple of blocks from here. I'd warn you about going in there, but if you're asking for it by name, sounds like you have some business to attend."

Chapter 9

Kip stepped outside into a cool breeze, the wind off the river bringing an extra nip to the air. Following the directions Trase had given, he walked through two narrow, paved roadways. He wondered if they were tight streets or just alleys, as there were no markings or signs. They were cold and dirty, shaded with no direct sunlight to disinfect the mold that gathered in the corners and crevasses. The buildings surrounding him were equally worn as his new living accommodations. Built just after the uprisings, they now slowly decayed under years of weathering and lack of maintenance.

As he passed a particularly rotten area, he stopped to examine the graffiti painted on the wall, which read RESIST NIRVANA in large, red lettering. Underneath there was a circle surrounding the words "Citizen One" with an X through it. Although the intent of the signage was clear, he wondered who would do this and why. It seemed dangerous and without reward. If caught, the artist's social score would certainly get hit, but more likely they'd be sent to reeducation camps for challenging Nirvana's leadership. And for what possible gain?

He continued down the alley, thinking that there was no explaining the full spectrum of the human condition. Each person has a lifetime of differing experiences that shape and mold them into who they are today. From serial killers to teachers and Citizen leaders to zookeepers, an individual's day-to-day occurrences, specifically their failures and successes, shape that person into who they are and how they view the world. So, while painting graffiti on a wall could never make sense to him, he hadn't walked a mile in the shoes of the artist. If he had, maybe it would be clear.

Kip exited onto Lotus Street, a main thoroughfare of Pubtown. He scanned the nearby businesses and found The Tavern two doors down. Standing outside for a moment, he studied the square brick building. The bottom floor held The Tavern, the upper floors appeared to be housing with front porches of a similar scale to Kip's new home. The bar's double doors were shaded by a torn and weathered awning. A small wooden sign with "The Tavern" hand-painted on it hung on a single wire hook.

He tried to see into the bar, but the windows were covered with little to no light streaming out. He wondered if the place was even open. As he considered the question, two men in dirty and worn laborer clothing exited through the front doors. The sound of rustic music seeped out. The two men hesitated, staring at Kip. The man on the right gave an uncharacteristic nod before they both stumbled away.

It was now or never. Although anxious, Kip knew it had to be now. He entered through the doors and stepped back in metaphorical time. Standing in the rundown entryway, he allowed his eyes to adjust to the dim light and smoky haze. The room was sizeable, with maybe a dozen round tables set up on a sagging plank floor that showed dark blotchy stains. Kip's bet was years of blood and vomit. The brown paneled walls were mostly bare except for a painting of the building in its heyday. At the far end, a serving bar spanned half the room and was lined by a series of wooden bar stools spaced neatly in front. The place reeked of vape, old alcohol, and a musty, mold-like odor. Despite the room being mostly empty, the eyes of the patrons there were staring at him.

Kip continued to the bar, wondering if Tik could have possibly made a mistake. He took an open stool as far away from the other customers as he could. A petite woman with green eyes, braided red hair, and a hardened smile strolled over. She stopped halfway to pour a drink, then continued to him and slid the glass in front of him. It was green with a horrible smell.

"What's this?" Kip asked.

"You must be new around here," the woman answered.

"That obvious?"

She wiped down a drying glass with a smirk. "Yeah."

"What do I owe you?"

"Nothing, first drink here is on the house," she answered. "Oh, and the drink's called the Green Ooze or just Ooze. It's the only thing we serve. Has a bit of an aftertaste, but also quite the kick. It'll grow on you . . . not literally." She laughed at her own joke.

Kip sipped the beer-like liquor. With a bitter, nutty finish, his first reaction was to spit it out. Not wanting to be rude, he swallowed hard, gulping it down, hoping it didn't come up on its own. "That's good. What is it?"

"You're a horrible liar." She gave a wry smile. "It's roasted fermented Green. About the only thing that is plentiful around here." She put the glass away. "What brings you in?"

Kip considered asking about Ann but waited, thinking it better to ease into that conversation. "I'll be moving in down the street tomorrow; thought I'd check out the area."

"New to the neighborhood. What do you think of our little slice of heaven?"

"Not the best place I've been, but also not the worst." He tried to say it with a straight face. Worried he failed in his bid, he quickly changed the subject. "I was walking here and saw a sign for 'Resist.' Resist what?"

She stared at him for a few seconds, then walked away to the far end of the bar and a patron who'd just finished his drink.

Kip almost called her back but thought it better to wait a few minutes to ask his question, so he went back to his Ooze. As he took another draught, two men walked up, settling on either side of him. Kip glanced at the one to his right. A giant of a man wearing a torn shirt and stained pants with a hint of a used diaper smell leaned against the bar. An intimidating large scar ran up his neck to just below his chin.

On Kip's left, the man who tried to pick his pocket earlier inched closer. "Well, if it isn't Cupcake. What brings you in here?"

Kip refocused on his drink. "Just thought I'd have a drink, no crime in that."

"No crime in that, if it's the truth. Who are you?"

Kip met his eyes. "I'm new to the neighborhood. Who are you?"

"I'm the Pubtown welcoming committee. My friends call me Ell, and this here is Bear."

Kip faced the giant, who gave a bearish growl.

Ell never broke his stare. "I'll ask you again. Who are you?"

"I'm a person who's not looking for trouble," Kip responded while lifting his Ooze, struggling another gulp down.

"Look at me when I'm talking to you." Ell leaned over and spit into Kip's Ooze.

Kip complied, facing him. "You know, surprisingly, your drool can only make this crap taste better."

Ell swung at his head. Kip dodged backward, avoiding the punch. The back of his skull blasted into Bear's hovering face, exploding his nose. The giant fell without Kip so much as throwing a punch. Ell swung again. This time Kip closed fast, and the swing went behind him, Ell's bicep catching Kip in the shoulder. Kip knew he had the advantage of size and strength. He grasped Ell's shirt and lifted with all he had, then pushed forward. Ell hit the bar with a crack to his lower back. He started to go down; Kip kneed him in the gut to make sure. His assailant crumpled to the floor.

Bear started to rouse, blood dripping down his face. Ell was up. He pulled a knife and flashed it at Kip. For the first time in his life, Kip lost control. He reacted, grabbing the nearest chair, and swung it as hard as he could. It hit Ell's face with devastating force. The only thing dropping faster than the knife was Ell's body. Bear was up and rushing him. Kip spun, swinging the chair again. This time it shattered across the giant's head, sending him tumbling.

Both attackers staggered to their feet. Kip was ready for the next assault; the knife still lay on the floor. At that moment, the front doors opened, and two Security Force Officers walked in. Ell and Bear leaned on the bar, pretending they were drinking patrons. Kip stepped on the knife with his shoe, covering it, then bellied up to the bar himself.

The officers made their way over. "Afternoon, Citizen."

96

"Afternoon, officers," Kip responded, keeping the blade hidden.

The barmaid scurried to their side of the bar. "Can we help you?"

The shorter of the Security Officers took an interest in Bear's bloody nose. "What happened to you?"

Ell answered. "We were horsing around right before you came in. He tripped and hit his head on that chair, shattered it. But he's okay, right big guy?"

"Yeah, I got unlucky. A little too much Ooze and these guys." He showed them his gargantuan shoes.

The taller officer came over, seeming to take an interest in Ell. "I'm Officer Pit and this is Officer Ya. We had a report of someone matching your description damaging a Security Force vehicle a few blocks from here."

"I don't know what you're talking about. I've been here for hours."

"I can vouch for him; he's been here the whole day," the barmaid said.

"And you are?" Ya asked.

"I'm Ann, the owner of this place," she answered.

Kip took note.

"How about anyone else not invested in the bar?" Pit focused on Kip. "Were you here with him?"

"Yep, don't know him, but he's been here as long as I have. And you missed it. This big guy falling, that is, it was like a tree in the forest."

Pit reengaged with Ell. "We're going to check your video."

"Sure," Ell responded.

Kip's pulse quickened, afraid of what they'd see.

The officer removed the circular device from his belt. He held it next to Ell's head. His personal information popped up first, including his 523 social score, and then the video came running in reverse. It showed nothing but the view from the bar stool for as long as the officer rewound.

He stopped after a few seconds. "Okay, your story checks." Pit gave a hard stare, focusing on Ell. "But I do find it interesting that you didn't even glance over when your friend hit the chair."

Ell shrugged. "When you've seen it a dozen times, it's not that interesting."

The officers turned for the door. "Have a nice day, Citizens."

As they exited, Ell menacingly pointed at Kip. "This isn't over."

Kip kicked the knife back to him, sliding it across the floor. "Yes, it is. You won't see me again. It was a mistake coming here."

"Why are you here?" Ann asked. "We don't see newbs very often."

"A friend of mine said to find you. A guy named Tik said you can keep me out of trouble."

"Based on what you just did to Ell and Bear, I'm betting you can take care of yourself."

"Thanks for the drink, Ann. Best of luck to you."

"Best to you," she responded.

Kip winked at Bear, who scowled in response, then to Ell, who methodically raised his middle finger and held it up. Kip laughed at the gesture and headed for the door, leaving the bar.

Walking to the bus stop, he was passing a dank alley where an unusual low hum resonated, when a disheveled man in need of a bath came from the shadows and stumbled into him. Unsteady on his feet, Kip held the drunk up. The reek of Ooze saturated the man's clothing.

The man leaned in close and whispered, "Follow me. Someone you know wants to speak with you."

"What?"

"Shh, play like you're helping me walk."

Kip slid under the man's arm and escorted him deeper into the alley. Once in its shadowy recesses, the drunk started walking on his own. He turned to meet Kip's eyes, "My name is Jun, and this is a tough thing to ask, but you got to trust me."

"Trust you how?" Kip asked.

Jun held up a black, hat-like cloth. "I've got to blindfold you for a few minutes. I give you my word, you'll be fine."

"I'm telling you now, if I feel unsafe, the blindfold's coming off."

"I understand and don't think that you will."

Jun placed the thin hat over Kip's full head. He raised the bottom so his mouth could breathe. "Now I'm going to just grab your arm and walk you through this. Try to relax."

The next minutes were nerve-racking, Kip wondered more than a few times what he was doing as he zigged and zagged. Completely blinded and escorted by a stranger, he shuffled forward in the most dangerous area of Nirvana. What was he thinking?

Jun was a man of his word. At every step, every turn, and even a few low ceilings, he warned Kip then guided him through. When they finally stopped, Kip could only discern two things. First, there was the same smell of ammonia that permeated Bear's clothing, and second, an audible hum was ever present in the background. Jun helped Kip sit down, then removed the blindfold. Across the table in front of him, Ell and Ann sat with three pints of Ooze.

Chapter 10

"What do you want?" Kip asserted, not trying to mask his anger.

"We'll ask the questions, and if we're satisfied with your answers, we'll tell you what you came for," Ann responded, her voice calm and reassuring.

"What I came for . . . I don't know what I came for," Kip shot back.

"Hold still for a moment," Ell said. "And so you know, that hum you're hearing blocks all recordings from your implant. No one will be able to download this meeting." Ell held a circular disk like the Security Force had near Kip's head. He then placed it on the table so Kip could watch. The video scrolled in reverse at one hundred times speed, the last few hours from Kip's life. They passed his meetings with Trase and Tik, continuing until it stopped after five hours, then went to static. Ell pressed a few buttons, and the picture slowly reemerged and started replaying. It ran this way until Sky came into focus. Ell stopped scrolling.

"Who is this?" Ell asked. He then added, "Be honest, nothing you say or think is being recorded."

"How are you doing that? Our implants only record five hours," Kip responded.

"We'll ask the questions, you answer, and if we believe you, we'll tell you what you came for," Ann repeated.

Kip wavered, wondering why they wanted to know about Sky. "She's my partner from the Changing."

"You just met her?" Ell continued.

"Yes . . . well, at the Games actually, I sat next to her, and we talked. We met again at the Changing to see if there was a connection."

"And was there?"

Kip hesitated to answer.

"We couldn't care less about your bedroom adventures; we just want to know about her."

"If you keep scrolling that video, you'll see for yourself. But yes, we decided to partner. And I trust her; she's an honest person."

"Okay," Ell said, then continued to speed through Kip's life. They flashed past the Changing Festival, and on to the Games. Ell stopped at the Punishment scene where Kip refused to participate.

"Why didn't you do it? It would've been so easy for you to just swing. You don't know that guy and you owe him nothing."

"Because it didn't feel right." He met Ell's eyes. "Because I believe he is a victim of the system, just like I am now. And I refuse to punish—no, torture—someone who I'm not sure committed the crime."

"How did you know that?" Ann asked.

Kip stared at her for a moment. "I could tell by his eyes. Like you, you have honest eyes."

Ann motioned for Ell to continue. Ell scrolled back days upon days and into the last weeks of the more mundane times with Blu. Periodically he'd pause the tape to ask a question about someone Kip had interacted with. Like his questions on Sky, he paid particular attention to Blu. In all cases, they moved on until finally the screen faded to static.

"Why did you help Ell and Bear in the bar with the Security Force, especially after they came at you?"

"I almost didn't. I guess it was a little bit of self-preservation, afraid they were going to come for me next. But mostly I don't think people should be arrested and charged for a bar fight."

"What about damage to a Security Force car?" Ell continued.

"I don't condone that, but that falls into the I-can't-confirm-it-happened bucket."

"You asked me about the Resistance graffiti on the wall. Why?" Ann asked.

"Two reasons. I was trying to be polite and change the subject from this hell hole you call home. It was awkward, I know." Kip's glance flashed between the two, watching for a reaction.

"Anything else?" Ell asked, with no change in his demeanor.

"Nothing being recorded, right?" Kip watched as Ann shook her head. "And because there's an appeal to me to resist the State. I've found the Security Force to be fair in implementing our laws, but our leaders who make the laws are self-serving narcissists who only crave power for themselves. It's one of the reasons I didn't punish Rock. I don't trust our Citizen leaders."

Ann stood from her chair, switching off a machine behind her. The louder humming continued.

"What's that?" Kip asked.

"It's a high-tech lie detector. It measures subtle changes in the body as you speak."

"And?"

"You didn't hear any buzzers or bells, so you were telling the truth," Ell answered.

"Meaning, now we'll tell you about us," Ann added, pushing the Green Ooze to Kip.

Kip hesitated to take it.

"Take it. If I wanted to poison you, I could've done it upstairs."

Kip took the ale and sipped it, then spoke to Ell. "First question, how'd you fool the Security Force with your implant video? You weren't anywhere near the bar."

"Ell knows his electronics. He can do a lot more than that," Ann answered.

"That was easy," Ell said. "Only a few people in Nirvana know an implant is hackable and programmable. I have several false feed images in my unit that give me the alibi I need. It's just a question of which one they'll see."

"And my unit's video just now?" Kip asked. "Those are usually limited to five-hour increments."

"Yes, the implants overwrite their storage in five-hour increments. But the data underneath is not really destroyed until after thirty days. It's just a question of finding it, bringing it forward, and putting it together in the right sequence." He held up the silver disk. "This unit does that. Built it myself."

"Impressive. Would have never guessed it during your derelict impersonation." Kip paused, considering his next question. "Why are you doing this, the video, questions about Sky, the lie detector?"

Ell motioned to Ann to answer.

She obliged. "Because you show up in my bar asking about the Resistance, yet you're a friend of Tik's. So, either you're a crafty spy for Citizen One or truly an awkward newbie with a friend that is a friend of ours. We had to confirm."

"A spy? I think you've had one too many Oozes." Kip laughed; his two hosts didn't join him. "What, you're serious, me a spy?"

"Your gut is right on the Citizen Leadership and the people of Uptown. They're corrupt to the core and will do anything for power. But it's worse than even you can imagine. People of the Flats go missing and are found tortured and dead. Our elderly are sent to the Senior Resorts and always find their way to the infirmary where an infection forces a lost lung or a kidney, sometimes even worse, they take the heart." As she said *infection*, she used her fingers as air quotes. "The reeducation camps are the worst, a host of abuses and perversions of your worst nightmare." Ann's tone was dead serious. Kip knew she felt every word she said.

"We are part of a resistance," Ell added. "We're trying to expose the corruption and the abuses. Those in power fear us, and they'll do anything to expose and convict us. To shut us down."

"I'm not saying you're wrong, but why haven't I heard any of this?"

Ann leaned forward, and for the first time, she appeared angry. "Because they control everything, the media, all industry, including the food we consume, the water we drink, the drugs we take, even how we fuck. We're only fed that which they want us to eat, both literally and metaphorically."

Kip studied her face; her passion was real. He believed her. "Why come to me?" Kip asked. "My question in the bar was innocent."

"Because of what I saw upstairs, what you did at the Cleansing, and because Tik sent you here. You have a moral center. You're also honest and tough. And, with Tik out of commission for a while, we need somebody who's connected to the Elites," Ann said.

"I was an Elite. Not after yesterday."

"This is a long-term game we're playing. You want to get your status back, right?"

"Of course, and my job."

"In time, we can help with that."

"And why the focus on Sky and Blu?"

"Just shaking the tree, see if any apples fall. This is a high-stakes game we're in. We like to check out who you're connected with as well, especially partners. If we find anything, we'll let you know."

"Last question. How does Tik fit into all this?"

"He's a mutual friend and longtime supporter of our cause. I'm confident he sent you here because he suspected you had the same leanings. I think he was right," Ann answered.

"We're the ones who arranged for his kidney transplant. We're doing what we can for him," Ell added.

"Thank you for that. We haven't always seen eye to eye, but he's always been fair to me."

"What's it going to be? You interested in helping?" Ann asked.

"That depends," Kip said. "But say I wanted to, what would be next?"

"There is no 'next' right now, we just met. We'll do our homework, wait, and see what happens, and then figure out where you can help," Ell said.

"Meanwhile, do what you can to get your social score up. Having Elite status would be a big bonus. And if you need anything, I mean anything while you're settling in Pubtown, let us know. Lastly, we'll keep an eye out for you," Ann added. "You won't know we're there, but we will be."

"And if I want to contact you?"

"Use Trase at your house to deliver the message, and we'll get back with you as soon as we can."

"Trase? I would've never guessed."

"We're everywhere." Ell gave a grin.

Kip picked up his pint of Ooze, raising it in a toast. "Here's to being everywhere."

Ann and Ell lifted their glasses to join him.

After taking a big draught, he placed the glass down and said, "Wow, that tastes horrible."

His two hosts laughed before Ell added, "It grows on you."

Kip peeked at his watch. It was well past time to get going, and he didn't want Sky to worry. "I'm sorry, I've got to go. I'm moving tomorrow."

"We understand and hope you'll understand if Jun takes you out the same way you came in," Ell said.

"Don't speak of this meeting to anyone. Especially if you care about them. The leaders will use any method to extract information. By sharing, you put them at risk," Ann said.

"No one will know. That's a promise. Thanks for an interesting day."

"Watch your back," Ell said while standing.

Jun entered the room as if summoned. He pulled out the blindfold, then repeated the process with Kip until they were safe in the alley, where he bid his goodbye. Kip hurried to the bus stop, and, once safely on board, video-called Sky.

"There you are. I was worried," she said, her face beaming.

"I'm sorry; got delayed in transit, then delayed down here. You name it, I was delayed. How are you?"

"Great. It was a good day. Teaching at the school was fine, class behaved." She paused. "I love my kids, especially little Bug. She means everything to me."

"Bug . . . is that her name?"

109

"Yes, she loves ladybugs, so when she was able to choose her name, Bug was the perfect fit."

A nurturing warmth stirred in Kip. Sky's passion was truly contagious. "I can't wait to hear more about little Bug and your classes."

"When will I see you tonight?" Sky asked.

"About that—it's going to be a tough night. I need to do some packing for tomorrow. How about I catch you tomorrow afternoon, late?"

"Um, how about I come to your place, and we do that packing together? That's what partners should do, help each other."

Kip thought about her words and his feeling of isolation while with Blu. "Where have you been my whole life?"

"Where have you been?" she responded, a sweet kindness in her voice. "Be safe coming home. They still haven't captured Rock."

Chapter 11
Monday, January 7, 2075

Kip finished unloading the last of his items into his new Pubtown home. The clock on the wall read 10:45 a.m. Late morning, with still plenty of daytime left. Fortunately, there weren't that many boxes, as most possessions belonged to the house, thus the State. Beyond some clothing, some food, and miscellaneous household things, the move was routine and easy. As he finished putting away his cleaning supplies, a knock came to his door.

"Who is it?" he called.

"Trase. I'm here to welcome you in." Her morning voice was even more raspy.

Kip opened the door. The diminutive landlord stood smiling on his doorstep, a bottle in her hand.

"It's official, you're in. Welcome to the neighborhood." She extended her arm, offering the bottle. "Here's a housewarming gift."

"Thank you, that's very kind." He studied the dark bottle; an old cork stopper was lodged in its top. "What is it?"

"It's a bottle of fortified Ooze. A mutual friend said you'd like it . . . a lot. I don't know why. Stuff tastes awful," Trase answered.

Kip chuckled to himself. "There may be some exaggeration there. I found it tolerable." He examined the bottle. "But again, thank you. I'll tolerate this tonight." He placed it in his tiny refrigerator.

"Are you on your way out?" she asked.

"Yep, heading to work. Some stuff to check on there."

"You may want to stop on your way out and pick up another bottle of this yourself." She winked. "In case you're feeling wild and go through more than one bottle tonight."

Kip understood. "That's a good idea. Even if I don't drink it all tonight, better to have too much than too little."

"Good then. I'll see you later," she said, walking away.

Kip left, locking his door behind him, wondering if the lock really made a difference in this neighborhood. He made his way to The Tavern, this time entering confidently. Ann stood behind the bar; Ell sat on a stool in front of her. There were no other customers. Kip walked to the seat next to them and sat. Ann instinctively poured him a short Ooze, sliding it in front of him.

"Thought we were rid of you," Ell said.

"Just wanted to stop in and say I'm sorry for any problems I may have caused." He sipped the Ooze, grimacing.

"Not accepted," Ell shot back.

Ann walked over. "I think we can let things go," she said.

Ell slid in next to him, a little too close in Kip's opinion.

Ell flipped on the humming device that blocked the AST and whispered, "Just listen. We checked out Sky. She's a third-grade teacher and, at first view, appears clean. We found nothing in her job, her finances are next. Blu and Pinc are questions. They're friends with some people who we think are dirty. One of them is TF. Do not trust him, he's compromised. Thought you should know."

Ann leaned in. "Also, Tik had surgery this morning, and as of right now he's doing fine. In recovery as we speak."

Kip gave an unfocused nod about Tik, his heart fluttering due to Ell's feedback on Sky. "Thank you both."

"Nothing for you to do yet, so have a good day." Ell finished and moved to his old stool. Once there, he clicked off the AST blocker.

Kip took one sip of Ooze, then exited with a quick nod to Ann. "Much appreciated."

As Kip walked to the bus stop, his video phone rang, the name "Sky" flashing on its face. He pressed the button, answering, "Hey, this is a surprise."

"I know, I'm sorry to bother you. How was the move?" Her characteristic energy was missing, and she seemed distracted.

"Fine, in fact, pretty easy. How's class?"

113

"Okay so far, but I only have a minute. I was wondering if we could meet?"

"Sure, when? I'm at the zoo until five o'clock or so."

"The zoo is perfect; I'll be there at three o'clock. Meet me at the lion exhibit."

Kip was caught off guard. The zoo? He assumed she meant meeting after work at the bar for a drink or the dispensary for some Meds. "Yeah, that's fine. I'll be there." He continued, "Is everything okay? You seem a little stressed."

She glanced away. "Oh, it's just the kids today. And I'm sorry, I've got to go." She hung up.

He stared at his phone for a long moment, expecting a call back or a text. None came. File that under unexpected, maybe even weird. He hoped all was okay for her.

Kip pushed those thoughts away by the pleasant surprise that travel to work was smoother than he expected. Even the timing was not as bad as he thought it would be. When he arrived, Citizen Qu, Tik's current boss and the previous head of operations for the zoo, was waiting for him. He was an older man with gentle eyes and an easy smile. His thin muscular build gave the appearance of someone much younger.

"How was your move?" Qu asked.

"Good. Not keen on my location, but all in all, the move went well." Kip straightened his shirt, knowing he was going out to the public side of the zoo. "And how are things with the animals? I got here as soon as I could."

"Thanks for that. Pretty good shape, most of the pens have been serviced and cleaned. I have Jen with the monkeys now and Tom feeding the bears. He was over the top about that."

"Yes, he likes his bears." Kip chuckled. "I'll go take care of the lions?"

"Yes, that was the plan." Qu's face tensed. "Two things. First, off the record, I'm sorry about what happened. And I wish you the best. You've always been a good worker."

"Thanks Qu, I believe in times like this with one door closing, another door always opens. I just have to find it."

"If anybody can, it's you." Qu checked his phone. "All confirmed." He said to himself. "The second thing is Citizen One will be here today. Not an official visit, just wants to walk the zoo like an equal Citizen. So be on your toes and look good, and you may even earn some credits back."

"Wow, Citizen One. That sounds good, thanks for the heads up. I better go and take care of those lions then." He stepped over to his desk and searched the drawer for his key. It wasn't there. "Hey Qu, my electronic key is gone."

"It is? Probably Tik. Knowing you're leaving he gave it to Tom or maybe Jen. Here, take mine, and don't forget to give it back. I'll need it to close tonight."

"Thanks, I definitely will."

115

Kip made double time to the lion's pen. Once there, he corralled them into the back cages, using some fabricated mystery meat that smelled of raw flesh as a lure. He put the lions' medicine inside the steak, centered it in a wide metal container, then slid the container in through the feeding slot. Within seconds, he heard the lapping of their sandpaper-like tongues working the meat. With them occupied, he cleaned their enclosure, including draining and refilling their drinking water tub. By the time he had completed the work, Leo had long finished his meal and now batted at a knotted rope. Sinbad and Anastasia were happily sunning themselves. He opened the back cages, allowing them to roam free in their savannah-like enclosure facing the zoo patrons. Leo stopped on his way through as if to say hi. Kip stepped near the cage, "Hi buddy, I'm going to be leaving soon. Wish I could take you with me. Let you run free." The lion's yellow eyes followed him. "They're going to take real good care of you. And I'll come back and visit. I promise." Leo answered with a muted roar, almost as if in recognition.

Time was getting short before Sky arrived. Kip cleaned up in the locker room as much as he could, remembering Blu's statement about Tik and his smell. As he finished dressing, Jen came in to do the same. She appeared excited. "I heard Citizen One is in the park, just strolling the grounds. He's with Citizen Eight. They may want me to show them the monkeys."

Kip froze. "Did you say Citizen Eight?"

"Yeah, why?

"He's the ass—I mean . . . judge who cited me, forcing me to lose my house and this job. Not my favorite person at the moment."

"Maybe best to avoid him."

"Best to avoid them both. After my actions at the Punishment, it's unlikely that Citizen One is a fan." He ran his fingers through his long hair, staring in the mirror. "Not as good as a comb, but it'll have to do. Hopefully Sky won't notice."

"You're very handsome. She's lucky to have you," Jen said.

"Thank you for saying that. I don't feel that way as of late." Kip glanced over. "And good luck to you. Hope you get some face time with Citizen One, maybe even earn some credits."

"I'll be happy if I don't lose any."

"Just relax, you'll be fine." His watch alarm buzzed. "Sorry, I've got to run. Sky should be here."

Jen waved goodbye in response.

It was already three o'clock—Kip was late. He hurried to the lion's enclosure at a near run. As he approached, he saw Sky on a bench, scanning the area. He waved, but she was focused on something behind him, so he made an exaggerated signal with his hand. Seeing him at last, she waved back. Her brow furrowed.

"Hey, thanks for coming by," Kip said, breathing heavily and sliding in next to her on the bench.

"No, thank you for meeting me." She scanned the area again before locking in on his eyes.

"You okay? Something seems wrong and frankly, you look nervous."

"I'm fine." Her tone was short.

"You sure? While meeting me at work is fine, it seems urgent, versus just talking at home tonight."

She started to answer, but as she did, Citizen One and Citizen Eight came around the corner up the walking path. They walked casually, chatting as friends do. A handful of Citizens surrounded them, taking pictures, along with some groupies who just wanted to be close. Two Security Force guards walked several yards behind. Rage was nowhere to be seen.

Citizen One glanced over to Kip and gave a polite nod but showed no evidence of recognition from their meeting at the Punishment.

Sky's eyes never left them as they walked by. After they passed and the crowd faded with them, she grabbed Kip's hand, a stress in her voice. "Usually, I wouldn't bother you here, but there's something I need to tell you and it can't wait."

"Sure, no secrets between us. We'll figure it out together."

Her eyes started misting as he finished these words. "You are such a good person. Which makes this harder."

He squeezed her hand. "What is it?"

"Just know, I've never felt the way I feel about you. But I haven't been honest, and I want to start over."

Kip watched her lips quiver; she was on the verge of tears.

At that moment, a woman just up the path and out of view screamed, "No!"

A man's voice followed with, "He's attacked Citizen Eight!"

A jumble of cries followed. "Stop him!" "He's escaping!" "Help, security!"

Kip stood and started toward the screams. As he did, a brown-skinned man with long black hair sprinted past him. The man brushed his shoulder, dodging the other visitors, almost knocking him down as he made his escape. From the fleeting view Kip had, it appeared to be Rock.

Nirvana security chased him. They blew past Kip, lasers drawn. He then heard the familiar whine of the drones from above. Forgetting about Sky for the moment, he instinctively went after them, knowing he could help.

He sprinted down the path, jumping a fence that bifurcated the park, trying to cut off the savage at the entrance, his most likely escape point. Rushing through the monkey house, he exited the other side into an isolated feed storage area, arriving just as a member of the Security Force cornered the fugitive against a fence, his laser raised at the Savage's head. Kip only had a glimpse at Rock, but he appeared shaken and scared, a far cry from the stoic man in the ring. Rock raised his shaking hands in surrender. The security guard fired a laser blast. The energy pulse exploded into Rock's face, blowing his head off. The decapitated torso fell, thumping onto the ground.

"What the fuck!" Kip reacted.

The Security Force Officer pointed his weapon at him. "Don't move!" The officer reached down, patting the victim's body, appearing to search for weapons. He removed a bloody knife and stuck the blade in the ground. He then removed something unseen from the dead savage's pocket.

As a team from the Security Force arrived, the officer who shot Rock stepped to Kip. "I'm Security Officer Finne," he said while holding a small electronic device near Kip's head, assumably evaluating his health. Once finished, he commented, "You're fine." The officer then pushed Kip in the shoulder. "Come with me," he ordered.

Chapter 12

Kip wondered if he was being escorted voluntarily or forcibly marched. The Security Officer's hand was locked in a vise grip on his arm, pulling him back to the scene of the crime. Officer Finne refused to provide any comment except for, "Keep moving."

For his part, Kip wasn't too worried. His firsthand view of the events could help the investigation and possibly earn him some much-needed credits. He was pushed past the bench where he and Sky talked. She stood, hand covering her mouth, tears rolling down her cheeks. Kip mouthed the word "go," to her.

She seemed to shake her head in a "no" motion as he passed.

When Kip arrived at the scene, Citizen One was seated on a bench, blood covering his silky clothes. On the ground nearby, Citizen Eight's body lay mostly covered by a sheet. A man in a doctor's uniform had lifted the end of the covering and was examining the hidden corpse. All other Citizens had been removed from the area except for a few new Security Officers, a Security Droid, and Qu. A moment later, Sky was escorted to the group, a Security Officer by her side. The Security Droid opened his compartment, exposing the video screen, where a judge in purple robes came into focus. His name, "Citizen Thirty-Five," shown on the screen below him.

Citizen One spoke. "Citizen Eight was a great leader and, more importantly, my friend. We will not rest until we root out those who were involved in this conspiracy to murder me. By the grace of Nirvana, the savage missed me. Sadly, his aim was lethal to Citizen Eight." He focused on Officer Finne holding Kip. "Where's the savage?"

"He's dead. He came at me with the knife. I had no choice but to shoot him."

"No, he didn't!" Kip shot back. "I was there, I saw it. He had his hands up."

"Kip," Sky said, subtly shaking her head, her eyes begging him to stop.

Citizen One stood and walked to Kip, studying him. "I know you. You're the one from the Games. The one who refused to punish Rock. What's your name, and why are you here?"

"I'm Kip, and I work here."

"You work here? How convenient. And did you know Citizen Eight?"

Kip hesitated to answer.

"What are you hiding?" Citizen One asked. "We'll find out. No stone will be unturned."

Kip knew an answer from him would be better than none, "He just ruled on my case. He penalized me twenty social score credits and one hundred bank credits for breaking curfew with an illegal weapon."

"And why were you out with a weapon, breaking a curfew that's in place for your own safety?"

"Because somebody tried to break into my house. I was protecting my partner."

"And who tried to break into your house?"

Kip glared at Citizen One. "You know who."

"I don't know who, and please answer for the record."

"It was Rock, the savage."

"And what happened when Citizen Eight penalized you?"

Kip seethed, "I lost my house and my job."

"And did that make you angry? I mean, you seem pretty angry now."

"No, I didn't agree with it, but I was determined to make up for it."

Citizen One spoke to Sky. "You must be his partner. What's your name?"

"Sky," she whispered.

"It's okay, you're safe, dear. Do you remember the event in question? The break in."

Sky gave a reluctant nod, her hands visibly trembling.

"And what did Kip say in response to Citizen Eight's penalty?"

Sky hesitated, reluctant to answer.

Kip recalled the night, his anger, and his words. "Sky don't lie! Tell the truth, don't get in trouble for me! They have it."

"It's okay, dear. What did he say?" Citizen One prodded.

Sky was barely audible, her voice cracked, tears running down her face. "He said he hoped Citizen Eight got what was coming to him."

Silence hit. Kip burned inside, his rage seething just below the surface.

Citizen One was the first to speak. "So let me summarize. The man you didn't punish, who came to your house for an unknown reason, just killed the man who punished you, forcing you to lose your house, your job, and possibly even your partner. Maybe I need to rethink these events. Maybe Citizen Eight was the target." He thought for a moment, considering the sequence. "No, the savage came for me first. You were trying to get us both, two birds with one stone, I think the saying goes."

"No," Kip shot back. "Check my implant; I was working at the lions' pen and then with Sky. When I saw Rock running, I tried to help capture him. You'll see it, you'll hear it in my thoughts." He was starting to panic.

"You're right," Citizen One responded. "The whole reason we have AST is for times like this." He motioned to Officer Finne. "Please, let's see what's on it."

Finne removed his metallic device and held it to Kip's head. He scrolled the video, holding it so Citizen One could see. Nothing. Only static filled the screen. He continued scrolling through the full five hours—nothing showed.

Citizen One stepped to Kip, studying him. "How did you do that? How did you erase your video?"

"I—I didn't," Kip stammered. It then hit him like a bolt of lightning. He rushed Officer Finne, grabbing him. "He did it! Back when he shot Rock, he scanned my head. He erased my video so you wouldn't see him shoot an unarmed man! Arrest him!"

A second Security Officer pulled Kip away, and the two cuffed his hands.

"Is this the truth?" Citizen One asked Officer Finne.

"No. Not a shred of truth to it," he answered. "Check my implant."

Citizen One took the machine and held it to the officer's temple. He watched the video which backtracked through the events there, the walk from the enclosure, and then the shooting. It showed Rock attacking Finne with a knife. And while there was a short blurring of the video, there was no evidence of the officer holding anything to Kip's head to erase his implant.

Citizen One addressed the screen in the security droid, "Your Honor, given the evidence we've seen, I would ask conviction and sentencing to Pine Mountain Maximum Security Prison until this animal can be put to death."

The judge made a note, then returned his eyes to the screen. "This is all very troubling. Citizen Eight was my mentor, my friend. He will be missed as a beacon of law and order for this city. While I see motive and opportunity with this young man, I don't see any direct evidence of his involvement and, unfortunately, the assailant is dead."

Officer Finne stepped forward. "Sir, I found this on the savage." He handed Citizen One a small black device. Citizen One held it between his two fingers. "What is this?"

Qu stepped in, examining it. "That's Kip's electronic key for the zoo."

"It was found on the savage?" Citizen One reemphasized.

"It was."

"I haven't seen that for two days, ask him." Kip motioned to Qu with his head. "I told him earlier today."

"Well, earlier today he mentioned it was missing," Qu said. "That can be confirmed, the conversation is on my implant video."

"It's obvious he staged that." Citizen One clenched his jaw, his frustration showing, "Isn't this proof enough? How much more do we need, Your Honor?"

The judge considered the question. "The key could have been stolen; it's all circumstantial. You need direct evidence he gave it to Rock or was some other part of the conspiracy. Go and talk to people, check the AST system top to bottom, build your case. Give me something more airtight and you'll have your conviction and death penalty. I'll give you six months to do it, otherwise I'll be forced to let him go." He then focused on Kip. "Young man, I abhor what I believe you've done. The only thing keeping me from sending you to Pine Mountain is the law, which we abide by at all times. Given your actions, however, I can send you to reeducation. I hereby remand JU450625 to Elysian Fields Reeducation Center. All your social score credits and bank credits are frozen, your partnership is dissolved, and your housing forfeited until such time we revisit these charges. You are canceled from civilized society until this matter is resolved."

Sky gasped, "No!"

Kip faced her, his heart breaking. "Wait for me," he whispered.

Citizen One grimaced as he said, "The Law has spoken."

Chapter 13
Tuesday, January 8, 2075

The fortified bus bounced along the broken country road. Kip sat, rocking back and forth, electronically chained to the unkept man sitting next to him. A good ten years older than Kip, the man hadn't shaved or bathed in weeks, his pungent smell having a nauseating effect. In an odd twist, Kip was now eagerly anticipating arriving at Elysian Fields.

As his mind wandered, Kip's thoughts returned to Sky and the events that unfolded at the zoo. After sentencing, she was escorted from the area with Qu holding her. He'd always remember the confusion and sadness in her eyes as she walked away. Would he see her again, or would that be the final memory of what was the most intimate relationship of his life?

The answer to that question relied entirely on the resolution to his deteriorating situation. The Security Force wasted no time in collecting him, despite technically not being under arrest. His "detention" for reeducation meant the State had similar rights for his restraint and control as prison but not for implementing corporal punishment. Post zoo, he was immediately taken to a group holding cell in an underground bunker-type building where he remained cuffed, despite the other nine detainees being allowed to move freely. The barred, concrete area had four metal benches, a single common toilet, and a water fountain for the detainees' hydration and dehydration needs. Just outside the cell, multiple video screens faced the group. The jailers played a constant stream of State propaganda videos, highlighting all the benefits Nirvana provided. The start of his reeducation had begun. Kip ignored them as best he could.

An officer came to the cell around five p.m. and served a sealed portion of Green to each person. Kip ate alone on the last seat of a bench. A couple of the other detainees tried speaking with him, particularly a young bald man, the last to arrive in the cell, who made repeated attempts. Kip was polite, but kept his interactions short, deciding it was best to keep to himself.

At night, the group sprawled out to sleep where they could. It was cramped, cold, and awkward at best. Kip didn't get much rest.

This morning, after a similar breakfast of Green, they processed individuals in a terse exchange, which included a DNA sample before being put on this bus. Kip suspected it wasn't an accident that he was seated next to who he was.

He swiveled his head, glancing at his co-guests also being sent to Elysian. That was the euphemism they used for the prisoners of reeducation; they were "guests" for enlightenment. He noted the mix of both men and women, most appeared haggard and all in need of a shower. Once again, Kip observed the individual who had engaged him in the cell, staring at him. Of medium build and height, he had a shaven head, a muscular physique, and a feral vibe. Kip refocused his gaze forward—best not to send messages, one way or the other.

They continued driving for a few more hours, approaching the border of the Outer Boundary and the edge of Nirvana's territory. The farther they traveled, the more inhospitable the terrain became. The landscape went from a greenish meadow and woodlands to a barren, desert-like red rock formation, complete with bluffs and canyons. And if possible, the road appeared to transition with the landscape, transforming from bad to miserable. Although still technically paved, the sun's heat and winter's cold created heaves that shook the bus and sent Kip bouncing into his aromatic seatmate.

When they finally arrived, Kip felt sick. Between the motion and the smell, he knew that a few more minutes locked in there and his Green would have come up.

They pulled through a chain-linked fence gate with barbed wire curled at the top and into a large prison-like enclosure with rows of barracks. The area the bus parked was paved but most of the ground inside the fence was just brown dirt and finely crushed rock.

The guests unloaded from the bus and filed into a single line. A solitary guard in full police riot garb guided them out, pushing them forward. Only a few of the new guests were restrained, the others had free use of their hands and legs. A slick, electric SUV with blacked-out windows and off-road tires was parked yards from the bus.

Once everyone had exited the bus, the guard ordered, "Face forward, stand straight, and pay attention!"

A nondescript man with a scruff for a beard gave a low chuckle to the bald man who had tried interacting with Kip earlier. Kip couldn't hear their conversation.

But the guard also heard the laugh and stormed toward the bearded man. "Do you think this is funny? Do you? You know what's funny?" He removed a sleek black baton from its holster on his waist. Kip heard a quick whine of the baton powering up. The guard pressed its tip to the man's chest. An electronic buzz discharged, blowing the man back. He hit the bus with a thud before slumping to the ground, a thin stream of liquid oozing from his mouth.

The guard crouched down in the man's face, overexaggerating his words. "Ha, ha, ha, you see now, that's funny! You don't listen and I get to tase you and see you drool." He stood up, face beet red, and walked down the line of guests. The guard shouted, "You're in my home now, and when you're in my house, you'll obey my rules. If you break my rules, there will be consequences." He stopped in front of Kip, his nose an inch away, spittle flying from his mouth as he continued, "Do you want a consequence?"

Kip didn't make eye contact. He stared straight ahead, past the guard. "No, sir." He answered in a firm voice.

"I'm not going to have problems with you, am I? Because if I do, the taser will be the least of your problems. Do you understand me, dirtbag?" the guard said, ice in his voice.

Kip continued his stare forward. "No sir, I'm here to learn."

The guard glared for an overexaggerated moment. "That's too bad. I was hoping to get acquainted with you." He stepped back, making his way down the line. "I'm Security Officer Mace. You may call me Security Officer, Officer, or Sir. Do not use my name. Do not make eye contact. You respect me or there will be consequences. I am not your friend. I am your teacher. Is that clear?"

Some in the group answered, "Yes, sir." Others remained silent.

"When I ask you a question, you answer me!" He repeated the question. "Is that clear?"

In unison, the group yelled, "Yes, sir!"

"We'll make something of you ingrates yet." He motioned to the blacked-out vehicle. The rear door opened. A slim man with angular features emerged. He wore a black uniform with an emblem of a small eagle on his chest. He had black polished paramilitary boots and while walking toward them, put on a black beret with the same eagle emblem.

133

"I am Citizen Fifty, Comandante of Elysian Fields." He spoke in a direct but matter-of-fact tone. "I am the lead educator for your time here. If you listen and do what you're told, you won't have any problems. I'll even say you'll have an enjoyable time learning about the benefits and value you have as a Citizen of Nirvana." He inspected the closest guest to him, then raised his index finger and brushed her cheek. The woman didn't flinch, managing to stare straight ahead. "If you don't," he paused for emphasis, "well, let's just say Officer Mace will enjoy getting to know you." He walked down the row, studying every face as he passed. "Each of you has a story that put you here. That story can be erased and rewritten if you follow our simple rules. Do what you're told, study your lessons, work hard, keep your hands and body to yourself, and tell the truth. That's it, pretty simple really." He stepped to Kip. "Are you the man that conspired with the savage to kill Citizen Eight?"

Kip kept his gaze ahead, past the comandante to the horizon. "I'm the man accused of conspiracy to kill Citizen Eight, but I didn't do it."

The comandante motioned with his hand to Office Mace. Mace stepped forward and hit Kip with the taser wand. A bolt of excruciating pain tore through his torso, forcing him to lose control. Every muscle in his body jerked at the same time, propelling him away from the baton. He hit the ground hard, lights flashing in his mind, chest burning, and lungs paralyzed.

He couldn't breathe, his heart raced, and his body was on fire. He had no idea how long he lay there gasping for air, but slowly and painfully, his motor functions returned until only his chest hurt and his head throbbed.

When he was finally aware, the comandante stood over him, saying, "Tell the truth, it's one of our rules." He spoke to Mace. "Put him in the cage."

Mace smiled. "With pleasure, sir." He leaned down and grabbed Kip by the shirt, pulling him up.

The bald-headed man shouted, "What the fuck? He didn't do anything."

Mace stood up, letting Kip fall. He strode over to the man. "What did you say?" Mace hit him with the wand.

The question was rhetorical as the man could not possibly answer as he flew back then collapsed to the ground.

As both men lay semiconscious, the comandante spoke. "Put them in the cage together."

Chapter 14

At the end of the new guest line, Kip limped into the compound of the barrack-type buildings, his body slowly recovering from the jolt he received outside the bus. There were at least thirty structures in the yard. Each was the same, a windowless bunker with solid black shingled roofs. Made of brownish corrugated metal, he estimated each building ran thirty yards long and half as wide, with doors at each end and one in the middle of the side. The majority of the group was directed right to the closest door. Kip and his newfound acquaintance were both stopped by the guards and sent left to the next structure over. Kip felt uneasy about this selection.

They entered the building through the side door and into a narrow corridor, traveling the few steps to its center where the walkway intersected the main hall that ran the length of the building. The guard pushed them right into the main corridor. On either side of the hall, cage after cage of imprisoned guests for enlightenment were jailed. With at least two guests per cell, the occupants invariably sat or lay on the floor. All the inmates appeared worn and beaten down.

"Look ahead," the guard warned. "Don't go eyeballing the other guests."

Kip did as he was told, not wanting to meet the wand again.

They continued down the row until the guard ordered, "Stop." He stepped in front of Kip to open the door to their new home, a five-by-five cage just tall enough for Kip to stand in with two narrow bunk beds, a drain in the floor and one open toilet. The bunks were little more than sheets of metal that folded up to make room for the occupants. There were two neatly placed thin blankets on the upper bunk.

The gate opened, Kip entered first, his new roommate following immediately behind. They barely fit standing next to one another. Once in, the door clanged closed behind, and a wave of claustrophobia rolled through Kip.

The guard stepped in front of their cross-wired metal doors. "I'm Officer Tak. I run this wing of Elysian. We have a few rules, so listen carefully, as this is your only warning. Failure to obey will result in severe punishment for both of you. We won't differentiate over who did what." Tak's gaze went from Kip to his roommate. "First, you follow all orders, no matter how crazy they sound. If I tell you to jump, you jump. If I tell you to roll in the mud, you roll in the mud. Follow all commands." He paused, ensuring the first rule was understood. "Second, you eat what and when we feed you. There will be no saving for later and no one trades food for favors. Third, when lights go out, so do you. There is no talking after lights-out. See that camera?" He pointed to the corner of the cage. "We're watching and listening. If we have to, we'll pull your video to confirm." He paused, studying them both. "Last, everybody works to support themselves. No freeloaders here. Either at school, at the hospital, in the fields, or in the mine. No exceptions. You're here for reeducation and the fact you're already in isolation means you have one strike against you. Work hard, pay attention, learn, and you can work your way out of here. Nod if you understand me."

Kip nodded; his shaved-headed roommate did as well.

"Good, you have one minute to take off your clothes. Fold them and place them neatly by the slot." He pointed to a small grated flap in the door just above the floor. "You better be naked by the time I get back."

Kip flipped the upper bed vertically, giving them more room. He hung the blankets on the wire frame of the bunk.

"What the bloody hell is he doing?" his new acquaintance asked.

"My guess is prison clothes," Kip answered. "But I don't want to find out the penalty if I'm not naked." He continued removing his shirt.

"Yeah, neither do I." His cellmate started removing his clothing. "By the way, my name is Ben. Guess we're in this together."

"I'm Kip," he answered, taking off his pants and then removing his socks and underwear. He had just finished folding

139

them when Officer Tak returned holding a hose. He collected their clothing, pulling them through the slot and putting them to the side in the hallway.

"You. Move forward to the door," he said, pointing to Kip.

Kip stepped forward, stopping a foot away.

Officer Tak opened the hose, firing its stream on him. The freezing water blast shocked him, temporarily driving away the pain from the wand.

"Arms out," Tak commanded.

Kip complied.

"Turn."

Kip turned, doing what he could to maintain his composure. A single minute seemed like an hour, almost breaking him until finally, he was complete.

"Step back, next guest forward," Tak ordered.

Ben had a less difficult time withstanding the water pressure and temperature. From Kip's view, he appeared to be rigidly disciplined, almost zoning out of his body as the water washed away his metaphorical sins.

Once complete, Tak stepped forward, a blue spotlight held in his hand. "First guest, step forward."

Kip did as he was told. The guard moved the light up and down his body and legs. Once complete, he ordered, "Turn." He repeated the process on his backside. Then ordered, "Switch." He repeated the process with Ben.

Once complete, he put the light out of view and stepped back to the cage. "Use your blankets to clean up the water in this cell. If you do a good job, we'll give you dry blankets. If not, it'll be a cold, wet night. I'll be back in thirty minutes to check on you."

Still naked, the two men dried off first, then went to work drying their cell. The excess water had already run down the center drain, but the side and rear cage bars had water spray all over, not to mention the bunk beds and toilet.

Ben started on the toilet while Kip did the bunks before moving to the walls. Each man worked feverishly to beat the deadline.

"Any idea on the blue light?" Ben asked.

"We should be careful talking; they could scan our thoughts."

"Not here," Ben said, "Too far from the main AST network. They'd need to recreate the whole system. They will scan your implant, though, for cause. So don't give them a reason to."

"Good to know." Kip wiped the spray from the bunk bed. "I'm guessing the blue light's a disinfectant or an anti-lice device, but . . ." He shrugged.

"How about that cold water?" Ben added, almost laughing.

"It was freezing, but you didn't seem too bothered."

"No, I've had much worse," Ben answered.

Although Kip thought that answer was either odd or intriguing, he didn't pursue the conversation. They continued working in silence until Tak returned. By all measures, the cell appeared both dry and immaculate.

"When I tell you to stand, I want you at attention, side by side, in front of this door."

They nodded.

"Stand," Tak ordered.

Both men took their positions in front of the door.

Tak studied the cage from the outside. After a moment of silence, he leaned over and grabbed a bundle of clothing and shoes off the floor. "This is for JU450625." He pushed the bundle through the slot.

He leaned over again. "This is for FB211927. Get dressed. I'll be back in five minutes."

Kip was ecstatic to put on clothes. Between the cold water, damp air, and wet hair, he was chilled to the bone. The clothes provided were thin, dark pants with a small, single pocket, and a pullover shirt of the same material. They included a pair of matching socks and black slip-on shoes with a hard sole. There were no laces, no zippers, and no buttons on any of the material. A single word in large lettering was placed on the shirt: GUEST. Kip dressed quickly, rubbing his hands up and down on his arms and legs for warmth. Ben didn't seem bothered by the cold or the rough amenities.

"I tried to speak with you in the city lockup. You ignored me. Why?" Ben asked.

"Because I didn't know if I could trust you."

"That's good. Keep that attitude. Don't trust anyone. Especially in here. They'll sell you out for a few privileges."

Officer Tak returned promptly. Once more, he opened the slot and slid a single box unit through. "This is for JU450625." He then pushed the second box through. "This is for FB211927."

They stood at attention until Tak ordered, "You have fifteen minutes for dinner. When done, push the closed boxes through the slot." Then he spun and walked away.

Kip was famished. He opened his meal box. His heart sank when he saw the contents—a single crust of stale bread and a small container of Green. A small bottle of water was his drink, and there were no utensils or napkins of any kind. He joked, "A feast for a king."

Ben had already ripped into his Green and was using his fingers to scoop it out. "I've had worse." He said, devouring his bread.

"You've said that a couple of times. How could it have possibly been worse?"

"Was in the Guard, fought in the Wilderness Campaign until they tossed me." Ben took another scoop of Green. "And keep your voice down. They're always listening. Don't make it easy on them."

"Tossed you for what?" Kip's voice was just above a whisper.

Ben studied him as if deciding how much he wanted to share. "Insubordination. It's how I ended up as a guest at the five-star Elysian Fields Resort."

"And that was worse than this?"

"I spent many a night in the open air under subzero conditions, wondering if a person was sneaking into camp to slit my throat. There were other nights with no blankets, no fire, no food. We ate bugs and bark to survive, knowing the next day you were inevitably getting into a firefight with no certainty you'd make it through the day." He shrugged. "You tell me."

"I'm sorry, I had no idea."

"You'd be amazed at what the human body can endure." He leaned over, meeting Kip's eyes. "Listen to these words and own them. To survive hardship, any hardship, you must get your mind right. You got to be tough, prepare for the worst and hope for the best. Recognize it's going to be bad, and it will *hurt*. But know that whatever it is won't kill you. Keep reminding yourself of that whenever you're being tested."

"But what if it does kill you?"

"If for some reason you don't survive, there was no use worrying anyway. You're dead." He gave a wicked grin. "Take the water hose. Cold? Yes. Uncomfortable? Yes. But it's not going to end you. Again, be stronger than what life provides. What doesn't kill you makes you stronger. Remember that too."

Kip finished his Green, licking his fingers, never realizing how good it could taste. "Appreciate the advice." He focused on Ben. "Why'd you do it?"

"Do what?"

Kip leaned in close. "Get thrown in here."

Ben's eyes came up from his Green.

"I don't know you well," Kip continued, "but from my early observations, you're a disciplined man. The water, being in the Guard, the survival tips. You speaking up when they zapped me was sloppy—you knew what they'd do. Being uncharacteristic of a disciplined man, it must've been intentional. You wanted to be in here. Why?"

Ben gave a small nod, impressed. "To protect you from what's coming down." He stood up. "We better get our boxes out. Tak will be back soon."

Kip handed his box over. Ben slid them through one at a time, placing them in neat order before returning to his seat.

A different officer came forward, picked up the two containers, and ordered, "Stand."

The two men complied, moving side by side.

145

The officer surveyed them both. "I'm Facility Officer Finna. Which one of you is JU450625?"

"I am, sir," Kip answered.

"Very good. You both have five minutes to finish any business,"—the officer pointed to the toilet—"then it's lights out. We'll be seeing you at five a.m. sharp. When the alarms go off, you get up and you have one minute to get ready, then stand by your door. When it opens, you file into the hallway. Stay in line, single file. When ordered, you proceed forward. Nod if you understand."

Both men nodded.

Finna started to walk away.

Kip stepped forward. "What about dry blankets?"

Finna came back. "Did I tell you to speak?" He stepped closer. "You will answer when I ask you a question or I tell you to speak. You do not ask questions, you do not speak to me, you do not make eye contact with me. You only answer me. Do you understand?"

"Yes, sir," Kip answered, staring ahead.

"Your penalty for disobedience is wet blankets for the night. Do it again, and it'll be for a week. Enjoy them." He laughed and strode out of sight.

With no hesitation, Ben pulled down his pants and sat on the toilet like he'd done it in public a thousand times before.

"I'm sorry," Kip said, "I had no idea."

"Don't worry about it. He was never going to give us dry blankets. They try to mind-screw you. Remember, always plan for the worst. If it comes out better, that's a bonus."

"I'll be more careful anyway." He fixated on the cell next to them, giving Ben privacy where there was none. "What did you mean to protect me from what's coming?"

"Did you kill Citizen Eight?" he whispered, cupping his mouth from the camera.

"No, definitely not. I was set up."

"Exactly. You were set up, and they tried for a quick death penalty, right?"

"Yes, but they didn't have sufficient evidence, because there isn't any."

"Well, whomever is pulling those strings has you in here now. And I'm betting they're not planning on you walking out. The only way to make his murder go away is to make you go away. Got it?"

Kip considered his words, a heavy pressure building in his chest. "I only have six months and then I'll go free. They won't find anything."

Ben stood and flushed, his voice masked by the running water. "*Always plan for the worst.*" His words were slow and methodical to emphasize them again. Ben pointed for Kip to use the toilet.

Kip squatted. "Why would you help me? I don't know you," he whispered, then stood and flushed.

While the water ran, Ben came close. "Because we have a mutual friend who runs a bar and shares the same beliefs."

He stepped back, jumping on the top bunk. "You're bigger than me, so you get the bottom."

Kip slid into his bed, the cold steel pressing into his back. The ambient dampness of the cell smothered him. With no pillow and no blanket, it would be a long night. It was time to get tough. "One more thing, I met another Security Officer Finne the day I was taken into custody. I wonder if they're related. It could be why he asked about me."

Ben whispered back, "They are twins, thus the same name but ending with *A* and *E*." He rolled, finding Kip over his bunk's edge, exasperation in his eyes. "Always assume the worst."

Good advice, Kip thought, his mind's eye returning to Sky. He wondered where she was and what she was doing. The lights clicked off. Darkness covered the room.

Chapter 15
Wednesday, January 9, 2075

Kip lay awake, cold and uncomfortable. With lights still out and no windows to gauge the night's moon, he was unsure of the time. He had dozed on and off, but restful sleep was a premium that evening and he knew the day would be long. He listened to Ben's rhythmic breathing, envious of his cellmate's ability to block out the cold. There was truth in Ben's words about hardship and the human psyche. All too often, we let a minor setback destroy a promising life or relationship, possibly a career, when in the end, that's just life. No person in the history of the world has escaped tragedy and hardship. But how you respond to such events will define you as a person. You can cave to life's pressures—throw in the towel, rationalize your defeat as you sit in misery, reliving the horrors of the ordeal time and again. Or you can fight every day. Choose to move forward and work your hardest to overcome these inevitable challenges. Then, win or lose, wake up and battle again the next day. Kip would fight. Every day.

His thoughts were interrupted by flashing lights and a siren blaring. He rolled out of bed, slid on his shoes, and moved to the door. Ben was slower out of his bunk but equally efficient in dressing. In under a minute, they stood ready, waiting for the next signal. It came quickly. The door swung open. Kip took two steps to the center hallway. Glancing right, he saw the other guests facing the northernmost door in a single-file line. Kip and Ben mimicked the others.

Kip noted that there appeared to be a full house in the building. Two guests vacated each cell and filed into the line. The two men across the hall slid behind Ben while two women one cell down moved in front of Kip. One by one the cages emptied, crowding the hall. When the shuffling had finished, a single order came through the loudspeaker: "March." They moved in unison, maintaining their distance through the end door and into the cold morning air. The blast hit, causing Kip a full-body shiver.

Expect the worst, he thought to himself as he marched, a reminder to start the day.

The group walked single file between buildings to a structure at the end of the compound. They entered between double doors into a cafeteria-type room. The guests continued one by one past a counter where another prisoner handed out boxes. After receiving his, Kip tracked the line sitting in order. Ben slid in next to him.

Kip observed that no one opened their box until every inmate was served and seated. Once the last inmate sat, a light flashed on the wall, switching to green from red. As if in coordinated fashion, the inmates all opened their boxes and started to eat.

Once more the cuisine was a morning helping of Green and a single slice of bread with a water bottle for drink. No one spoke. Kip opened his meal and ate the bread. When done, he opened the package of Green and tipped the food into his mouth, reluctant to use his fingers. He chewed while stealthily glancing at the tables around him. There were roughly one hundred inmates, split 70 percent men and 30 percent women, which seemed about the right number for the isolation building. Most were thin, appearing sickly. These inmates tended to keep their heads down while eating, hoping the nightmare might go away. A few, like Ben, appeared young and healthy, consuming their food quickly with head held high while watching the propaganda video on flat screens placed around the room. Lastly, more than a few seemed to be predators. The best way Kip could identify them was by the destructive leer in their eye as they studied the people in the room. They were watching for a weakness to exploit.

Kip caught two of these men staring at him. He quickly turned away, only to glance back. Their gaze hadn't shifted. One was tall and unshaven with black hair, wiry features, and dark circles around his eyes. The other was more robust. Thick from head to toe would be a better description, with a round head sitting on a tree trunk-like neck. His short brown hair appeared awkward and out of place for his build. The latter guest continued his stare, finishing with a wink.

Kip looked away, deciding to focus on the video. They were presently playing a montage of historic places in Nirvana, emphasizing the beauty and culture of the city. It was narrated by Citizen One. Most guests ignored the propaganda with its monotonal droning. Those inmates that were paying attention were the ones hoping to get bonus points from the guards. Kip scanned the room and noted that more than a few of the guests were living in their own minds, oblivious that the video was even playing.

With no sure way of knowing, Kip guessed that breakfast lasted twenty-five minutes or so. When complete, the green light flashed back to red, accompanied by that irritating buzzer. Each guest rose by seating position, cleared their area, and filed by the large wastebasket to throw away their trash. They then went to the drop area to return the reusable material. It was all quite efficient.

They walked out of the building and across the compound into a similar structure. On the way, Kip noted a large group of guests milling around on the far side of their enclosure. The group appeared less structured and able to move freely about their area. He refocused on his situation when he was shoved in the back.

"Keep moving," Officer Finna ordered. "You'll never see the general population."

They filed into a large lecture hall, each person taking the next seat available. Once the group was situated, the lights dimmed around them but brightened on the podium in the front of the class. A moment later, a mousy man with wire-rimmed glasses and unkept hair stepped behind the podium.

"Welcome to your morning reeducation. As a reminder, there's no talking and you must pay attention. Failure to do so will mean loss of your daily privileges. Today's topic is social score. What is it? How is it used? And how a good Citizen can optimize theirs."

The lecturer prattled on and on, detailing the social score and its benefits. As he spoke, an officer walked the circumference of the seating area, focusing on the guests. If anybody dare fade from listening, he was there as a reminder to refocus. On two occasions, a male inmate whispered and got caught. In both cases, he was pulled from his chair, shackled, and sent away. The lecturer barely broke cadence as the man was hauled out of his classroom. Kip could only imagine what happened next, so he stayed focused, reminding himself, this is a breeze. Although he didn't agree with social scoring, if tested, it would be an easy A for him.

The class lasted a couple of hours, ending with a question-and-answer session. It was here where the same people watching the video at breakfast asked question after question, trying to earn points out of their isolation. Kip started to rethink the ease of the class, becoming impatient with the idiots and suck-ups. After a brief mandated bathroom break, they thankfully finished.

The group left the building the way they came in. Officer Finna made a single pronouncement. "Time for work."

As Kip walked, it occurred to him that he had been up more than three hours and not said a word. They filed directly into the cargo area of a beaten-up transport carrier with an ever-vigilant armed guard hovering over them. The carrier was designed to move items of war, including soldiers, past the Outer Boundary and into the Wasteland. The vehicle had large knobby wheels, a caged flatbed, and a throaty mechanical growl under the hood. It looked at home in the rugged terrain it now traveled.

Once the guests buckled in, the truck started to roll. It was here that Kip got the best view of Elysian Fields and the surrounding area. Set in the first of a series of connected valleys, the reeducation center was named for the eternal resting spot of the chosen few from Greek mythology. The irony being that it was the opposite of heaven. The camp had a rectangular layout. He estimated that it was a mile long and half as wide, with a heavy-duty fence lining the entire perimeter. The fence structure was a visible deterrent for anyone considering escaping with a thick base of smooth, solid slats tapering to a spiked top with razor coils, at least double the height of any man.

The dirt road on which they now traveled ran parallel to the fence. From his elevated perch, Kip could see the whole of the reeducation area. It was divided into compounds by hardy chain-link fences topped with razor wire coils. From his perspective it appeared there were six compounds with five symmetric ones holding barrack-like structures like the one in which he was housed. He surmised that each compound held a general population and a smaller isolation group.

The sixth and largest area contained a substantial two-story brick building with a sizeable parking area. The lot was half-filled with what assumably were the staff's cars. Ben tapped Kip's leg and nodded toward the structure, making sure Kip saw it. If Kip had to guess, he'd say it was the facility's hospital.

They continued their travels along the perimeter fence, dust from the road kicking up into the wind, until the vehicle stopped at the rear gate. Built with heavy, tempered metal; it had thick rivets and reinforced brackets. It also had spikes projecting from its front, appearing as if built in a medieval horror story. After a quick conversation between driver and guards, the doors slowly swung open, allowing the carrier to leave. As the truck groaned forward into the desolate land, the gates creaked closed behind them.

Once out of the facility, they rolled into a small valley with pale dirt bluffs rising above the road on both sides. These hills were speckled with sizeable black holes, each representing

155

a shaft from the iron ore mining that took place there. Kip had once read that these excavations had been operating for fifty years and ran deep into the mountain. Unfortunately, the veins were thinning and there were rumors of an underground river that flooded the ore-rich lower levels whenever rain fell. With all that said, the camp still sent guests to work there every day, despite the risks and less ore being mined every year.

The vehicle ground past the mines and continued deeper into the harsh territory, over a small rise and into the neighboring valley. As they crested the hill, Kip saw fields of Green, the hybrid between algae and spinach, spanning acre after acre in a much wider and longer basin. Planted in rows hundreds of yards long, the Green flowered low to the ground with new growth replacing the harvested leaves which was used to feed the Citizens of Nirvana. Kip marveled at the size of the operation. There must've been a thousand rows in this quadrant alone.

They drove to a spot at the end of one field, and the truck ground to a stop. Officer Tak was the first out of the cab, making his way to the rear of the truck. He opened its gate and with his wand out entered the caged flatbed housing the prisoners.

"This is for the new people. You work for your food. You don't work, you don't eat. One person per row. Pick mature leaves only, we don't want to kill the plant. You finish your row, you're done for the day. We'll be inspecting. Anyone slacking will be penalized. Anyone trying to escape will be shot on sight.

Know Officer Bon is an expert marksman." He pointed to the burly guard at the rear of the truck holding a laser rifle. "Lastly, keep talk to a minimum. I don't want to hear the sad stories that landed you here." He waved them out. "Okay, that's it, everybody work!"

Kip followed Ben out of the truck. They were each assigned a row. When Kip came to his assigned row, they handed him a sack with a strap to wear on his shoulder.

"Put the leaves in the sack," the guard ordered.

"Yes, sir," Kip answered with his first words of the day.

Chapter 16

Kip watched the others who had already started picking. Most had dropped to their hands and knees and were crawling through the dirt, picking the midsize leaves from the bottom of the stalk, then depositing them into their bag. A few were in a crouch position and one shorter guest just bent from the waist. Given his height, Kip dropped to his knees and began picking. Kip soon realized the physical process numbed the mind. It was all body with no thought required, giving Kip plenty of time to live in his head.

His thoughts returned to Sky and found that she gave him an inner strength and focus. He remembered her sad face on the fateful day at the zoo. What was it she wanted to tell him, to come clean on? He couldn't imagine her hiding anything. She had been so open and giving. But the truth was, he really didn't know her that well. A booted toe jammed into his leg, bringing Kip back to reality.

"What do you think you're doing!" Officer Finna's rough voice commanded. "You're missing half the leaves. Start again, at the beginning, and this time, pick them all."

Kip glanced up, then over at Ben, who was already well in front of him.

"Don't worry about him!" Finna hissed. "You go back and do it right." He finished with a harsh kick into the ground, sending dirt and pebbles into Kip's face.

"Yes, sir," Kip answered. *Expect the worst.*

The rest of the day proceeded in similar fashion. Under sunny skies, Kip would work his way forward, only to be sent back ten to fifteen yards by Finna or some other guard. They weren't going to make it easy. Kip knew they were trying to break his spirit and he wouldn't let them.

The group stopped for a few minutes in the late afternoon for some water and a crust of bread. Kip's hands were raw and his knees bruised from the small rocks on the ground. Ben was dead on. He'd need to get his mind right to do this every day. The break was over all too quickly and he was back picking, his leaf bag slowly filling. Its weight soon became another issue to deal with. He'd pick and drag, pick some more, then drag that heavier bag with him. It was a slow torture.

By early afternoon, most of the inmates were done. Kip and a few others under the glare of the guard's wrath continued. The men who were staring at Kip at breakfast were now finished for the day and began harassing him.

"Hey new guy, want some help?" the thin angular man said.

"Oh wait, we can't. It's against the rules. Meaning we're stuck here waiting for you," the thick man added. "Move that sexy ass. I want to get back."

Tak walked over, hand on his wand. "You guys hunting for trouble?"

The angular man glared at the officer. "No sir, just trying to motivate our young friend here."

"Take your motivation to the back of the wagon and sit quietly," Tak ordered.

The thick man scowled, then grumbled something under his breath. "Going Officer sir," he added.

With the other guests all finished, Kip continued picking, completing his row at least thirty minutes behind Ben and the stragglers. His hands were beyond sore, with broken blisters on most fingers. His back ached, his knees were numb, and he had a metallic taste of dirt in his mouth. He threw his filled bag into a second truck bed that had arrived midday, then climbed into the back of the carrier's flatbed. The only seat available was a spot next to the angular man and across the bed from his thick friend. Ben was three seats over. Kip had no sooner strapped in when the carrier started to roll, rocking those in the bed.

The thin man leered at Kip, then offered a fist. "I'm Ped, and this is Bane." He motioned to his friend across the bed. "We'd like to make your acquaintance."

Kip didn't make eye contact, leaving Ped's fist out there. "That's okay. I have enough friends."

"Are you being rude to Ped, because that would make me very angry," Bane said. "Bump his fist."

Kip ignored him.

Bane leaned over. "Hey new guy, I said bump his fist." Ped's hand extended farther.

Kip leaned close to Bane. He stared him in the eye and whispered. "I wouldn't bump his fist if he was holding my pardon papers."

Bane leaned back, laughing. "Oh, I get it. You off a Citizen Leader and now you're a tough guy." A devilish grin spread across his face. "Yeah, we know. But did you know that tough guys always get what's coming to them?"

Ped leaned closer to Kip. "I was only trying to be neighborly, seeing how you're new here."

Kip closed to within an inch of his face, his eyes lasered on Ped's. "Go fuck yourself, neighbor," he hissed.

Ped leaned back, now sitting upright. "Okay tough guy, you don't want to be friends."

The rest of the ride back was made in a tense silence. Kip didn't care that Bane stared at him the whole time. Ped maintained his distance while Ben watched closely, quietly being jostled in his seat.

When they pulled to the gate and the doors were creaking open, Bane leaned in and whispered, "I'll be seeing you later."

Kip remained silent, not acknowledging the thug with a word or gesture. But a consuming anger welled inside.

The carrier ground to a stop, the back gate swung open, and Kip filed out first. Bane and Ped were right behind. Ben exited a few seconds later.

As they filed into the yard, Tak approached from the cab. "You have thirty minutes of yard time. Make the best of it."

Ben strolled over. "Just a heads up, your two new friends are the muscle in here, so be aware. I was warned in the flatbed while you were still picking." He kept walking, like he was stretching his legs.

Kip surveyed the yard, finding Ped and Bane. They were being reprimanded by Officer Finna. As Finna walked away, Bane brushed the ground with his toe, as if moving a rock. He bent down and picked up something from that spot, cupping it in his hand. He scanned the area for watchers, then strolled away, head slumped down. Ped followed a step behind.

Kip started to walk the fence in the opposite direction of Bane. Ben trailed him by a few yards, both keeping to themselves. Kip was studying the mines on the closest bluff, wondering what it would be like to work underground in the darkness, when he caught a blur out of the corner of his eye. Bane was rushing him.

The bowling ball of a man lunged and slashed at his neck. Kip reacted on instinct, head moving backward, blocking with his arm. The swipe missed its target but nicked his forearm. He could feel the warm ooze. Bane made a second, vicious slash at his face. This time Kip was ready, and he dodged the blade. Bane fell sideways, off balance from the miss. Kip stepped in and kicked, connecting in Bane's groin. The blow landed hard and doubled his assailant over, an audible groan expelling from deep in Bane's chest. Kip moved fast and drove his knee with full force into the thug's face, his nose exploding in blood. The attacker crumpled to the ground.

"Hey!" Ped yelled, rushing toward him.

Kip spun, preparing to fight, but there'd be no need. He watched as Ben cut off the skinny man's path. Ped threw a punch, which Ben blocked easily. His new friend retaliated with a series of punches and elbows that ended with a devastating fist to the throat, Ben's military training evident. Completely overwhelmed, Ped slumped to the ground, unable to breathe, grasping his neck. Ben stepped in and gave a finishing kick to his ribs.

"Fuck you, perv!" Ben hissed.

Officer Tak rushed over. He started to check Bane, but the thug kicked him away. Tak changed tactics and now attempted to restrain him. Bane pulled his hands back from the officer's cuff and elbowed the guard in the face, sending him to the ground. In a frenzy, Bane started pummeling the guard like a crazed animal. He dispensed blow after blow, while screaming some indecipherable words on, "killing him" and "torture." Without thinking, Kip took two steps and launched his full weight and fury into Bane. He struck Bane's head with an elbow, stunning him. Kip pulled the thug off Tak and threw him on his back, then seized the advantage. He wrestled to the top of Bane and then threw haymakers, one after the other. With each blow thrown, Kip could feel his fist hit bone, then teeth, then eyes. Each delivered with a crushing crack. And with each blow landed, his fury rose, a retribution for the injustices served on him repeatedly. He would no longer be bullied by man or the system. Bane had either given up, been knocked out, or was possibly even dead. The only thing definite was his fight was gone. Kip couldn't care less. One more shot was all he needed.

Kip felt a heavy tug on the back of his shirt. It was Ben pulling him off. The guards were now responding.

Officer Finna was the first over. With no hesitation, he hit Kip with his wand. Once again, Kip felt the burn, the pain, and the loss of control seizing his body. Whether it was adrenaline or his body's acclimation to the pain, he never blacked out or lost his mental acuity. Watching Finna stand over him, he physically came back quickly from the shock.

With his wand still drawn, Finna ordered Ben, "On the ground, face down, hands to the back of your head!"

Ben complied without a word. Kip started to roll over, trying to get up from his hands and knees. Finna kicked Kip's hand out from under him, collapsing him back to the ground.

"Stop it!" Tak yelled.

Kip rolled his head, eyes moving to the sound. Tak was now up, his face swollen and bloody. Kip got to his knees again. This time, Tak grabbed him under his arm and helped him to his feet.

Using his radio, an arriving guard called for medics for both Ped and Bane. In under a minute, two gurneys were there, loaded and carting the men away toward the large brick building.

"You. Stand," Tak ordered Ben, who was still on his knees.

He complied.

Tak held the small blade used by Bane between his fingers. "Where'd this come from?"

Kip's eye darted to Finna, then reengaged with Tak's. "I—I don't know for sure, sir. Bane came at me with it. I was lucky to dodge it." Kip had trouble getting the words out.

Ben added, "For god's sake, examine his arm. He got cut in the first slash, then he settled it. He was defending himself."

Finna stepped in. He pulled his wand again and put it in Ben's chest. "You shut up." He then moved the wand to Kip. "I think he's lying, sir. No way he's still standing if Bane had a blade. Let me get to the truth."

166

Tak pressed his hand in Finna's chest, sending the message to back off Kip. Tak then stepped forward, taking Kip's injured arm, rotating it to examine the bloody wound. After a moment, he refocused his attention on Officer Finna. "I'll take this man to the infirmary. You get the other guests to dinner and into their cells."

Finna glared for a moment, jaw clenched. Then answered through gritted teeth, "Yes, sir." He holstered his wand and pointed to Ben, "You're not injured, you're with me. Move it, scumbag."

Tak waited for the other guards to leave. He gently moved Kip's arms behind his back and restrained them with nylon cuffs. He spoke in a gentle tone. "I'm going to say this once. Thank you for what you did. He would have killed me."

"No problem, sir."

Tak studied his face for a moment. "This doesn't mean we're friends, it doesn't mean I like you, and it doesn't mean I owe you one." He paused, starting to escort Kip forward, "What it means is I believe your story about the blade and will get to the bottom of it."

"Thank you, sir."

"No need to thank me. It's my job." Tak gripped Kip's arm. "One last question," he said. "Earlier, you said you couldn't be sure where the blade came from. What's your guess?"

"It wasn't forged here, meaning it was brought in by someone with access." Kip's eyes met Tak's.

"And?"

"And I'd start with Officer Finna."

Chapter 17

Under the setting sun, they walked side by side to the large brick building. Kip could see that Officer Tak was struggling. With his adrenaline wearing off, the full extent of the guard's injuries was coming to bear. Tak's face was now swollen with two black eyes forming, and he spit blood for most of the walk.

With the front door in sight, Tak started to wobble. Kip leaned in. "Cut me free. I'll get you inside. I promise I won't do anything."

Tak met his eyes. Kip could see he was fading. "Okay, but I'm trusting you."

Kip rotated, providing Tak access to his bound hands. The officer removed his knife and cut the nylon bands, almost falling over in the process. With his hands now free, Kip grabbed the knife from Tak's limp hand and slipped it into his own pocket. Then he slid under the guard's arm, allowing him to lean on his shoulder. He wrapped his bloody arm around the man's waist and started supporting him to the door. By the time they entered the building, Tak was barely conscious, and Kip was pretty much carrying him.

They started down a nondescript hall. The building interior was white with bright lights and miscellaneous equipment stored along the hallway walls. An antiseptic smell wafted throughout the area. The corridor ran the length of the building, with multiple rooms on either side and security cameras strategically placed on the walls. All doors were closed, ensuring the secrecy of the procedures happening within. Kip followed the main hall, crossing an intersection that led to another wing.

He stopped at the first orderly he came to. "Do you have a gurney or wheelchair? This guard needs help."

The orderly hopped up, pressed a button, and a buzzing sound filled the room. "Yeah, hold one second." He grabbed the nearest chair and slid it under Tak. "Put him here. I'll grab a gurney."

A few seconds later, a doctor in a white lab coat entered the room. He rushed over to Tak. "What happened?"

"He was attacked by a guest," Kip answered. "Got beaten bad. His condition deteriorated on the way here and is totally out of it now."

Tak spoke in a low voice, clear he was struggling, "I'm okay . . . just a little dizzy."

The doctor pulled down Tak's lower eyelid and shined a light into his eye. "Were you part of the fight that injured the two guys that just came in?"

"We were," Kip answered.

The orderly returned with a gurney. He and Kip helped Tak onto it.

The doctor saw Kip's bloody arm. "What happened to you?" He grabbed Kip's hand, rotating the arm to better examine the wound. "You're going to need stitches. But I'll get to you last. The other two guys are in bad shape. And the officer here most likely has a concussion." The doctor motioned to the orderly. "Can you clean his arm, then put a wrap on it? Try to stem the bleeding until I can get to him."

"Of course, Doctor." The orderly put his hand on Kip's back, guiding him away.

"Hold it," Tak said. "He needs to be secured until he's treated and then transferred back."

"Of course, we have a secure wing here," the doctor answered while connecting wires to Tak's chest. "Although our officers are tied up with the two guests who came in earlier."

"He's not a high risk," Tak said, barely above a whisper.

"Okay, secure him in room 3 in the Alpha wing," the doctor said, as he read Tak's blood pressure. "The guy in there is restrained and hasn't said a word since he arrived. Bind this guest's good hand to the bed bracket. I'll get to him as soon as I can." He spoke to Kip, "Be patient, I'll be there ASAP."

The doctor wheeled Tak away.

"This way please," the orderly said, taking a step forward. "And I'll ask you to behave. There are guards on their way over now."

"If I wanted to cause problems, I could have left him out there," Kip said.

As he finished, they passed an unconscious prisoner lying on a gurney with his smock open, a newly stitched incision on his right side. He was chained to his rolling bed, an IV drip attached to his arm. There was a chart attached to the foot of the bed that read "Kidney Infection." The orderly paused to check the patient's pulse before continuing.

"I know, I noted that. And your help will be reported. But I feel like I have to say it, if only to remind you." The orderly stopped, flashing his ID card in front of a black sensor mounted on the heavy metal door. The sensor light blinked and the lock popped. He opened the door and held it for Kip. Once through, he slammed it shut behind them, waiting for the lock to reset. They walked down to room 3, where the same process was repeated. They entered a double room with two small beds and a dresser holding medical equipment splitting the two. The curtains were partially drawn around the far bed, with the shaded image of a patient resting clearly visible.

"I'm going to bind your good arm to the bedframe bracket."

Kip offered the orderly his good arm.

He gently took Kip's wrist, looping the nylon over it, then attached the other end into the fastener before pulling the nylon taunt. "I'm sorry to do this, but they have a rule for everything. We need to follow them."

Kip said, "I understand."

"Okay, let's see that cut."

The orderly put on gloves, pulled out some disinfectant, and wiped the wound. In the big scheme of things, Kip had gotten lucky. The slice ran a few inches long, but the depth was shallow, missing the heavy muscle and bone.

"Oh yeah, this will require more than just a few stitches, and you'll probably have a scar. But fortunate for you, it's not deep. You'll heal fine."

Once sterile, he wrapped the arm, then cleaned up the waste. "It'll be a few minutes before the doctor gets to see you. That short guy is in bad shape; he may not make it. So, relax, lie down if you want and be patient. There's some water on the counter if you want a drink and a bottle under the bed if you have to urinate."

Kip nodded.

"Alright, I'm going to leave you then until the doctor is ready." He gave one last pull on the nylon cuff, then exited through the heavy metal door. Once closed, Kip heard the lock click in. He sat on the edge of the bed, taking stock of his body. All things considered, after a day in the fields, being hit by the wand, and a fight for his life, he felt well. His hands were sore, and his arm burned, but otherwise he was okay. He started to think about Ben, what happened to him after he left with Finna. His thoughts were interrupted by the person in the other bed pulling back the separating screen. Their eyes met, and Kip saw the light of recognition in his new roommate's face.

Kip didn't recognize him immediately. With dark skin, shaved black head stubble and a lean frame, the only thing that seemed familiar were his dark eyes. Kip slid out of bed and took a step toward the man. Studying his face, he tried to place him. When it came, it hit hard. It was Rock from the arena pit. But how could it be? That man was dead.

He inched even closer. The man just stared, saying nothing.

Kip reached out and grasped the man's shirt. He did not flinch as Kip raised his shirt sleeve. It was there, the unusual tattoo band Kip saw on the man in the pit—the savage.

"You're the man named Rock, from the pit. You refused to kill a man for others' entertainment."

"I am, and you're the gentle soul who would not harm an innocent stranger to entertain the mob. Thank you for what you did. It took great courage. What is your name?"

"I'm Kip . . . well, my friends call me Kip. To the State, I'm JU450625," he answered awkwardly. "I'm sorry, but how are you here? I saw you die by a laser blast at the zoo."

Rock shook his head. "Smoke and mirrors from your leaders. I've been in custody since my victory at the pit."

"But you escaped the hospital. You came to my house. You killed Citizen Eight. I saw it all."

"You saw what they wanted you to see. They killed me off publicly so they can do this privately. But fate has brought us together so you can know the truth." Rock tugged on his cuffs fastened to the bed. "I have been locked away, first in the city for a few hours and then in solitary confinement at Elysian Fields. They just moved me to this hospital and keep me cuffed to this bed."

Kip felt lightheaded from the news, the lies, the manipulation. *How deep does it go?* His thoughts immediately went to Sky. Was she okay?

"We have to get you out of here. You're proof that they're lying. That I had nothing to do with the death of Citizen Eight."

"There's no escaping. And I'm scheduled for a kidney infection any day now."

"What does that mean?"

"It means the operators here are harvesting prisoner organs, and I'm about to be the next donor."

"How do you know?"

"It's an open secret they like to torment me with. And a profitable business they sell to the Elites." He gestured to his large frame shackled to a hospital bed. "I hate to say it, but in all likelihood, this is a glimpse of your future."

"All the more reason to get out of this place."

Rock raised his cuffed arm. "We have these, the locks on the doors, and about thirty guards to get past. How?"

"I don't know yet, but can you move? I mean, like get up and run?"

"Yes, I've chosen to not play their games, but I'm fine. What are you thinking?"

Kip reached into his pocket and pulled out Tak's knife. "I'm thinking I can get us out of these cuffs, but haven't figured out the rest."

Rock smiled. "I have the rest of the plan that, even if it fails, ensures you'll be safe."

Chapter 18

The lock clicked and the door swung open. The orderly walked in with a pleasant enough smile, barely glancing at the silent patient in the next bed.

He approached Kip, who lay resting in his bed. "How's the arm? The doctor says he has fifteen more minutes, then he'll be ready for you."

Kip waited to answer until the door closed and the lock clicked shut. "The arm is okay, but would you mind examining it again? It kind of burns."

"Sure, let's see what's going—"

Rock's hand covered his mouth, the knife's blade at his throat.

"I'm so sorry. He took me off guard!" Kip pretended.

The orderly raised his hands, mumbling through Rock's suffocating grip, "Let's everybody calm down. There's no damage done. . . ."

Rock slid his arm around the man's neck and started to squeeze. The orderly flailed, trying to break his grasp. His head soon slouched, his eyes rolling back.

Kip started to freak out. "Is he dead? Did you just kill him?"

Rock laid the body out on the floor and started to undress him. "Get out of the bed. We need to strap him down."

Kip rolled off the mattress. "Why did you do that? He was a good guy."

"First, he's not dead, he's just unconscious. And second, this nice guy is one of the people who was going to remove my kidney. He traffics human organs for money. So, forgive me if I don't share your sentiments."

Kip had no response. Who was the real savage here?

Rock finished dressing in the hospital garb. They put the orderly in Kip's bed and tied him to the bedframe, securing both hands and then gagging his mouth. He covered him with a sheet. "This will buy us more time."

He snapped up the orderly's ID card and attached it to his belt. "Turn around," Rock ordered.

Kip complied. "What are you doing?"

"Plausible deniability." Rock loosely attached a set of cuffs around his wrists. He grabbed Kip's arm like he was escorting a prisoner. In the hospital scrubs and a stethoscope-like gauge placed around his neck, he appeared every bit the medical worker. "If things go bad, you claim I forced you."

Using the orderly's badge, Rock unlocked the door and walked out, Kip by his side. They proceeded, unnoticed, past multiple guards and hospital workers, then through the security door and into the main hospital area. They were well on their way to a quiet escape when the ER doctor, reading an electronic chart, came hurrying around the corner, almost bumping into Kip. "What are you doing? I want you in room 3 of the Alpha wing." He turned to Rock. "Who are you? And where is Orderly Gan?"

"I'm on the cleaning crew. Gan had an emergency, asked me to take the guest to room 3. Guess I wasn't paying attention," Rock answered.

"Let me see your badge," the doctor ordered.

Rock held up the badge, his finger covering the picture.

The doctor leaned in to read it. "That's Gan's badge!" he blurted. "Guards!" He lurched forward, trying to grab him.

Rock pushed the doctor's hands away and swung, connecting clean on his chin. Kip could hear the punch's crack and watched as the man collapsed, hitting the tile floor with a slap.

Rock grabbed Kip's arm, hurrying him through the corridor. The exit door was in sight but still a dangerous ways away.

They were running down the hall when a familiar guard emerged. Officer Finna ordered, "Stop!" then pointed his laser weapon and pushed the trigger button. A red light blasted from the gun barrel. Kip dove, the flash splitting him from Rock's side but missing them both. The wall behind them exploded, spraying brick like tiny missiles.

Rock tumbled away, rolling to his knees. He threw the small knife at Finna. The blade hit with precision and lodged in the officer's right shoulder. Rock rushed the stunned guard, sweeping his legs and sending Finna to the ground. His laser weapon clattered away on the floor.

With catlike reflexes, the savage scooped up the rifle and sprinted for the door. Kip slid his hands from his bindings, running right behind.

They burst through the exit and into the night air. Sirens were blaring, and a small army of guards assembled behind them. Kip recognized the parking area for staff and guards.

"This way!" he urged, sprinting to the first truck he saw, a heavy-duty emergency vehicle suited for all-terrain use. He hopped in the driver's seat.

"What's your plan?" Rock asked.

"I drive, you shoot is all I have right now!" Kip snapped, firing up the engine.

He pressed a button, putting the vehicle into drive, then hit the gas. As the truck shot forward, he watched in the side mirror as the doors to the hospital flew open and a platoon of guards surged out. A bandaged but lucent Tak emerged in the front, Finna by his side. They aimed, then, without hesitation, discharged their lasers.

The rear of the truck exploded in a fireball. Kip slammed the accelerator harder, trying to keep the flames behind them.

Rock leaned out the window and fired back, sending the guards scurrying for cover and buying them a little more time.

Kip sped down the main road toward the rear gate they had used earlier in the day. Word of their escape had obviously spread—occasionally a guard stepped forward from the shadows, firing their weapon to try to stop the vehicle. Kip kept his head low and his foot down, the incoming laser blasts just missing the cab protecting them. Rock showed no fear. Leaning out the window, he returned fire with a hair-trigger, forcing the attackers back into hiding. Kip glanced in his mirror. A swarm of vehicles with flashing lights were now behind them and gaining.

He scanned forward. The prison's rear gate was coming up ahead. The gate guards had taken defensive positions and were waiting for the truck with weapons ready. Kip knew he couldn't break through the fortified structure he'd seen that morning. There was only one choice. "Scatter the guards on the right side, then blast the wall," Kip said.

Rock came in close, his eyes wild with anticipation. "On it!"

Kip shifted gears and floored the accelerator again. The vehicle responded with a gravelly roar, then lurched forward.

Rock fired at the windshield, shattering it, then leaned back and kicked it out. They were now clear for forward fire.

Kip grabbed his seat belt. "Buckle up. It's going to get rough!" Rock did the same.

They approached the gate at top speed. Rock laid down a barrage of fire any invading force would have been proud of. The guard's defensive positions were lit up with fireball after fireball, destroying their cover and most likely their lives. The guards remaining in the battle responded where they could, but hitting a moving vehicle at top speed under a withering laser assault was not in their skill set.

Kip stayed low in his seat, eyes forward, foot firmly on the gas. Rock started blasting the wall. Twenty yards from the gate, as Kip watched the guards evacuate their positions, he veered the wheel right.

"Hold on!" He screamed as the truck carried its full momentum and plowed into the reenforced fence. They hit with a devastating crunch, lurching Kip forward only to be snapped back by the belt, almost breaking his shoulder in the process. The truck punched through the barrier, its tires getting hung up for a moment on the residual standing base, but then the rear wheels caught, and they shot through the punched hole and sped into the desert landscape.

A round of laser blasts from the reassembling guards followed them out. A few landed in the bed area with a thunderous impact.

"We're not clear. They're opening the gates," Rock said, his eyes fixed on the side mirror.

Kip did the same and saw the swarm of flashing lights leaving the compound and speeding after them. He spun the wheel and drove off-road, heading for the nearest cliffs.

"What are you doing? The bluff's impassable. There's no escape there," Rock said.

"We'll lose them in the mines. We just need to get there."

The off-road heaving jostled something under the hood that ended with a loud bang. The truck's engine started grinding. The crash through the gate had taken its toll. The chase cars were now in the open at top speed, their gap closing quickly. Kip plowed through the rough terrain to the base of the hills, the grinding noise getting progressively louder, until the truck finally seized to a halt.

Kip snapped off his belt and jumped out. "Let's go, this is going to be close!" He sprinted for the steep hill.

Rock raced behind him, pushing him to move faster. They reached the rise and began the climb toward the lowest mine entrance, about thirty yards up. As they scrambled through the rocky terrain, the chase cars were now skidding to a halt near their abandoned truck. The officers sprung from their cars, giving chase on foot. A few laser blasts hit nearby, exploding into the dirt and just missing Kip's feet.

He pushed harder, legs burning and lungs searing as he churned through the breaking dirt underfoot. Kip was now at the mine's entrance. He offered a hand to Rock, who grabbed it and tugged himself up. Once safe in the mine's mouth, Rock twisted and lit up the hillside with his laser. From Kip's perspective, it appeared Rock intentionally missed, keeping his return fire close enough to not wound, but to send a strong message: stay back. The guards dove to the ground at first, but eventually had to slide down the hill and take cover behind their vehicles, away from the terrifying assault.

The two men rushed into the mine shaft. Just behind them, laser blasts from below exploded into the rock walls. They entered a circular tunnel that was illuminated by the moon's light, the shadows soon fading to complete darkness the farther they progressed. The shaft had a beamed roof barely over Kip's head, holding the weight above, and it ran deep into the bluff's hard rock. The floor was a sandy stone covering hard rock, the perfect recipe for a misstep or twisted ankle. Kip led as they stepped with care, moving forward at a steady pace.

"Careful in front. There could be a shaft down that's not boarded," Rock whispered.

They were well into the tunnel when the grading shifted down. Kip swiveled to inform Rock of the shift, but saw the glimmer of light reflecting off the wall.

"The guards are in the tunnel," he whispered.

"We have to get off the main shaft and into the depths of the mine," Rock answered.

Kip couldn't have agreed more. He took a few more steps, then stopped as the first branch off the tunnel appeared. Kip took a deep breath. The air seemed stale; there was no movement.

"I'm guessing a dead end. Keep going," Kip said.

"The lights are getting closer," Rock answered.

"I know, so keep moving," Kip shot back. "We'll get off this shaft."

Kip pushed onward as fast as he could. They came to a second branch heading up, and the air seemed cooler and less stagnant.

Kip made the call. "This way."

In the distance behind them, a voice echoed, "You two take this shaft."

With one hand on the wall, Kip made his way up the smaller tunnel. It seemed to have crested and now graded gently downward. The lights behind them faded behind this peak.

As he continued, something besides the scuff of boots and Rock's breathing became audible—the echo of rushing water. Having no choice but to trust the mine engineer who built this place, he pushed forward, faster, feeling his way through the darkness.

A drop of moisture hit his face. He stopped. "I think there's a river here."

Rock's brow furrowed. "We're too high up, no way."

A light flashed just behind them; the guards were closing.

185

"We need to move," Rock hissed.

Rock strode forward with fearless abandon, passing Kip and taking the lead. He progressed a few yards into the darkness when he tripped, the stumble sending him down. Kip watched helplessly as the shadowy figure of Rock slid down a steeply inclined floor. Rock grabbed at the tunnel walls in an attempt to stop his momentum, but there was nothing to hold. He disappeared from Kip's sight, descending into a black hole.

All Kip could hear was the word "No!" then silence and what sounded like a distant splash. At that moment, a beam lit up Kip. He spun to see the source, but the light blinded him.

"Freeze where you are. You have a laser pointed at your head." It was Officer Tak's voice.

Kip raised his hands, not able to see anything but the spotlight and the shadowy outline of Tak's head.

"I don't know everything that's going on, but nothing fatal has happened yet. I'm imploring you to come back with me now and sort it all out. Before it's too late. That includes what happened in Nirvana. I'm guessing there's more to your story." Tak inched forward.

"I can't. I won't survive to clear my name. You saw what happened in the yard."

"I did, I saw it," Tak said, his voice calm. "I'll protect you; you'll be safe. You have my word."

"You don't get it. You can't protect me! This goes all the way up to Citizen One. Just back off and let me do this my way."

"You know I can't do that! I can't let you go."

"Tak, listen to me. That man I'm with supposedly killed Citizen Eight and then was killed by an Officer Finne in Nirvana. He's my proof I'm not part of anything, and that it was all a setup. Give me a few days. If I'm wrong, I'll turn myself in." He peeked over his shoulder at the black hole Rock went into. "But if I'm right, Nirvana itself may fall."

"I can't do that," Tak commanded.

"You have no choice." Kip twisted and leaped as Tak's laser blast sailed over his head, collapsing the ceiling above. He plunged into the black hole, rocks cascading all around him. He slid down the rock face like a giant slide, picking up speed the farther he fell. He bounced a few times. He scrambled to grip something, with no luck. He was moving too fast. In absolute blackness, he slid, bouncing off slick rock, skin scraping and hands clawing for any hold. Until the ground ended and he tumbled into a free fall. He twisted in the air, afraid of what he would land on. An agonizing second later, it came with a slap. An icy chill encased him as he spun in the water, his mind shrieking from the cold. He couldn't breathe even if he wanted to, as the black water held his body. Collecting his wits, he kicked to what he thought was up. Fortune was with him, and his head burst through the water's surface.

He bobbed up and down, thrashing back and forth, clearing his head. He tried to calm himself. A moment later, he succeeded in relaxing, easing his strokes while breathing in the air, cherishing every breath. He rotated in the black water, trying to get his bearing, but found no identifying marker in the darkness.

He heard Rock's voice. "This way, this way! Hurry!"

He focused on Rock's voice and began swimming toward it. Kip did a few more strokes when something in the black water brushed his leg.

"Quick, there's something in the water," Rock urged from the shore.

Kip swam faster. Whatever it was seemed agitated as the surface started to swirl and bubble. His hands hit ground. He started to crawl onto the mucky land when a slimy tentacle gripped his leg, pulling him back toward the black lake. He clawed at the beast, trying to peal its grip from his leg. This only seemed to make the creature angrier as multiple arms surged from the water.

They started to wrap around him when Rock fired from his laser. The first blast hit the limb holding Kip, and the rest of the flashes rocketed into the water, hammering at the black blob just below the surface. The creature screeched, almost bursting Kip's eardrums as the sound echoed through the chamber. Whatever it was released him, sinking below the surface to avoid the weapon. Kip scrambled onto the muddy shore, crawling over the driftwood and debris that lined the water.

Rock offered him a hand as he passed a particularly large tangle of branches and wood that had washed onto the sandy riverbank. They hurried away from the water. Once a safe distance on shore, they stood in the darkness, watching the bubbling black river. They could just discern the thick arms of the creature when it slapped the water's surface, then disappeared.

Chapter 19

"What the hell was that?" Rock asked.

Still breathing hard, Kip answered between gasps, "If I was a betting man, I'd say a pretty damn old octopus."

"A what? How would that get here?"

Kip took a deep breath before answering. "Historians say that after the uprisings, the zoo was emptied and lots of animals escaped to the wild. My bet is that this big guy somehow got into the river system, managed to survive in the freshwater, and found his way down here. It's been sheltered with no natural predators and feeding on whatever floats by. Including me."

Rock's eyes narrowed. "It's unnatural. Let's get out of here before it decides to evolve onto land."

"Go where and how? It's pitch black and we have no light. The only way I know is following the river out. It must flow into the Cascade." Kip wiped the dripping water from his face. "But that creature is in there. There's no way."

"We can't just stay put. The soldiers will eventually find us—plus we need food and water." Rock squatted, using his hands to probe around on the ground. "One problem at a time; first let's get some light."

Rock felt his way closer to the river, grabbing dry wood and leaves piled in the shoreline debris that they had just crawled through. There were ample quantities. After a few moments, his arms were more than full. He stepped back to Kip and higher ground, piling the material in a campfire fashion.

"Step back, this could go up quick."

Rock adjusted his laser settings to the lowest energy pulse. He then shot two blasts into the heart of the dry material. To Kip's great surprise and delight, a small fire sparked immediately. The kindling smoldered with a small orange glow. Rock dropped to a knee and blew the embers into flames.

"Excellent," Kip said.

With the area now illuminated, they quickly gathered wood and leaves and piled them on. Soon, a bonfire blazed, the light dancing high off the walls of the cavern.

Kip heard a slap and saw ripples in the water. He stepped farther away from the pool, not knowing if the newfound light would attract the creature from its dark domain. He walked toward the outer edge of the cavern to search for a way out and found two possible choices. One tunnel appeared more promising, looking as if the ground had been packed from foot travel. The other was higher off the ground and the floor was less worn.

Rock busied himself with finding an appropriate limb for a torch. He ripped a wet sleeve off his shirt, squeezed it dry, then

192

tied it in a tight bundle around the top of the sturdy wooden branch. He repeated the process with his other sleeve, making a second one. "Kip, tear up your shirt to build some torches. We don't know how long it'll take to get out of here and can't lose the light."

Kip returned to just outside the fire and began ripping his shirtsleeves.

"There are two possible ways out," he said. "We need to get a flame over there to choose the right one."

"That's good. We need to keep moving. They'll keep hunting for us and will eventually find their way down here."

"Hopefully they have to cross the river and with this guy waiting . . ."

When they finished making the torches, Rock lit one of his, holding it high. Its bright flame worked to perfection and revealed a sandy ground transitioning to a reddish hard stone the farther he walked from the river. Kip followed him, staying close behind.

Rock traveled the path to where Kip had just searched. Bringing the torch down, he studied the ground leading into the tunnels. "There are signs of some foot travel, although not recent." He crouched down and touched the base of the open shaft. "But this doesn't appear to be a mining cut, looks to be a natural fissure."

"So not created by the guys chasing us. That's good."

Rock took a step toward the other potential shaft. Kip grabbed his shoulder, stopping him in place. The two watched as five glistening black arms the size of small trees slid silently from the water, each tentacle writhing toward the fire. The giant black mass controlling the arms broke the water's surface and slithered onto shore, into the morass of rocks and wood. The creature was an ill-defined hulk with a dark, oily sheen to its skin. It heaved itself forward, wriggling toward the light, and stopped when it was within reach of the flames. With a single swing of a trunk-like tentacle, it smacked at the fire, spraying the wood and embers high into the air while making an ear-piercing screech.

In less than a second, the main light in the cavern extinguished. The only glow remaining came from Rock's torch. They continued to watch as the leviathan slithered farther out of the water, past the shore debris, toward them and Rock's light. It seemed eerily adept at land travel, its tentacles darting back and forth, searching for obstacles in its quest for the remaining light source.

Kip didn't hesitate. "Let's stay with this tunnel."

Rock held up his torch, the light fading into the blackness ahead. "I don't think we have much choice."

Rock took the lead and plunged forward, Kip staying close behind.

The shaft they traveled ran uneven and was not worked stone. With no other signs of construction, such as the support braces typically seen in a mining tunnel, Kip was confident in Rock's speculation that this was a natural fissure. This created some problems walking. Although the path graded slightly down, the gap between floor and ceiling narrowed and widened, making navigation difficult. At times, Kip had to crouch, or worse. After crawling at one point to squeeze through a pinch point, his mind started racing. What if they were heading deeper into the mountain to another cavern, with another unknown creature intent on their demise? Even worse, what if the tunnel led to a dead end? With no way out, eventually the torches would burn, and they'd be stuck in complete darkness with only their sense of touch to navigate. Having no food and water, how long could they inch their way forward? Three days, maybe four? His head hurt, and a heavy feeling weighed on his chest.

Rock stopped. "Are you okay?"

"Yeah, why?"

"Because I'm feeling negative energy." He held the light up so Kip could see his face. "Keep your thoughts positive. We'll find our way out. Negative energy never helps, it only hurts."

"How did you know? You can actually feel my energy?" Kip asked.

Rock studied his face. "You've been civilized; you need to leave that city and its programming." He started forward again. "We'll discuss this when we're clear of the mines."

They traveled in silence for what seemed an eternity. Kip did his part to keep his mind right, believing in his soul they would get out. Rock had to light his second and then third torch, indicating time's passage and their methodical progress. But ever since Kip's stay at Elysian Fields, his wristband had been taken, leaving him no connection with the outside world, including information as trivial as the exact time.

Kip stayed close, watching Rock's backside and adjusting based on his step. They continued through the winding path, which at times appeared as a natural fracture in the rock and at other times to be hewn, albeit not with mining tools. When the third torch started flickering, Kip handed Rock the fourth and final one. "This is it."

Rock held the last torch to the dying flame. It didn't spark.

Given the diminishing light, a suffocating black gloom started creeping in around them. Kip scanned the tunnel ahead, staring for a long moment. It appeared less dark. Not like sunlight, but the ambient darkness seemed grayer. He tapped Rock on the shoulder. "Keep at that. Once it's lit, come join me. I'm going to check something out ahead."

As Kip walked away, Rock said, "Don't go too far. I don't need you falling down another shaft."

Unsure if Rock was joking or serious, Kip ignored the comment and continued creeping forward, hand on the tunnel wall guiding him onward. He rounded a small bend. Although

196

the path continued in front of him, the right wall of the tunnel abruptly ended and opened to a giant cavern blanketed in a soft moonlight shining through a crease in the ceiling. The path hung like a balcony, halfway between the larger cave's ceiling and floor. Kip peered out. In the soft light, he could see rudimentary shelters scattered on the floor and the orange glow of fires emanating from within.

He rushed back into the tunnel. He stopped Rock, who was holding the burning torch. "There're people here. Put it out."

"Too risky. Once it's out, it'll be difficult to relight."

"Trust me on this one."

Rock bit his lower lip, considering the options. "Hold this and stay here." He handed Kip the torch and crept forward, much like Kip had done, until he reached the edge. He stood motionless, peering down on the village from the perch, then appeared to study the path ahead. A moment later, he returned.

"It's still chancy. The path reenters a tunnel on the other side. We don't know what that section will bring."

"But if we bring the torch out, we'll highlight we're here and we don't know their disposition to strangers showing up in their hidden town," Kip said.

"Don't be afraid of the unknown. Yes, there is a risk, but trust that goodness will show itself."

"Not a question of goodness showing itself, it's not revealing yourself until you have to. To be able to make a better decision on whether they're friendly or hostile," Kip added. "We can always try and light the torch again if needed."

Rock considered the argument. "Okay, I will acquiesce for now."

He dropped the torch, covering the flame with the sandy rock on the floor. The tunnel fell into darkness. They stood for a moment, eyes adjusting to the diminished light.

"I'll lead," Kip said, moving forward. "This was my idea."

The two continued down the path, through the overlook section. It narrowed and only one person could pass through at a time. Kip found himself hugging the wall, staying clear of the path's ledge and a certain plummet down. Once past this choke point, the tunnel expanded to the widest they'd seen. Kip maintained a slow but steady speed, eyes down on the trail but one hand always on the wall guiding him. Although dark, it wasn't the black they'd encounter by the lake. It felt more like nighttime, with his vision being limited to a short distance. They walked this way for minutes when Kip saw a stair below his feet. The step was roughly hewn from the rock. He crouched, peering down into the darkness, and could see a second step directly below. One by one, they paced down a total of thirteen stairs— Kip counted them as he went—until they reached a small flat landing area. He stopped. Rock came up from behind.

In front of them was a narrow ravine, maybe fifteen feet wide. Scanning down, he could only see the ledge wall for a little way and then black. Crossing the ravine were two thinly braided ropes, one situated a few feet below the other. Kip found the rope's anchors on this side. They were attached to the bedrock by what appeared to be metal eyehooks crafted by skillful human hands. He picked up a small stone off the floor and dropped it into the ravine. It fell for more than a few seconds, then plinked in what sounded like water.

"Maybe the drainage from the river," he whispered.

Rock nodded, then motioned that he would go over the rope bridge first.

Strapping the blaster over his shoulder, Rock pulled on the upper line, gauging its tightness, then stepped on the lower one. He went no more than a step out, testing his weight. It all held fine. He shimmied forward, hands gripped apart, feet sliding together then spreading on the lower rope. On two occasions, he leaned backward, then overcompensated his weight forward, practically flipping himself over. At both times, he eventually righted himself, finally stepping onto the far landing area. He motioned for Kip to follow.

Kip gingerly stepped on the line, grasping the upper rope with a viselike grip, then slid forward. He made slow and methodical progress, thinking, *This isn't too bad*, when he hit the halfway point and the maximum flex of the rope. There he started to waggle back to front, then front to back, trying to balance. His heavier frame created more of a problem. He had just righted himself, settling his equilibrium, when the lower rope snapped. His feet plummeted with the broken cord. Luckily his hands were locked on the upper one. He jerked hard, almost losing his grip, then started bouncing up and down, his heart pounding under the risk that the single rope wouldn't hold. He dangled this way, swaying for a few seconds, all the while trying to stay silent. Once the motion began settling, he let go with his back hand and swung it forward, gripping the rope in front of him. He continued this monkey swing until he neared the landing. Rock reached out and grabbed his torn shirt, pulling him in. Kip clutched his arms as his feet hit solid rock. He gave a loud exhale of relief.

Rock raised his finger to his lips, requesting silence. Kip held his breath, listening for any sounds or noises. None came. A moment later, Rock released him, a grin on his face. Relieved, he gave Kip a light slap to his back.

With Rock leading, they started down the path again and navigated another set of narrow stairs. Kip noticed that with each step taken, the shadows lightened and the tunnel became more illuminated. He was about to warn Rock when they moved around a slight bend that exited into a small cave-like room with a sandy floor. Standing in front of them was a skinny man holding a torch high and an archaic pistol in his other hand. Its barrel was aimed directly at them.

Chapter 20

The diminutive man appeared shaky, his gun twitching back and forth. He had pale skin and a scraggy beard, and his thin face emphasized his large eyes. He stood in his matted clothes, blocking their way.

"Why you here?" the stranger asked in a broken, guttural tone.

Kip raised his hands slowly, no sudden movements.

Standing closer to the man, Rock answered. "We're lost in the caves and finding our way out."

"We mean you no harm," Kip added.

"You with bad men who dig in mountain?"

Rock shook his head. "No, we're not with them. We're not like them."

The man stared, his gun still pointed at Rock's chest. "You fight them?"

Rock hesitated. "We do. We were running from them when we fell in the black lake at the end of this trail."

The smaller man smiled. "You survive lake monster. . . ."

"Just barely," Kip added.

"You great warriors?"

Rock held his hands up in a calming fashion. "Please put your gun down. We're only trying to get out."

"Torg will let great warriors pass." He began walking in the direction they were heading, sliding the gun into his belt, his torch lighting the way.

"Is that your name? Torg?"

"We talk later," the man said, striding forward.

The three walked single file, continuing down the path at a brisk pace. Kip heard a rock tumble behind him. He twisted his head to see another man, like Torg, carrying a rifle and following a few paces behind. The farther down the path they traveled, the more men came from their hiding spots to escort them. Each had a similar build and all carried weapons of various types. Some had spears, some had clubs, a few held old guns, and at least one held a newer laser weapon. Kip wondered where they had been hiding and how long they'd been following. Did they watch him break the rope over the cavern? Were they waiting for him to fall?

They continued down the winding path until the tunnel opened onto the floor of the large cavern they had seen from the ledge above. The group had traveled into the heart of the village.

Kip could now discern the houses were little more than shacks made from whatever material the builders could find. Mostly stone, there was also wood in the form of trees and boards, and even some sheet metal. Given their location inside the cave, where rain was not an issue, the roofs were little more than branch coverings. One by one, Torg's warriors peeled off. Torg kept going, leading Rock and Kip to the largest of the shelters. They entered it through an open portal with a wolf skin for the door.

He motioned to the two men. "Sit. We eat, drink, and talk."

Kip studied the sizeable room. In one corner a fire burned in a stone pit, and in the other, what he assumed was a family huddled together, caring for a sickly woman lying in a bed of straw and covered with furs. The elder woman of the caregivers rose and walked over.

She had petite features with the same large eyes as Torg and a wiry build with graying black hair. She stared at Rock and nodded, then repeated the greeting with Kip.

"This is Jenja, my mate," Torg said.

Jenja gave another small bow to her guests, then shifted to Torg.

Torg addressed her in a gentle voice in a language Kip did not understand. "*To grat esin, dris forn parge es frin tage.*"

"*Ba,*" she answered and walked away.

"Wait here. Torg back soon." He stood, not waiting for an answer, and stepped to the bed. There he clasped the hand of the sickly woman. He pressed the back of his free hand on her forehead and held it there a moment. He leaned over and kissed the woman's cheek. She didn't respond.

Kip watched as he comforted her—tucking the furs in tight to her shoulders and caressing her cheek with his hand. It was a caring he was unaccustomed to. In Nirvana, people were treated by the city-run clinics, isolated and alone. The only aspect more antiseptic than the medical process was the emotion of it all, or better said, lack of emotion. Even partners didn't usually attend medical treatments, just the patient and only an actual human doctor if the computer robotics could not attend to the ailment.

Torg returned, shoulders slumped, a furrow in his brow.

"What's wrong with the woman?" Rock asked.

Torg slowly shook his head. "Hot for two days now. Why unknown."

"May I examine her? I used to care for my people," Rock asked.

Torg hesitated, as if considering the prudence of granting the request. Warily, he gave a small nod. "*Ba.*"

Rock moved to the group, taking a moment to examine the sick woman's face and eyes. He moved the blanket around and examined her petite arms and legs. He stopped to focus on a small swollen scratch on her shin. "How long has this been here?"

Torg whispered something in his language to the group huddled around the woman. All shook their heads or said "*Na.*"

He spoke to Rock. "Unknown, maybe a few days. Why, only small scratch?"

"This redness is bad. It means an infection has entered the bloodstream. She will likely die if not treated. Do you have salt and cottonwood bark?"

Torg's eyes narrowed, giving Rock an inquisitive look. "Yes, both."

"Pack the wound with salt. It'll draw out the source of the infection. Crush a small amount of the bark and mix it with water. Then, force her to drink it. There's a substance that grows on the inside of the bark, a mold that will fight the infection in her blood. Keep treating her until she gets better, or . . ." His voice faded away.

Torg studied Rock's face. "*Ba*, I will try your medicine."

Jenja returned carrying three mugs of brown liquid and a hunk of crusty bread. She placed the mugs on the table and placed the bread in front of Torg.

Torg spoke softly to her in their unusual language. Kip couldn't hear what was said, but she nodded, "*Ba*," then rushed off.

Torg returned to the table, taking his seat. "Sit. Now we drink."

Finished with his triage, Rock sat as well.

Kip watched as Jenja returned with a bundle and began Rock's recommended treatment. Torg said, "Drink." Torg took a

205

deep draught from the liquid, then watched for Rock and Kip to follow.

Rock complied immediately, drinking from the mug. If it had any taste, you couldn't tell from his reaction.

Kip followed likewise, taking a gulp of the liquid. He swallowed hard, forcing it down, almost gagging in the process. The bitter liquor tasted hardened, and the singe of strong alcohol burned his throat. As unlikely as it was, the drink was far worse than the Ooze at The Tavern.

Torg laughed. "You no like Torg's brew?"

"No, I just wasn't expecting it." Kip took a smaller sip, hoping to prove his ability to ingest the liquor. Rock did the same.

"What you names?"

"Rock." Rock tapped on his chest, then pointed to Kip. "Kip."

"Rock, Kip, good. What happened with you and mountain diggers?" Torg got right to the point.

"We were held by them and fled. They chased us into the mines. In making our escape, we fell down a shaft and into the black lake. I made it out. The creature attacked Kip."

"I got lucky. He used the blaster to break the creature's grip." Kip pointed to the weapon.

Torg touched the gun on the table, then eyed Rock. "Mountain digger's weapon."

"I took it from a guard during my escape. I am not a mountain digger."

"Then who you?" He motioned to both.

"We were prisoners and escaped from their jail," Kip stated, feeling honesty was the best approach now.

"Why you prisoners?"

Kip motioned to Rock to answer.

"I was the leader of my tribe, the Omasus, in what the mountain diggers call the Wastelands. We've been at war with Nirvana since my people escaped during the uprisings. Now, they hunt us. They come to our lands to kill our women and children." Rock gripped his drink in anger. "We fought back, raiding their fortress, winning a great battle and killing the commander of their army. In retribution, they slaughtered most of my village, then hunted me down. They butchered my soldiers, but took me as a prisoner for their Games."

"You . . . you Rock of legend? I hear of you from many travelers." With a closed fist he pounded his chest. "You welcome here, always," Torg said, then shifted his focus to Kip. "Why you prisoner?"

Kip thought for a moment. "I am accused of helping Rock kill a leader of Nirvana. I didn't, and he can confirm he didn't kill anyone." He motioned to Rock. "He wasn't there when it happened."

"Then why they claim this?" Torg held a skeptical stare, his eyes studying Kip.

"Revenge, I think. I was set up by Citizen One for refusing to punish Rock at the end of their Games." Kip took a sip of his drink.

Rock nodded his agreement. "I agree. You embarrassed Citizen One."

Torg studied Kip for a moment longer. Seeming to accept the story, he took a draught, then broke off a piece of the crusty bread. "You eat."

Kip waited for Rock, who broke off a small chunk. "Thank you for the bread. I am hungry." He took a bite, then after swallowing continued, "Torg, how long have your people been here?"

Torg finished chewing and took another gulp. "After great uprising, we escaped, wandered Outer Boundary until we find Arapi, our home." He held up his hands, palms to the sky. "We safe. Our nation grow until mountain diggers come. They take from us, hunt us, kill our people. We hide in caves then fight back, kill invaders, and take their weapons." He fingered his archaic revolver, then smiled at Rock. "They avoid Torg's people now."

Rock raised his glass in a toast to Torg's pronouncement. "Here's to evading the mountain diggers." All three men drank in response.

As Kip placed his glass down, Jenja approached. She stopped in front of Torg. *"Tsin guto di quntin."* She said with a hint of excitement.

"Ba, gud," Torg responded, eyes wide. Jenja stepped back to the bed.

"Rock medicine is helping. Thank you," Torg said to Rock. "Now, talk over, time for sleep." He guzzled the last of his drink.

Rock shadowed Torg's actions, draining his cup. Kip did the same, the strong alcohol burning as it went down. He noticed the alcohol's effects and felt fatigue finally setting in.

Torg stood and motioned to the door. In concert, Rock and Kip rose and moved toward the exit. Rock paused before leaving to take one last glance at Jenja and her sickly patient. Jenja smiled in return, then went back to wiping the woman's head.

Torg pulled back the wolf skin door covering. "You go to room, sleep night, we talk in morning." He offered his hand to Rock.

Rock grasped it and shook. "Thank you for helping us. We will not forget your kindness."

Torg offered his hand to Kip, who also took it. "Nor your brew," Kip quipped.

Torg offered a hearty laugh as they stepped through the door, where a thin man with matted hair and dirty clothing was waiting. His eyes were also oversized, the same as Torg's. Saying nothing, the man gave a small wave, signaling for them to follow. They traveled single file on a small path that wound between boulders and the Arapi huts. Kip followed last and had to work to keep up. They finally stopped at a small wooden structure, no bigger than a shed. The man pulled a door covering back and motioned for them to enter. Rock went in and Kip followed. Their guide let the door covering drop behind them and was gone without a word.

The single room was dimly lit by a small fire in a tiny circle of stones. Next to the fireplace was a plate holding two clay mugs with water and a slab of the same bread. The room was sparsely furnished with only two furs laying side by side on the floor. Each had a thick bed of dried grass under it. Rock went to the closest skin and lowered himself to a sitting position. Kip did likewise on the open fur.

"More bread?" Kip offered, an uncomfortable feeling in his chest.

"That may be our breakfast; I'd hold off," Rock answered. He studied Kip. "You appear troubled. Why?"

"Is this place safe? We've assumed it is, but what's stopping them from charging in while we're asleep?"

"It's safe. People like Torg are true to their word."

"How do you know?"

"Experience. When you get outside the city, you learn to read people." He lay down. "He could have killed us in the caves, but didn't. Instead, he offered us food and drink. And did you see the way he tended to the sick woman? That's a man who cares about life, who wouldn't take one lightly."

"I did notice. It was foreign to me. I'm so used to everything being done by the State, so minimally and antiseptically, I might add. No one cares if you live or die. They just do the minimum required so you don't die on their watch . . . if you're lucky."

"It's different out here. It's people you rely on—family, friends, community. Not the nameless, faceless Citizens of the state. There's a sense of belonging that comes with caring for another human being, of helping. You don't do it because you have to or it benefits you, and not because they may help you in the future. You do it because you feel empathy and commitment. You want to see another soul get through their struggles to survive, because you know what it's like. And even more so when you find that perfect person, that perfect family, you'll know love and what it does to you."

Kip thought about the word *love*. What was it? He'd never really known it. Everything in Nirvana was selfish, all about self-care and gratuitous self-gain. It's not about the betterment of an individual or society, no matter what Citizen One claims. Sky's commitment to Bug came to mind—that was something beyond care. He then considered if that was why he kissed Sky. Was that love creeping into his life?

He lay down on his mat, his mind and body exhausted, the trials of the day winning. "Thank you for all you did at the lake, on the rope, and in the hospital."

"You help people, people help you," Rock said as Kip closed his eyes.

Chapter 21
Thursday, January 10, 2075

Kip woke to a heavy shake of his shoulder. Rock was on a knee next to him, an urgency in his face. Torg stood in the small doorway, his bulging eyes fixed on him. "You leave, hurry, mountain diggers come. Torg goes to fight."

Kip rolled out of his small bed. The aches of his body and the fog in his mind told him he hadn't slept long. "I'm up. Let's go."

"Can we help against the mountain diggers?" Rock offered his laser gun.

"No, you keep, and better you leave, not seen here with Arapi. Go!" Torg handed him a cloth bundle and a canteen-like skin containing liquid. "Take bread and water. Gift from Jenja, mother doing better. Rock medicine strong."

"Thank you, Torg. Good luck with the fight."

"Which way out?" Kip asked.

Torg pointed away from the way they entered. "Path out of Arapi that way. Cross bridge over river and enter forest. Cut bridge, no one follows. Torg's people will hide in caves." He started to leave, then stopped. "Beware of spiders, they follow light. Now go! We hold them as long as possible."

Rock immediately started moving in the direction of Torg's guidance. Kip hurried after him. He swiveled for one last look to see Torg dashing into the darkness, then heard pops like gunfire and a laser's buzz followed by lights in the back of the cavern. It appeared that the soldiers were on the ledge they had traveled the day before and were returning fire at the Arapi.

Rock never hesitated, gaining speed as they traveled downward and wound their way out of the city. The first light of day had arrived and its rays creased through cracks in the cavern's ceiling, providing a fuzzy illumination of the area, allowing them to move much faster. Kip did all he could to keep pace and was soon sprinting.

Rock found the path out in short order. Another natural fissure in the mountain created a tunnellike path with a sandy floor and yellow sandstone walls. It flowed fairly straight and Rock pushed their pace. Kip's heart pounded and his lungs were on fire, but he'd keep pace even if it killed him. The trail dipped down, passing through a small subcavern where the roof was veiled by the darkness above. Rock slowed as they navigated through a boulder patch, swerving through them easily. Kip followed through the area with no problems. They continued for a few more minutes at that pace, when, rounding a corner, the ambient light brightened and they came to a ten-foot crack—a doorway out. Rock skidded to a stop. Kip almost piled into him, but Rock held up his hand and pressed it on Kip's chest.

"They could be out there waiting for us."

Kip peered through the cave's opening. The path out graded down. Under the morning sun, he could see what appeared to be a rope bridge in the distance that crossed a canyon-like chasm. On the far side, dense green pine trees sprawled as far as the eye could see. He couldn't pinpoint the water flow, but suspected that a river ran through the gorge by the soft resonating sound of rushing water. He took a second survey of the forest; it appeared to be an ideal place for getting lost.

Rock poked his head out and scanned the hills on all sides around them. From his casual reaction, Kip suspected he saw no one.

Rock took a step back toward Kip and whispered, "We're at the base of the mountain. I don't see any soldiers. Unfortunately, lots of cliffs and boulders above us to hide in."

Kip scanned the terrain in front of them again. "This path runs to the bridge that crosses the gorge," he said and tapped the laser in Rock's hands. "We'll cross, then blast the bridge. No one follows." He watched for Rock's approval. "Then we lose ourselves in the forest."

Rock nodded. "Agreed, sprint at full speed, no hesitation. If they're smart, they'll lie in wait until we're clear of the cave, then fire when we're out in the open."

"That's what I would do."

"You lead, I'll follow," Rock grunted. "Anybody shoots, I'll be firing back. So don't wait for me, you just go."

"Okay. If we separate, I'll find you in the forest."

Kip edged to the cave's opening. He readied himself for the sprint to freedom. He eyed Rock, who was holding the laser in the firing position.

Kip gave a quick nod. "See you on the other side."

"On three," Rock said. "One . . . two . . . three!"

Kip blew from the opening, running as fast as he ever had. He raced, dodging right then left. He'd only gone a short way down the path when he heard the first hiss of a laser weapon firing. The blast exploded close on the left, jettisoning pulverized rock fragments into his face and body. Kip ducked below a boulder and looked back to the cliffs above. He saw the repeated flashes from soldiers firing round upon round from their weapons, their blasts fortunately off the mark.

Rock stopped at the same boulder and spun to fire back. His blasts hit just below the soldier's line. The mountain exploded into the enemy ranks, followed by screams of pain.

"Run!" Rock yelled.

The same scene replayed over and over where dozens more hisses erupted, blasts hit, then the heavy buzz of Rock's rifle returning fire. Kip followed Rock's direction, sprinting forward, never slowing or going backward. If someone was going to hit him, they'd have to do it with him sprinting at full speed.

Not an easy task, especially with their distance increasing with every step.

Kip was fast approaching the bridge when he heard a new whistling sound. A mortar was fired. It exploded with a devastating impact, with the ground literally shaking as if it would break. Kip twisted back just in time to see Rock collapse. He skidded to a stop, then dashed back to his friend. By the time he arrived, Rock was struggling to get up, his leg injured but not bleeding.

Kip slid under Rock's shoulder and pulled him to his feet. Putting his arm around him for support, the two returned toward the bridge and their escape. Rock limped as best he could, Kip helping to support his weight. They passed a massive boulder, the sentinel of the bridge. Under heavy fire, they arrived at the bridge's wooden beam buttress.

Kip noted the bridge was built with four lengths of thin rope bound together with separated slatted boards to walk on. Designed for a single traveler, it spanned a rushing river that had carved a deep and rocky gorge. The bad news was that the bridge was, at best, rickety. The good news was that once they traversed it and cut the ropes, nobody would be able to cross for miles. The forest would be their refuge.

Kip grabbed Rock's laser and pushed him onto the narrow span. He urged, "Go, I'll hold them."

Rock started to protest, but it was too late. Kip had already spun and pulled the trigger. Blast upon blast ejected from the barrel, drilling into the hillside. As Kip raged, the return fire quelled, his attackers pinned down by the viciousness of his assault. He kept the gun pounding, screaming, "Ahhh!" out of anger or maybe fear. The gun's muzzle started heating, a faint reddish glow on the metal tip of the barrel.

Then a whistle came, and a mortar exploded just in front of the giant boulder he hid behind. The stone took the brunt of the blast, but enough of the concussive hit made him feel like a truck had smacked, lifted, and blew him back onto the bridge. With his ears buzzing, Kip struggled to his feet, suddenly confused. He could see but couldn't hear Rock at the other end of the span, holding his arm out, urging him to do something. Kip stumbled toward him. With his laser hanging by a strap over his shoulder, he grabbed the guide ropes with his hands and took a slow step forward. Step by step, he deliberately headed toward the man pleading with him to "Move!" Was that what he was saying?

His head pounded in excruciating pain. The vibrations of laser fire buzzed past him, the blasts just missing him, but scorching the bridge. Then he felt a thump and burn in the back of his shoulder that knocked him forward. The singe of his flesh drowned out the agony in his head. He dropped, his body landing on the bridge slats, his head and right shoulder hanging off. He saw Rock limp toward him. Kip reached out; his friend was only feet away.

Another round of laser blasts hit the guide rope near his feet and it snapped. The bridge twisted in response. He slid down the slats, frantically grabbing for anything. For a second, his hand locked on the other secure guide rope, but the weight of his body was too much for his damaged shoulder to hold. The rope slipped away. As he fell, his eyes again caught Rock's as his friend's hand reached to save him.

But Kip slipped away. "No!" Rock screamed.

Kip tumbled, twisting in the air, trying to right his feet below him. It was a futile effort. He plunged into the silence of the gorge for what seemed an eternity, expecting the inevitable impact on river stone but hoping for water. He hit with a crack, a sharp flash of light filling his brain. Cold flowed all around and within him until things went gray. A darkness consumed him and time lost all meaning.

****

Kip stood motionless in a black purgatory. Unsure of his location, he waited in a brooding silence, knowing only that the smothering darkness surrounded him. Although void of all light and sound, he could feel something, a burning vibration stirring in his chest. He tried to touch the area, to scratch or massage it, to quell the odd sensation, but he could not. His hand couldn't find the spot of origin.

KP Boudreaux

Suddenly, the sensation changed, and Kip felt the vibration in his chest strengthening. A prick of white light appeared in the distance, breaking the black monotony. Intrigued, he followed as the dot grew. The prick became a ball, the ball became a disk, the disk a molten planet, the planet a sun. The suffocating black was slowly forced out by this warming light. It washed through him, illuminating all and destroying the darkness, providing a comfort and safety he had never felt before.

The white light vibrated, changing. Subtle hues appeared—reds, blues, greens, and shades in between—and brightened before swirling together and then apart in a kaleidoscope of colors and shapes. Kip watched as these glows coalesced into an Earth-like planet, and the planet separated between land and water. Another shudder came, and a wave of color gave rise to an evolution of plants and then animals, small at first, then morphing to the behemoths of the plains and finishing with man. Kip now stood in a lush forest, hardwood trees with giant green leaves filling the area. The vibration in his chest now churned hard, Kip could feel his energy attracted—no connected—to all around him. An invisible tether linking him to the energy of all plants, animals, and earth. All of it starting and ending with the white light.

A horned owl flew near Kip, circled, then landed on a branch near his head. The animal perched motionless, yellow eyes locked with his. Its brown feathers started ruffling. The owl blinked, and a new transformation began. Its large eyes and small face morphed into a human's, with delicate features and long black hair. It was Sky! She was here, only her eyes stayed yellow.

Kip reached for her. She reciprocated, gently taking his hand, yellow eyes never straying. Kip couldn't fully understand it, but the emotion of that moment overpowered his essence, consuming every inch of his being, like a fire burning in his soul. It strengthened him; it gave him purpose. It was love. Kip knew it. Kip also knew this wasn't Sky.

"I miss you," Kip said.

"And I you," Sky answered.

"What do I do?"

"You learn . . . by following your heart. It will lead you down the right path, even if it's the more arduous one."

"And all this?"

"An awakening." Her voice was reassuring. "A glimpse into the universal reality and the interconnection of everything. Remember, it all starts with the white light. Embrace your spirit, trust there is more, share your love for all to see, and don't be afraid to ask the hard questions. This knowledge will provide strength in difficult times."

"Who are you? You're not Sky."

"I am the beginning and the end and all that lies between. I am the white light, I am love. And you may call me Yahweh." Her eyes softened. "Trust yourself, Kip. Open your heart and

221

trust your inner voice. It will find that which you seek. You will know my love."

"I will, I feel this in my heart." He sensed their time was near. "It's time to say goodbye, isn't it?"

"It is."

"Will I see you again?"

"Oh yes, you will see me in many forms. Some you will recognize and some you won't, but trust I will always be there with you." She released Kip's hand and touched her finger to his forehead. "Remember."

A surge of happiness welled within him. She slowly dissipated, and the world around him started to unravel. Like time being rewound, Kip watched as all the interconnected threads of all life—all matter, all energy—recoiled back into the single prick of light. And then the darkness returned.

****

Something cold smacked into Kip's hurt shoulder, sparking white flashes through his mind. He rolled away from the pain, inhaling a mouthful of equally cold water in the process. As the churning current tossed him about, he struggled to right himself. Another boulder and another blow to his body, not as hard this time, pushed him right, which allowed his head to surface above the torrent. He gasped for air, managing to renew his breath before being pulled under again. He was fighting hard, his strength waning, his lungs about to explode when something grabbed his shirt and pulled. His head surfaced again. Through blurry eyes, he searched for whatever was holding him. The churning water beat into him, crushing his body but also lifting it high in the water. Finally oriented, he twisted his head to see his drenched friend hanging out over a boulder, stretched as far as he could reach. His two wiry arms held on to Kip's rifle, its strap still intact.

Rock heaved and Kip slipped from the power of the current, the water's roar echoing in his ears. Rock slid back on the boulder, steadied himself, then pulled on the gun again. This time Kip moved from the center of the rushing water into a slower pool-like area. Rock readjusted, then pulled one last time. Kip gripped the boulder, and with a weak heave, slid onto the dry stone. He lay there, his head pounding and shoulder screaming with pain. Not moving, he rested with his eyes closed and heart racing, but enjoying the feeling of warmth from the dry stone, savoring every breath.

He wasn't sure how long he lay there or what Rock was doing. He didn't care. As his body quieted, the sounds of the nearby forest became clearer. Birds were singing, the water churned, and the insects buzzed. The smell of the forest filled his senses. He rested in this quasi-solitude until he could no longer feel the throbbing in his temples.

Sensing Rock was still nearby, Kip rolled onto his back and opened his eyes. The man who rescued him sat cross-legged in silence, just watching, allowing him the time to recover.

Chapter 22

"Thank you for saving me," Kip said. "I was out of it; I'm surprised I didn't drown."

Rock closed his fist, lightly tapped it on his chest, then extended his open hand, palm down, toward Kip in what was a clear signal of friendship. "You risked your life to save me on the bridge. I am honored to help you."

"How did you get down into the ravine so fast?"

Rock smiled. "I jumped."

"Are you crazy?" Kip's voice raised as he lifted his head to better see his friend. "That had to be a hundred feet."

"Let's talk later. If you're up for travel, we need to leave." Rock stood. "The bridge is out, meaning that unless they fly in soldiers, the guards will have to travel well downstream to cross. Which should give us time to lose them in the woods."

"Where are we?" Kip asked.

"This has to be the main branch of the Cascade River," Rock answered. "My guess, we're near the edge of the Outer Boundary. My land is a few miles past that mountain range." Rock nodded his head toward the rolling mountains that lay in the distance, then offered Kip his hand.

Kip grasped it, and with a gentle pull from Rock, painfully rose from his lying position. With his gun still over his shoulder, he stood for a moment, taking stock of his body. His head really hurt. He touched his forehead. A swollen lump wept a warm bloody ooze. When rotating his injured shoulder, a biting sting shot through his arm.

Rock moved Kip's shirt to the side to examine the damage. "Looks like they wanted you alive. There's a burn, but it doesn't penetrate the skin. Blasters must've been on low."

Kip rotated his shoulder again. It was painful to move, but stable. The better news was that his legs were okay, if not a little sore. He could walk.

"I can travel. I won't be fast, but I agree—we need to get into the woods."

Rock didn't respond with words. He answered by stepping toward the forest, scouting for a dry path over the stones jutting out of the river. Kip followed, noting Rock still carried the semi-dry bundle given to him by Torg. At least they'd have food and drink for the night.

With care, they crossed the boulder field in the river and the smaller rock that made up the shore until they passed the tree line and entered the forest. The trees were giants, with ruddy brown bark that fed a green canopy of branches laden with pine needles and cones. The forest floor was a thick layer of the same needles with little to no ground growth, which made walking easier. There was no actual path and only wisps of sunlight reached the forest floor, giving a dusky feel to their hike. As they penetrated deeper into the forest, the air grew thicker, with no wind to speak of. Kip became concerned that they'd lose their direction. All the trees were alike, and they had no visual of the sky to gauge the location of the sun or moon—all navigational beacons were lost. Their only guide was the trail of disturbed needles they left as they walked.

Despite Kip's trepidation, Rock seemed confident. He walked with a disciplined stride around the unending wooden pillars that obstructed their path. If he felt any concern, he did not show it.

For the most part, the only animals heard or seen were the calls of birds, the hum of insects, and the occasional web strand from a spider. At one point, Kip thought he heard an odd rustling in the distance. Thinking it was a large predator, he tried to discern the location or source but could not.

They continued this way for what Kip guessed to be hours. As the light of the forest dimmed, he began feeling the wear from his earlier misadventures. He lagged farther and farther behind Rock, forcing his companion to slow or wait.

On the last such occasion, Rock said, "You seem like you've had enough."

"I have. I need to rest."

"We're far enough in and it'll be night soon. They'll have a hard time finding us now." Rock scanned the immediate surroundings. Seeing nothing threatening, he added, "I'm going to do a quick walk around the area. You rest. I'll be back soon."

"Will do, but don't go far."

Rock handed him the food Torg gave him. "Hold this just in case. Try to eat sparingly. We don't know how long it must last."

Kip took it, eyeing Rock, his last statement feeling ominous. "Be careful out there."

Rock took a step away, then stopped. Doing an about-face, he said, "No fire tonight, too risky."

"I don't think I'll be awake long enough to start one."

Kip found a relatively soft patch on the ground with no roots or embedded rocks. He gathered pine straw and hastily made a giant oval ground nest. He lay on his back, eyes toward the treetops, watching as the limbs swayed back and forth under a soft breeze. He focused on the sounds of the forest—the insects buzzed, the birds chirped, and a subtle clicking sound echoed from the treetops. Kip comfortably dismissed the noise as limbs brushing against one another. This was the last thought he remembered.

* * *

Kip woke to a tug against his arm and then a shake of his body.

"Wake up! Say something," Rock urged.

Kip shook his head. It ached . . . no that wasn't right, it throbbed. His temples were pounding. His eyesight was also blurred. What was happening? He felt a clingy ropelike substance peel away from his head and his vision cleared. Rock pulled away another clump that was pinning his arm to his body.

"Can you talk?" Rock asked.

"Yeah, I'm okay, a little woozy," Kip answered, still confused. "What's happening?"

Rock pointed to the trees. "Spiders," he answered as he peeled away another strand of web from Kip's torso and stuck it on a trunk.

Kip's eyes went to the treetops. A multitude of black spiders the size of small dogs with orange stripes on their bellies weaved their webs between the limbs of the trees. A few of the more aggressive ones were low on the trunks, their mandibles clicking open, then closed.

Rock grabbed Kip's arm and pulled him to a standing position. "We must go. Soldiers are coming."

Rock pointed back into the forest. Kip saw the intermittent dance of flashlights in the distance, the beams flashing behind the tree trunks cutting the night's darkness, fortunately they were still a ways off.

"Which way?" Kip asked.

"Stay close," Rock whispered. "I have an idea." Facing the beams, he put his hand to his mouth and shouted, "Run, Kip, run! Soldiers are here!"

Kip pushed him. "What the hell are you doing? You're going to get us killed."

Rock gave a devilish grin and raised his hand again, shouting, "This way Kip, move!"

The flashlight beams changed direction and started moving toward them, bouncing their way through the forest. The soldiers' voices became clearer with each running step.

Rock pushed Kip in front of him, "Go, now, that way!" He made no effort to conceal his voice.

Kip rushed through the trees as fast as he could. The darkness prevented an all-out sprint, but he was moving fast, much faster than he thought was safe. Unfortunately, the soldiers were gaining, their voices only a short hilltop away. Their lights now dimly illuminated the area. Kip tried to keep to the shadows. He stepped around a particularly thin and wiry trunk that was heavy with low-hanging branches and got a face full of spider webs. He ripped away at the thick strands clinging to his face and hair. He brushed his scalp with his fingers, feeling for anything moving. Fortunately, there was nothing.

Rock watched in what seemed to be amusement. "Stay there, I'll lead them in," he said, followed by, "It gets hairy." He finished by shouting, "Where are you, Kip? I lost you!"

As the soldiers' voices moved toward them, Kip heard the clicking noise in the treetops increase in volume. Their forest hosts were either noticeably irritated, or worse, hungry.

Rock moved ahead, navigating through the thick trunks with their course bark and under or around the thick webs crossing them. He then moved slowly and methodically back toward Kip, using the light available to his advantage. Occasionally, he'd give a call or yelp to ensure the soldiers were following them. Kip was baffled by the strategy but trusted the man.

Rock slid to a stop. He reached and pressed his hand on Kip's chest to ensure he didn't move. He brought his finger to his lips, calling for silence, then pointed above their heads. The treetops churned with motion and agitation, the unusual clicking noise of the spiders peaking in a crescendo. Rock crept forward, pulling Kip with him as he navigated the safe path through the maze of webbing. The soldiers were close. Kip could hear their curses as they started running into the spiderwebs, their flashlights lighting up the silklike strands in a ghostly display.

Something heavy crashed onto Kip's shoulder, then rolled off and fell to the ground. The blow startled him more than hurt, but when the unknown thing started crawling back up his leg, he full-on freaked out. A large black spider with orange striping on its thorax raced up his pant leg, going for his arm, maybe his neck. He tried swatting it off, but the freakish little

231

thing's grip was locked in. Kip grabbed its spiked hind leg, avoiding the pincers, and ripped the spider off his hip. He slammed his armored attacker into the nearest tree with a crack, and it let out a ghoulish squeal. He felt confident the blow killed the arachnid as it dropped to the ground, motionless. He booted it away, just to be sure, then hopped back a step, overwhelmed with fear—and creepiness.

Rock grabbed him by the shirt and pulled him from beneath the main swarm. The soldiers were literally feet behind them now, their lights illuminating the area where Kip and Rock stood.

Rock gave one more call. "Over here."

The thud of boots raced toward them. When the platoon was under the giant spider's nest, Rock sent a single blast from his gun into the treetops and the swarm. A loud hiss resonated as thousands of the creatures dropped into the midst of the soldiers. The downpour grew into an ankle-deep flood of eight-legged monsters, which was soon followed by shrieks of agony mixed with blasts from a randomly shot soldier's gun. The cries reached a painful climax before turning to muted grunts. Kip could only imagine the suffering the soldiers endured, wondering if the spider venom was deadly or just paralyzing, leaving them alive to be fed upon later.

Rock, however, didn't wait for the final act, nor did he seem too concerned for their well-being. He pulled Kip's shirt again, forcing him forward. Rock was not going to offer aid. As they moved away, the clicking of the spiders attacking their prey and the soldiers' grunts of torture slowly faded, those horrible sounds forever burned into Kip's memory.

Chapter 23
Friday, January 11, 2075

The muted gray of a cloud-covered sunrise had just broken through the treetops when a light breeze hit Kip's skin. He shivered, the dampness on the back of his neck drying, leaving a comfortable cool. They had had a slow and difficult hike through the remainder of the night in stifling conditions. The trees created a natural barricade to the wind, both high and low, meaning the stagnant air grew increasingly oppressive. Given this and Kip's extreme state of exhaustion, he began to feel lightheaded and, at times, nauseous.

Rock recognized his struggles when they occurred and either stopped to rest and gulp a mouthful of water or slowed the pace until it passed. In each event, he would set out again with renewed vigor, pushing them forward.

They heard nothing more from the soldiers who had attempted to follow. Whether the men had halted, been killed, or just gotten lost in the woods, he'd probably never know. But they hadn't seen or heard any signs of them since the spiders' massacre.

For his part, Rock was a consistent presence of strength. Leading the way in the walk, recognizing Kip's limitations, and motivating in moments of physical crisis. At all times, he exemplified honor and friendship. The more Kip observed, the more he was convinced this man was terribly wronged by the Citizens of Nirvana.

They broke the tree line at a rocky ridge that sloped downward into a narrow and deep valley. Kip paused, standing on a distinctive red-rock precipice, studying the beauty in the dense trees and the contours of the ground they covered. It appeared to be a green *V* carved deep into the earth with steep walls and a limited floor. Kip suspected the formation was bigger than it appeared, given the distance they were from it. He could also hear the low hum of water flowing from a river somewhere nearby, surely the one that had carved the valley. In the distance, a gray curl of smoke rose from an unseen fire burning near the valley's low point.

Kip waited for Rock, who met his eyes.

"I recognize this place." Rock pointed south. "This is the south fork of the Cascade River. It merges just north of Nirvana. My home is over that ridge and far into the next valley."

"Then where are we?" Kip asked.

"This is very old Navajo land, now occupied by the Shonto clan."

"Are they friendly?"

"Depends on who you are, but I know them. They will help us."

Kip readied to leave, but sensed Rock's hesitation. "What is it?"

Rock stepped past Kip and took the lead. "Stay in the woods, out of sight. We need to be careful we're not being followed. These people fight the mountain diggers too."

The two men trekked down the wooded landscape, traversing the hill while staying just inside the towering tree line. There appeared to be a narrow path in more open terrain that Rock paralleled but stayed off. The pace was slower this way, but Kip felt safer out of sight. He also noted that he felt more at home in the woods. This was a change from being in Nirvana. In the last days, nature's peace had grown on him.

They traveled this way for a few hours until the land leveled. Kip assumed they were nearing the valley floor as the river no longer hummed but roared. The ground here had a spongy feel and was covered with old leaves, holding more moisture in the soil. Kip was not surprised when they broke into the river's clearing. Both wide and deep, the water frothed between huge boulders and large stones, the crowns just cresting the water line. Rock moved to the edge of the water and stood on the small, rounded river rock. He first scanned the hillsides surrounding them, ensuring they were still alone, then stood motionless while studying the rocks and the water. Kip suspected he was mapping out a path that would increase the probability of a dry crossing.

Rock finally moved. "Follow me. There's only one part that may test us."

He hopped onto a giant rock that stretched into the water. At the farthest edge, he paused, then did a standing jump to another rock about three feet away. He landed gracefully, stopping his momentum, then motioned for Kip to come.

Kip followed easily, landed lightly and stopped quickly, not even bumping into Rock who shared the boulder. They continued this way, easily hopping from stone to stone, crossing slowly and methodically. Kip would check their surroundings prior to every jump, but the only life evident in the woods were birds and them. They had one last crossing to make. It was a leap of at least four feet onto a massive and steep boulder. Their landing area would be small, and they'd have to grip the stone as soon as their feet hit.

Kip volunteered to go first. "Let me go. If I fall, it'll be backward, and you can pull me from the water."

Rock nodded.

Kip studied the landing area, glanced to his friend, then readied himself one pace away from the edge of his boulder. He took the step to gain momentum, then leaped with all his strength. He jumped the water, easily clearing the gap, but hitting the boulder's face hard. He tried gripping with his feet, and his hands grasping for anything. With no luck, he started to slide. Not panicking, he pressed his hands against the rock and just before he entered the water, his right hand caught a grip that held him on the boulder's face. He hung by his good arm for a moment, steadying himself. Once stable, he swung right, getting a toehold, and was able to climb the face. Moments later, he was situated on top of the boulder and waiting for his friend.

"Soft on the landing. Handhold is here on the right." Kip pointed as he spoke.

Rock tossed Kip the gun before taking a step back, preparing the same way. When ready, he stepped and launched. Sailing faster and farther than Kip, he hit the boulder's face with a slap and let out an audible groan. The impact appeared to jar Rock, who started his slide down the face. He reached for the handhold, but his reflexes were slow, and he missed it. He was heading for the water when Kip leaned over as far as he could go and made a darting grab for his arm. Snatching it, he held Rock dangling just above the water, swaying back and forth. Once the swinging subsided, Kip pulled him up. Using his feet and free hand, Rock climbed, joining his friend on the top.

"Thanks for that," Rock said. "I didn't need another bath."

They were interrupted when a rock clacked down a nearby hill just inside the tree line. Kip turned to see a teenager dressed in brown, scrambling back up and into the trees.

Rock held up a hand. "Let me handle this."

"*Tu tinto, d'ah, po stug, mi numba et Rock,*" Rock called to the teen.

The teen poked his head from behind a trunk, obviously stunned to hear his native language. Rock stepped to the edge of the boulder and jumped down onto the small river stones that made up the shore. Kip followed. They walked single file directly toward their observer, who stepped down into the open.

The boy stood almost five feet, with fair skin and a mop of reddish-brown hair. He had a thin, wiry build with green eyes and light freckles on his cheeks. He carried a leather sack which was over-filled with mushrooms that practically spilled out from its open flap.

"*Tu wana spechen?*" Rock asked.

"I speak English mostly, sometimes the old language," the boy answered, his eyes never straying from the two strangers. "You know our language. Who are you?"

"I am the leader of the Omasus in the next valley. Do I know you?"

The boy studied Rock's face. "Yes, I know you."

"I have visited here before, but it's been many years," Rock answered. "Is Maja here?"

"She was, but I haven't seen her since early this morning."

"What is your name?" Kip asked.

"I'm Hant, and you shouldn't be here." His eyes darted to the gun in Kip's hands.

"We mean you no harm," Rock added. "We're in need of food and help. I think Maja will provide it."

Hant appeared uncomfortable, as if it didn't matter what choice he made, it would be the wrong one. "Okay, I'll take you, but I hold the gun."

"Do you know how to use it?" Kip asked.

"No, but I don't plan on using it and neither should you."

Kip clicked the safety on, then handed him the blaster. "Be careful with it."

Hant slung the rifle over one shoulder and his sack over the other, then walked away. "This way."

They hiked on a narrow path that threaded through the tree line. Paralleling the river, they stayed mostly hidden by the giant pines that were abundant in this area, thus avoiding open areas where a hiker or drone could see them. The sunset was in full glory when they entered what could only be described as the idyllic town. Carved out of the forest on the hillside, the quaint village overlooked the river. A packed dirt road with river-rock curbs separated the town with houses built on either side. Each home was a sturdy log cabin precisely located within a square patch of manicured land. A few of the houses on the hill side of the street were built into the valley's wall. To say the town was orderly was an understatement.

241

At the midpoint of the street, an open parklike area created the town square. A fire pit surrounded by large rocks was centered in an otherwise trimmed lawn. A few people wandered by, offering a smile or a curious gawk to the strangers, but all were heading somewhere too urgently to linger. The three travelers stopped at the square.

"Wait here. I'll be back," Hant said.

Still holding the gun and his sack, Hant continued down the street to the largest of the cabins before ducking into the front door. Rock and Kip waited patiently as the night shadows grew. Kip's belly rumbled, and his body felt weary. The muted sound of voices came from the cabin, then quickly hushed. The front door opened, and one of the biggest men Kip had ever seen walked out, holding the blaster.

At well over six feet with broad shoulders and a thick build, to describe him as a giant was insufficient. He had fair skin, wild brown hair, a thick beard, and the same green eyes as Hant. The light of recognition came across his face as he saw Rock in the shadows.

The giant bound up and extended his hand to Rock. "My old friend. It's been too long."

Rock's hand was lost in the giant's. "Moot, you're even bigger than the last time I saw you."

Moot patted his stomach. "Not in a good way. It's Maja's cooking." Moot offered Rock his rifle back. "And who do we have here?"

"This is Kip, a friend of mine." Rock put his hand on Kip's shoulder. "And if you don't mind, we should get off the road."

Moot's brow tensed with concern. "That sounds ominous. Let's get you and Kip inside." He strode away. "Follow me."

As they headed to the large house, people were exiting other homes and making their way to the square.

Moot noticed Kip watching. "Weather permitting, we build a community fire every night. It's a time we can all share our day and where people bring food to feed those that may be hungry. It's a communal sharing event."

"Is there a lot of hunger here?" Kip asked, trying to be polite.

"No, there isn't, but on any given day a family may be ill or have a bad hunt. It's one way we watch out for each other." As Moot finished, he entered his home and held the door for his guests. He made for the kitchen table and offered a seat to Rock and Kip.

"Maja will be out shortly. While we wait, can I offer you a drink and something to eat?"

"Moot, to be direct," Rock said, "Nirvana's soldiers are hunting us. I don't want to endanger your family or friends."

"I don't think giving you something to eat will endanger my family. And if it does, so be it. We must care for one another in the wilds."

Hant walked in, followed by a tall, lean woman with graying blonde hair. She had a wiry, muscular build and was wearing brown clothes made from animal hide. Her dark eyes highlighted her attractive, albeit weathered, face.

"Maja. *Cot no brend. Mat su gree*," Rock said, standing.

"Rock. It's good to see you again too," she answered. "Let's speak English for your friend."

Kip stood. "I'm Kip, ma'am. Thank you for having us in your home."

"Any friend of Rock's is welcome here," she answered, then motioned to the teen boy who had moved behind a seat at the table. "You remember our nephew, Hant. We care for him now."

"I didn't recognize him. He's grown up."

Kip gave a small nod to Hant.

"Please sit. We'll talk over food and drink," Maja said.

As if on cue, Moot left for the back room. A short moment later, he was back, carrying four big mugs filled with a dark amber ale. He set one in front of each person, the last for himself. He excused himself again.

"Please drink. He'll be but a moment," Maja said.

Kip took a big draught from the brew. He savored its subtle flavors—smooth, yet hearty. A far cry from Torg's brew in the cave or the Ooze served in Ann's bar.

Rock had also sipped it and was clearly enjoying the moment. "You still have the best beer in the Outer Boundary. You must tell me how you do it."

Maja smiled. "Top-secret family recipe. I could tell you, but then I'd have to kill you."

Moot walked back in, carrying three plates. Each platter held a giant sandwich with two slices of thick-cut bread and hunks of a light chicken-like meat with a healthy dose of ground mustard. Moot placed a dish in front of Maja, Kip, and Rock. He then excused himself and returned moments later with two more plates. He set one in front of Hant and the other at his place setting.

"Should we say grace?" Hant asked.

"I think we should," Maja answered. "Would you do the honor?"

"I'm sorry, what is grace?" Kip asked hesitantly.

Maja offered Kip her hand to hold, her other went to Hant. "We take a moment in every day to thank God for life's blessings." Maja nodded to Hant to proceed.

"Thank you, Yahweh, for this bounty we are about to receive and this beautiful place we call home. And please watch over our family, our village, and our new friends, Rock and Kip."

Kip watched as the family held hands, heads humbly bowed while they thanked their god for the ample but rough blessings they held. He couldn't help but think of Nirvana's description of these people—savages they were called.

Maja was the first to speak. "Thank you, Hant, that was thoughtful." She motioned to the food. "Please eat while we talk." She addressed Rock. "So, tell me your story. Why are you here, and how might we be in danger?"

Rock detailed his entire story from the moment of his capture in the Wastelands to the time they arrived at the river. He asked Kip to fill in his details that brought them both to Maja's doorstep. Maja, Moot, and Hant sat captivated, interrupting only to ask for details. By the time Rock was done, they had finished three mugs of brew and a few hours of time. Kip was feeling no pain, which was a good thing.

"Wow, that's quite the story. Do you think you lost the soldiers in the woods?" Moot asked.

"We don't know. They didn't follow us after the spider attack, but it doesn't mean they haven't picked up the trail, which is why you may be in danger," Rock said. "We'll stay the night and be on our way tomorrow."

Maja held up a hand in protest. "Let's agree that you'll stay tonight. We have places we can hide you, and you both need rest." She addressed Kip. "And you probably need a doctor.

We'll send out scouts first thing to see what we can find and then decide how long you should stay."

"I appreciate your hospitality," Kip said, "but the last people who hid us were attacked. And I'd hate for that to happen again. These soldiers work for evil men, people who kill to get their way."

"We are well aware of what you're dealing with," Maja said. "We've had run-ins with them in the past. Worse than you can probably imagine. But we do not run, we fight. And if it comes to it, we'll fight for you." There was metal in her words that was matched by the courage in her eyes. Maja stood from her chair. "Now, let's get you situated for the night."

Kip rose. "Thank you," he said to Moot, then followed Maja. Rock was behind him. They navigated through the back room that doubled as a kitchen and pantry where Moot had fixed the meals. A tall shelf full of dusty jarred goods completed the rear wall. Maja bent down and unclipped a concealed hook, and she easily pushed the shelf away from the wall, revealing a hidden door. She switched on a small flashlight that appeared to be Nirvana-built and led the way through a narrow hall. Kip guessed they were well into the side of the hill going underground. His intuition was soon proven correct. The tunnellike hall led to a larger wooden door with a heavy lock. Maja slipped in a thick key, jiggled it, then twisted it right. The door creaked open, and Maja went through. She crossed the room to its only dresser, struck a match, and lit a candle that was centered on its seasoned wooden top. The candlelight soon illuminated a small cave-like room.

Beyond the dresser, the sparsely furnished area had two small cots with thin pads laid on them. There was a set of clean blankets placed at the foot of each bed. At the rear of the room, a woven cloth that appeared both old and decorative hung, covering the wall. Maja pulled the cloth aside and revealed another small tunnel.

"This is your safe spot for tonight," Maja said. She lifted a clay pitcher from the table and poured a glass of water. "Water and some bread." She then raised the candle near the wall, illuminating a thin line tied to a bell. She placed a finger on the line and pulled it down. The bell jingled twice. "This line is connected to our kitchen. If you hear the bell ring, go out that tunnel and into the caves below. If you follow the path, it leads to the falls on the river. There are plenty of places to hide along the way." She placed the flashlight on the table. "Use this. It was taken from a soldier of Nirvana. Keep it safe."

In an unusual display of emotion, Rock stepped over and took Maja's hand in both of his. "Thank you for your kindness."

"It's the least I could do after what you did for my family," Maja responded. She then spoke to Kip. "I'll coordinate a doctor visit tomorrow morning to examine you."

"Thank you," Kip said.

Maja smiled back. "It's my pleasure. Good night to you both," she said and left the room.

Rock sat on the nearest cot.

"We're safe here. She'll guard us with her life," Rock said. "Sleep easy."

Kip went to the open cot. "That won't be a problem. I'm exhausted." He stretched out. "How do you know Maja? Sounds like you were close."

"We are. I intervened for Hant and Maja's sister when Hant was very young. They were gathering berries on the mountain when the soldiers came."

"Intervened?" Kip asked. "I'm betting you did more than that."

"They were going to assault the mother in front of the boy. I was hunting, happened upon the scene, and defended them."

"What happened?"

"Let's just leave it as I killed the soldiers. His mother was injured, so I brought them back here."

"You killed armed soldiers, risking your life for strangers you happened upon in the wilds? You could have been killed."

"They were innocents who needed my help. It was the right thing to do. Sometimes the right path is not the easy path. You must always take the right path, just like your actions with me in Nirvana's pit."

Kip thought about his dream with Yahweh and her use of the same words. "I'm learning that lesson now," Kip answered, closing his eyes. He thought for a fleeting moment about what drives a man like Rock, then drifted off.

Chapter 24
Saturday, January 12, 2075

Kip awoke. The throbbing pain had returned to his head. He lay for a moment, rubbed the sleep from his eyes, then massaged his temples. It was no help. The pounding continued. He glanced over to see Rock's empty cot. On the dresser, the candle was lit and now half burned. Next to the candle sat a bowl, a towel, and a clean set of clothes neatly folded.

Given it was a windowless room, thus lacking all sunlight, Kip had no idea of the time. His body felt battered but rested, making him unsure if it was morning, afternoon, or evening. He slid a leg out of bed, put a foot on the ground, then gave an audible groan while he stood.

He took a painful step to the dresser and found the bowl filled with water. Kip splashed it in his face. The cold felt good and helped to clear his mind. Using the towel, he dried off, then poured a glass of water from the pitcher and downed it. He refilled the cup, ate a small piece of bread and washed it down. He was just beginning to feel human again, when the door opened, and Rock walked in wearing Shonto clothing.

"You're up."

"Barely. What time is it?"

"Around two," Rock answered. "I was coming to get you; the doctor is ready."

"Good, 'cause I'm feeling like I was hit by a bus," Kip half joked.

Rock stepped close and put his hand under Kip's chin. He studied his face. "Your eyes are clear, but you've got bruising around your head. I'm betting the impact from the fall off the bridge." Rock walked away. "Get out of your prison clothes, the doctor awaits."

"Yes sir, with pleasure."

Kip quickly stripped out of his prison clothes. "May want to burn these," he said half serious. He dressed in the clean clothes and slid his feet into Shonto-made hide shoes. They appeared rugged and fit perfectly. "Let's go."

He trailed Rock out of their space, through the kitchen and into the main room where they drank beer the night before. Moot waited at the table.

"He lives," Moot said with a laugh.

"Just barely." Kip smiled.

Moot stood and went for the door. "Come, the doctor is waiting."

Kip followed Rock and Moot into the street. They were acknowledged by a handful of people milling about doing their business. All greeted the group with a hello, a smile, or a nod of the head. It was all quite friendly and polite.

They strolled under the warm temperatures of the midafternoon sun, going two buildings down. Kip noted the perfection of the day. The sun shone bright, and the birds' chirping interlaced perfectly with the occasional insect buzzing. More importantly, there was no sign of the mountain diggers.

They arrived at a sturdy one-room house built into the side of the hill. The town's school, with its trimmed front yard, had six children playing on the thick, green grass. Most were kicking a ball, like soccer of old, except two girls, who were playing a clapping game. Kip paused to take it all in. The town, the school, the children—the whole idyllic scene was sadly foreign to him. There was a simple beauty in this life, far from the controls of Nirvana.

The three men entered the school classroom where a thirtysomething woman sat at a table. With her brown hair pulled back, glasses sitting on her delicate nose, and her handmade dress sewn to perfection, she appeared every part the small-village doctor. Holding a book in her hands, she glanced up from her reading as they entered.

"Fawn, we're here," Moot announced. "I'd like you to meet Rock and Kip." He gestured at Kip. "He's the patient."

Fawn stood and offered her hand to Rock. "Nice to meet you. Your reputation precedes you." Then she spoke to Kip. "So, you're the bridge jumper?" She went straight to him. "Let's examine you."

"More like bridge faller." Kip chuckled.

The doctor smiled her silent response.

In a scenario similar to Rock's earlier examination, she studied Kip's head, pressing on certain bruised areas, then focused heavily on his eyes. She made him follow her finger, then shined a light in them, studying the pupils. She took out an old stethoscope from an archaic case and held it to his neck and then his chest. Lastly, she checked his ears, ensuring no blood in the canals.

"I'm betting you have a hell of a headache right now. Do you have any bruising on your chest or back?"

"I haven't checked . . ." Kip hesitated. Not knowing how much to reveal, he chose his words carefully. "We've been on the go."

Recognizing his unstated concern, she said, "You're safe here." She motioned for him to pull up his shirt. He slowly turned around so she could examine his torso. She first paused to examine the shoulder that was burned from the laser blast. "You got lucky." She reached in her pocket and removed a small circular tin and opened it. She dipped her fingers in the gooey solution and wiped it across the burned area of skin.

"What's that?" Kip asked.

"Disinfectant and topical pain killer." She pressed a white square bandage on the sticky wound. "When this falls off, you should be good. Try to stay out of the water."

She continued her exam, stopping him again mid-turn to feel a bruise near his liver. She pressed. "Does this hurt?"

He winced. "Yep. Not too bad though."

"You can pull down your shirt," she said while walking to an old wooden cupboard with open shelves on top, which were filled with jars of powders, leaves, twigs, and berries. "Anything else bothering you?"

"Not really, I mean, besides the headache," Kip answered. "What's the verdict?"

"The verdict is you're a very lucky man," she said as she pulled some leaves from a jar and placed them in a leather pouch. She handed it to Kip. "As far as I can tell, you have a concussion and a bruised spleen. But there doesn't appear to be any internal bleeding or worse, a hemorrhage in your skull. After a fall like that, it should have been much worse. You, my friend, have a guardian angel."

"A what?"

"A guardian angel, you know, a spiritual protector that watches over you."

Kip thought of his dream after the fall on bridge. *Is that what she was?*

"What's this?" Kip held up the pouch with the leaves.

"These are coca leaves, very rare. You may have heard of them. Chew them for pain as needed. They'll provide a euphoric high, so use sparingly. But they should take the edge off that headache."

Kip nodded. "Got it, thank you."

"I'd also suggest you take the next couple of days to rest. Let your body heal."

Kip motioned to Rock, deferring the answer.

"We'll be making that decision soon," Rock said.

At that moment, the children burst through the front door. They ignored the adults and sat at the center table, talking among themselves.

Fawn smiled at Kip. "I think your visit is over."

"Are you the teacher or the doctor?" Kip asked with a grin.

"Yes," she replied with a roll of her eyes. She picked up her book and stepped toward her students.

Rock pulled Kip's arm, heading toward the exit. Moot was already through the door.

Fawn peeked back to Kip and smiled.

"Thank you," Kip mouthed to her before exiting.

Chapter 25
Monday, January 14, 2075

For the next two days, Kip laid low at Maja and Moot's home. He slept on his cot in the rear cave, came out for meals or to take a discreet walk in the woods for exercise. The coca leaves were a big help. His headache slowly dissipated and his bruises were well on their way to healing.

Fawn came to visit him twice a day to check on his progress. On the afternoon of the second day, she declared him fit for "required" travel. Although happy for his improvement, Kip felt a tinge of disappointment and found he didn't want to leave this peaceful sanctuary. He appreciated Fawn's visits as she was engaging and easy to talk with, not to mention knowledgeable on all topics. He enjoyed the social interaction. Rock had left, and Maja's family were in and out with their daily routines of hunting, gathering, and maintenance, leaving him alone for much of the day. Kip was unsure of where Rock had gone, only that he would be "back soon."

"What's next for you?" Fawn asked, putting her stethoscope away.

Kip finished buttoning his shirt. "We'll likely leave either tomorrow or the next day, whenever Rock returns. Sounds like we're heading to his village." Kip hesitated. Being mostly alone or in Rock's silent company the last week, he found it easy to connect with the doctor, wanting to ask her more personal questions as their medical discussions waned. For her part, she seemed receptive to the conversation, cheerfully answering any questions he had. "What are you doing now?" he asked.

She raised an eyebrow. "School's over, I was going to pick berries. Heard there was an unusual amount growing in the field nearby. Why?"

"Wondering if you want to go for a hike, but berry picking sounds equally fun."

"How about both? But not too far. You still need to rest." She grabbed her case. "Let me drop this off at home."

They walked together in a quiet comfort to the school building.

"You live at the school?" Kip broke the silence.

"Yep, my place is in the back of the classroom, built into the hill. It's small but it's all mine." She motioned toward the house. "Wait here, I'll be right back."

Kip stood outside, enjoying the sunny day. The sun warmed his body and added to the pleasure of his current carefree existence.

A few young children walked by, escorted by their mother. Kip couldn't help but notice the caring mother-and-child bond, something he'd not seen in Nirvana. The smallest girl walked beside her mother, practically stepping between her legs, the security of love and safety in her stride. The woman beamed with joy as she taught her children the important lesson of self-sufficiency. All the children carried a small basket filled with blackberries, their faces adorned with big grins, clearly excited about the sweet reward for their efforts. The closest girl waved at him.

"What do you have there?" Kip asked her.

The young girl showed him the bounty inside her basket. "Yummy blackberries." She giggled, a hint of the residual juice around her lips.

"Mmm, they look great," Kip answered.

"Would you like some?" the mother asked. "We have plenty, and they've already eaten their share."

For the most part, the townspeople had stayed clear of him, respecting his privacy. Beyond the occasional hello on the street, they went about their business without asking questions or probing statements. In all cases, when he did interact, he found the people kind and generous, such as this sweet mother. A far cry from the "savage" label attached to them by the Citizens of Nirvana.

"Thank you, but we're heading out to pick some now. You enjoy those."

As Kip finished the sentence, he heard an unusual buzz, which raised then lowered in volume. It stabilized, then the whine raised again, and the back of his neck pricked. Then he saw it, in the trees over the river, now hovering.

Fawn exited the school, holding a basket. "Ready," she said to Kip.

"Get inside!" Kip pointed to the school. "Drone!"

The kids started to scream and run. The protective mother dropped her basket to corral the children and move them toward the schoolhouse. In her fear, the little girl tipped her basket over, losing her berries. She started to cry and tried to scoop them up. Kip didn't hesitate. He plucked her off the ground with the basket and ran for the school. He handed the terrified girl to her frantic mother at the door, who pulled her inside.

Fawn held the door open, rushing everyone in. "This way, this way," she urged.

Kip knew he couldn't go; it would put the others at risk. "Go!" he said. "I can't be with you."

The doctor reached out, touching his hand. "Then run and hide!" she whispered, her lips now quivering. She slammed the door and bolted it. Kip started to run as the whine of the approaching gunship vibrated in his chest. He sprinted to Maja's house and was just coming out with the gun when the ship opened fire on the schoolhouse. He watched as a single shell exploded into the building, followed by a detonation that rocked the ground where he stood. Half the building was blown away. The remaining section that was still standing was already engulfed in flames. Kip got hit by the concussive force of the blast, knocking him to the ground. He got to his feet, shaking. A combination of fear and fury consumed him.

The circular ship had just touched down, and a dozen soldiers rushed from its protected platform deck toward the burning schoolhouse. Out of their line of sight, Kip didn't hesitate. He opened fire with the blaster and caught the attacking soldiers unaware. At least six of them were cut down in the first exchange, either wounded or dead. It didn't matter. He continued the onslaught, moving his fire to those holed up in the ship. Surprised by the vicious counterattack, the soldiers hunkered down behind the fortified railings, safe for the moment from his gun. The ship's cannon that had just destroyed the schoolhouse returned fire. Kip dove behind a stone wall. The whistling shell sailed over him but found the house behind. In a replay of the school, the building exploded, and the blast pounded Kip forward into his protective wall. He was dazed and shook his head, clearing the cobwebs as the pounding of blasters echoed through the town. He peered over the wall to see Maja and Moot behind the closest trees, firing lasers at the attackers. Then a man sprinted toward the ship and threw a grenade onto its deck. The device ignited and set the ship aflame. Kip recognized Rock's brown skin as his friend started firing into the craft. The savage from the Wastelands had returned.

The remaining soldiers had no choice but to abandon the burning ship. Those that could, came out firing. Others stumbled or crawled as the smoke and flames forced them to evacuate. Moot, Maja, and Rock continued their assault. Kip joined them, aiming his blaster at the few soldiers nearest him. It didn't take long. The crossfire was too much, and the guns of the enemy were soon silenced.

Kip shot at the hovering drone. He missed. The machine elevated up and sped away, returning to its unseen master.

Moot and Maja came from the trees. They sprinted to the school as the townspeople gathered to fight the fire. Rock walked through the bodies of the fallen soldiers, doing the ugly duty of ensuring they were dead. Kip started to do the same and walked toward the nearest man, one of the first six he had cut down. The soldier was still alive and reached for his gun. Kip fired, literally blasting his hand off. The soldier now gripped his seared appendage, screaming. "Ahhh!" His face twisted in agony.

Kip closed the gap, kicking the soldier's gun out of reach. He grabbed the man's uniform around his shoulder and rolled him over onto his bloody back.

"Fuck you," the man hissed, blood streaming down his face, his body shaking.

Kip studied his contorted face. "I know you." He squatted down, pulling the man's helmet off to get a better view of his features. "You're Officer Finna. You tried killing me in Elysian Fields. You used Bane to do your dirty work."

With his grim task done, Rock had moved and was now standing next to Kip. "Who is he?"

"He was a guard at the prison. Tried to off me. He set this adventure of ours into motion. His killer wounded me to send me to the hospital the day I met you."

Finna glared at Rock. "I know you, you're the monster from the Wasteland."

"I am. The one that killed twelve Nirvana soldiers that were—doing what?" Rock paused. "Oh yeah, that were bringing 'medicine' to my people. You're a murdering liar!"

"Fuck you too!" Finna screamed louder. "You're both dead! We won't stop coming until your bodies are hanging in Nirvana's center! And then, before you've even rotted away, we'll come for your families." He glared at Kip and rambled. "Who's that pretty partner of yours? Sky . . . that's right, we know her well. Yeah, asshole, we know all about you. We've been playing you since day one."

Kip squeezed his blaster's grip, rage building inside.

Finna continued his insane rant. "Nice schoolhouse. Were there kids inside? Or maybe a pretty teacher. With a little luck, there were both! If there's one thing I love, it's dead savages."

Kip had killed before, probably on the battle at the bridge and no doubt a few minutes earlier. But that was reaction, something more basic for survival. It was out of necessity—kill or be killed. In this case, something just snapped inside, and his rage unleashed. Kip knew the world would be a better and safer place without the virus named Finna. He raised his blaster and pulled the trigger, blowing a hole in Finna's chest. The officer's dead body slumped on the ground. A black silence took hold of Kip's mind. He had crossed that dangerous line of becoming Finna.

Rock grabbed Kip's arm and pulled him toward the burning schoolhouse. "We need to leave."

Kip did not like the feeling he had inside and was glad to keep moving with Rock toward the group of people spraying water on the burning structures.

In a stroke of creative genius, the town had built a tank on the hill above the village and manually pumped river water up to it as needed. The tank gravity fed back to the buildings, providing drinking water and the protection system for firefighting when needed. It was a sophisticated design.

Moot was operating the hose while others threw buckets of water on the flames to keep them from spreading to the other buildings. They had successfully knocked them down enough for others to start collecting valuables from inside the at-risk structures. As far as Kip could tell, no survivors had been found—for that matter, no bodies either.

"Maja," Rock said as he approached her. "We need to talk."

Maja stopped throwing buckets of water. Soot soiled her clothes. She faced Rock, anger raging in her eyes.

"I'm sorry," Rock said. "I had no idea they would fire on a school filled with children."

"They are evil incarnate, the worst you can imagine. And they call us savages."

"You need to get your people out of here. You're not safe. Get lost in the woods, maybe in the caves below. The drone got away. They already know they lost the ship and will be back for revenge. Don't worry about the buildings."

"And what of you two?"

"We can't go to my village," Rock said. "They'll keep coming for us until we're dead."

Kip thought of Finna's words and knew he'd never see peace again. They'd keep coming for him and use Sky to do it. Kip seethed, "Then we go back to Nirvana and bring the fight to Citizen One."

Rock glared at him. "What are you thinking?"

"I'm not going to be hunted like a wild animal anymore, letting innocent people get hurt. If we're going to die, we're going to end it on our terms."

Maja didn't try to argue. "Follow the river south." She pointed in that direction. "It runs through Pubtown. Use the path in the caves behind our house. Its exit is hidden behind the falls. There should be a raft at our landing just south of there." She stepped in and hugged Rock. "Be careful. The river will be dangerous, and they'll be watching."

"What of the doctor and the children?" Kip asked.

Maja's face became grim. "No sign of them. There's a lot of rubble in the back where the house collapsed. I'm hoping they made it to the back tunnel and into the caves."

Chapter 26

Maja wasted no time gathering the villagers. She urged, "Leave now. Take only what you can carry! Go into the caves and hide until the danger passes."

"What about our home?" a woman cried.

"With any luck," Maja answered, "the troopers coming will see an empty village. With no one to kill or torture, they'll leave."

Kip said nothing, but suspected otherwise. At a minimum, they'd burn the town to send a message to those who aided their enemies. Unfortunately, he and Rock could not be here to find out or help in the evacuation. It was too dangerous for them to be seen with the villagers.

Kip and Rock stopped in Maja's kitchen and gathered some bread wrapped in leaves and then headed for the rear bedroom where they'd been sleeping. They grabbed the flashlight off the table, pulled the weaving back, and squeezed through the wall's opening. Kip reached back to straighten the cloth, covering their escape route as much as possible.

Rock held the flashlight out, illuminating the path in front of them. Holding the bread and gun, Kip stayed close behind and wondered how in his twenty-eight years of life had he never been in a cave and that now he was in his second one in days. There'd be time to reflect on the chances of that later, but for now, speed was essential.

The narrow path on which they trekked was smooth, packed dirt with tunnellike solid stone walls that appeared to have been carved by running water. Its height was just enough for the two men to walk upright. They headed downward, losing altitude as they wound through the hill, making their way toward the river. They had only traveled a few minutes when Rock stopped and switched off the beam. In the darkness, Kip could barely make out Rock's finger held to his lips, once again requesting silence. They stood, not moving or making a sound, when the glow of a light flashed ahead of them, followed by a squeaky young voice, the voice of a child speaking.

Rock moved closer and whispered, "We can't let them see us or know we're here. It would be dangerous knowledge for them."

"Agreed," Kip whispered back. "Is it Fawn?"

Rock shrugged. "Possibly, or the other villagers." He motioned for Kip to follow.

They crept down the tunnel and entered a cavernous space, the soft sound of water flowing now audible. Kip could now see that the voices and the muted light were coming from an elevated area off to their right, although no one was visible. He could see their light's reflection dancing on the walls and hear the scared whispers of multiple children, a sure sign they were heading deeper into the cave system. Rock grabbed Kip's arm, pulling him away from the hiding villagers and toward the sound of water.

A few moments later, when they were a safe distance away, Rock relit his beam and surveyed the area. They now stood in the middle of the giant cavern that could easily fit thirty of Nirvana's largest buses. The rocky ceiling was embedded with tiny crystals that sparkled when the light hit them. The floor was a combination of sand and large stone crafted by the erosion of water. At the far end of the cave, a cascade of white water covered an opening to the outside.

"That must be the falls and the river," Kip whispered.

Rock nodded, saying nothing in return but moving toward the opening. They were soon staring at the back side of the river falls, which produced a heavy mist that dewed on Kip's open skin. They continued on the path until they stood outside the cavern on a rock precipice behind the wall of water. Kip scanned the area, looking for the last segment of the trail that would take them to safety, but there was none. The path apparently ended here.

Rock hesitated as the heavy mist blanketed them, peering through the cascade, scanning the river and its shores for any sign of danger.

Kip studied the river as well, also listening. He saw no one, only hearing the roar of the water. "Where to?" he asked.

"I'm guessing through," Rock said. "Probably the only way this place stays hidden."

"So, we're getting wet."

"We are, unless you can think of a better way." Rock gave Kip a chance to answer, but nothing came to mind.

Rock set the flashlight down and said, "The villagers will eventually find it and use it." He leaned out, peering over the edge again. "See you down there, and don't lose the gun." He stepped back a few paces, then ran and jumped through the falling torrent of water.

Kip heard the splash in the river but couldn't see him surface. Waiting a few seconds for Rock to clear the landing area, Kip mimicked his preparation. Holding the bread in one hand and gun in the other, he stepped back, then accelerated. His foot landed solid as he leaped as far as he could. The water rush from the falls hit him hard, shocking his system. He entered the water with a slap, trying to keep his gear high and dry, but failed miserably as his body submerged into a deep pool. The ambient cold hit like a hammer, taking his breath away. The rushing current swept him sideways, pushing him forward, the bridge fall suddenly flashing in his mind. Using his arms, he finally righted himself and got his head above the waterline. He stroked toward the shore, able to gain a tenuous footing on the slippery river rocks. Then Rock was there again, offering a hand. Kip grabbed it and rose out of the cold. A chill rippled through his body as the gentle breeze caressed his skin. Despite its leaf wrapping, the bread was long past soggy. Kip let it slip into the river. His blaster was soaked again, but likely still operable.

As they emerged onto dry land, Kip peered upstream toward the falls and saw no sign of a raft or canoe. Rock was already making his way downstream. Striding along the shoreline, they came to a dam-like blockade of the river. The combination of boulders holding downed trees created an idyllic pool but, more importantly, signified the end of the river's rapids. The downstream water appeared glassy, ideal for raft travel.

Just below the natural dam, Kip spied a raft hidden under bushes and pulled partially onto the rocky shore. "There." He pointed.

They hurried down the shoreline, Rock splashing into the water the last few feet to free the craft from its tied mooring. He pushed it from under the bushes into the open water, then to the shore where Kip waited.

Sturdy and made from hewn trees, the raft consisted of two layers of brown barked pine logs. The logs that comprised the lower level were secured parallel to the water flow and the upper-tier was tied perpendicular to the lower level. They were lashed together with a thin braided rope that minimized the open space between the logs. Centered on top of the raft was a thin wooden pole, made from a young sapling, perfect for pushing through the slower sections of the river.

Kip stepped onto the raft and took the pole.

Wading, Rock pushed them into open water and jumped on. Kip poled the raft into the center of the current, where they started floating away in a peaceful silence.

A loud hum broke the tranquility, followed by a resonating boom. A fireball exploded from the upstream hillside where the town stood. Kip watched as black smoke rose, billowing high into the sky. The soldiers had returned with air support and, from the sounds of it, with a vengeance. The booms continued, growing fiercer by the moment and the smell of burning wood now filled the air.

Kip poled harder, pushing them as fast as he could, his muscles burning while sweat ran down his back. The sounds of war started to fade. Kip suspected this was driven by the distance they had moved and not by the ferocity of the continuing assault. That distance was still not far enough for him.

They rounded a narrow bend in the river, the blue water picking up speed and moving them close to the near shore. Kip noted that this was a particularly overgrown section, where mature trees from both shores interlaced to form a low ceiling of leaf-covered branches. The shore was overgrown with large bushes laden with heavy green leaves.

Rock said, "Push us to the shore now."

Kip didn't ask, he just acted. He had learned to trust his friend's instincts. He poled to the shore. They nestled in under the hanging wide leaves of the bushes which covered most of the wooden surface. Rock leaned over, tying the raft to the main stalk.

"Lie down. Hide under the leaves." Rock demonstrated, lying on the raft and pulling the wide bush leaves down.

Kip followed suit, pulling the branches over him so that only the outer log of the raft was exposed. "What are we doing?"

"Hiding until the drones pass," Rock answered. "The soldiers will come searching to see if anybody is downstream. It's just a matter of time. Keep yourself covered; their scans shouldn't penetrate these leaves."

Kip pulled the limbs down, holding them tighter. They waited. They lay in silence for what seemed like hours, the gentle gurgle of the river a dreamy companion, the far-off boom of a soldier's gun an occasional nightmare.

As predicted, a buzz sounded in the distance. Growing louder as it approached, the drone came speeding down the river. It paused at the tunnellike opening in the trees, the engine whining steadily as it hovered while making the decision to venture in or go the safer route above. The engine's hum peaked. The decision was made. The drone rose and buzzed away.

Kip relaxed, letting the branches go. He peered at Rock, who was grinning. "Think they saw us?" Kip whispered.

"Unlikely. It would have stayed longer to get a closer view," Rock answered.

"Good. What's next?"

"Rest, maybe even get some sleep," Rock said. "We should travel by night. Fewer eyes watching. So, for now, we wait to ensure the drones are gone and the sun sets."

As much as Kip wanted to sleep, he couldn't slow his mind. He lay, comfortably listening to the water flow, thinking about Fawn and her kindness, hoping that she and the family were safe. And then, he thought about Sky. For all that had happened, he still missed her smile, the smell of her hair, and the taste of her lips. But it unsettled him hearing what Finna had to say about her. What did he mean? And what did she want to tell him that fateful day at the zoo?

Chapter 27

Kip woke to the rustle of branches; the breeze was picking up. The sun had disappeared, and the shadowy darkness of evening now blanketed them. He stretched, not remembering falling asleep, only thinking of Sky and Fawn, hoping they were safe. When he rolled over, his back ached. The rigid beams of the raft were unforgiving. The snap of a twig breaking came from the shore. His eyes went to Rock's location, but his friend was gone.

The branches of the bushes separated, and Rock came through. He dumped a bunch of berries and mushrooms on the raft's beams, then grabbed its edge and pushed against the shore. The raft moved. "Heads up," Rock said as the craft slid from under the branches.

Kip held the leaves away so that their spiked edges didn't rake him. With the raft now free, Rock hopped on and began centering the food in the dry area of the raft. Kip was already holding the wooden pole, pushing on the rocky river bottom, navigating to the center of the current. Once in the flow, he casually stood at the back of the raft, occasionally poking down to straighten their course. Rock sat cross-legged in the front, nibbling on berries while watching the shorelines in a protective vigilance.

Under a full moon, they rode in silence. The only sounds were the natural ones created by wind, water, or wildlife. The moon provided a soft, illuminating glow that covered the rugged, picturesque terrain in gray shadows. It was bright enough to see deep into the wild countryside, but secretive enough to keep the landscape's details hidden. On occasion, Kip would see a flash of movement with a glimpse of white fur. He assumed it was deer or elk wandering the rugged land that nestled into the river's edge.

As they floated past a sparsely treed area, a pack of wolves started howling somewhere in the distance. Aided by the fact they were safely protected inside the river's boundaries, what started as unnerving became glorious by the yelping finale.

"It's beautiful out here," Kip said.

"Yes, very beautiful but also wild and dangerous," Rock said, still watching the shorelines.

"If it's so dangerous, why do people live in such isolation? I mean, they're raising families out here?" Kip paused. "By the way, do you still have family?"

"I did," Rock said, his jaw clenched. "Nirvana's soldiers killed them when they attacked our village. That's when I killed the twelve men. Not in revenge, but in the heat of battle when they attacked me. But, much like Maja's village, the soldiers returned in force and killed everyone they found. They murdered my wife and child, then captured me."

"I'm so sorry. I didn't know. . . ."

"You sensed enough to not swing at the Games; that's sufficient."

"That must be difficult to live with."

"At times." Rock swiveled to meet Kip's eyes. "Your next lesson outside your protected city existence is that life is hard, people die. You're at risk when you love someone. Loss and grief are always nearby."

"I'm not even sure what love is. Everything is so selfish in Nirvana. But love doesn't sound appealing."

"It is appealing. In the end, love is worth the pain. We all experience death—no one gets out alive."

"But they were young."

"Yes, but they led meaningful lives and impacted many for the better. Most importantly, I know I will see them again." Rock refocused his attention on the shores, vigilant in his watch. "You asked about danger and living in the wilds. Are your cities safe?"

"In some places, where the Elite Citizens live, but they're not in many other areas."

"So, why do you live there?"

Kip thought for a moment. "I guess I have food, medicine, shelter, and at least some safety."

"We have all that here and more. We have freedom. We think for ourselves, determine our own future, trust in one another, and help those in need. And yes, we must protect our families from the wilds, but the biggest risk we face are the soldiers from Nirvana." Rock tensed for a moment, studying the shore, then relaxed. "Out here, we don't have the State playing in our minds telling us what to do, what to eat, who to sleep with, and controlling our thoughts. We have free will."

Kip thought about Rock's comments. "We have laws. I guess it's part of being in a civil society." His response didn't even convince himself.

"Civil," Rock retorted. "You've seen Maja's village. Is that the savages you were told were in the wilds? Is the little girl picking berries less civil than the bloody Games in the arena?" There was an edge to Rock's tone.

"No, you're right. I'm not going to defend them. There are so many things I disagree with. The Games being one."

"So, why live in the city?" Rock probed.

Once again, Kip considered the question. "I guess it's perceived safety. My people trade their freedoms for the promise of safety. The concept that the Citizen Leaders will take care of you in times of a crisis."

"My experience is the Citizen Leaders cause the crisis, often intentionally, to drive a desired change in society or, more than likely, to consolidate their power. You're less safe with them than the pack of wolves you just heard." Rock chuckled, lowering the tension of the moment. "You will be sacrificed when it furthers their cause."

"Is that what's happening now? Am I being sacrificed?"

"What's happened to you could all be a coincidence, but my bet is it's not. You made Citizen One look bad. Plus . . ." Rock leaned lay back on the raft, his gaze momentarily going to the night sky.

Kip felt flush as anger flooded through him. Rock's words echoed with the truth. "Plus what?"

"Look up, tell me what you see," Rock said.

"I see stars."

"Is that all?"

Kip concentrated on the clear sky. Except for the moon's glow, it was a perfect night for stargazing. The longer he stared, the more the heavens came into focus. As far as the eye could see, millions upon millions of tiny specks of light radiated out. Each one represented a star like our sun, with who knows how many planets orbiting them. There was also a red planet visibly layered in front of a nebula-type cloud of gas. The sky's beauty was perfection, its origins a mystery. "I see a lot of unanswered questions. Where'd it all come from? Why is it here? Why are we here?"

Rock sat up, silent for a moment. "That's the answer I expected from the man who sacrificed everything by refusing to

279

join the mob in torturing a stranger. And that's why you're a threat to the Elites of Nirvana."

Kip spun his head to see Rock. "I don't understand."

"You think for yourself, you exercise free will even if it costs you, and you question the official narrative. You knew I wasn't the cold-blooded killer they represented, and you acted on it against their wishes. In short, they, the Elites, couldn't control you. And what they can't control scares them to the point that they must eliminate the threat in any way possible. In your case, they want to eliminate and make an example of you for all others who carry those traits."

Kip finally got it, the weight of the revelation troubling him. "I knew you weren't a killer. Your eyes, your actions in the ring, my inner voice—all told me you were a fighter, protecting something dear."

There was a long silence between the two men. Kip finally spoke. "So, where did it all come from?"

Rock's gaze returned to the sky. "The Shonto believe Yahweh, the Christians think God, the pagans believe in many gods working for or against one another. There are too many beliefs systems to describe them all. Even if I could describe them, I couldn't answer that question definitively. So, I'll answer the question this way. There is more to our existence than that which our senses deliver. Find the answer to what feels right to you and hold on to it. One freedom we have in the wilds is the freedom to worship however we choose."

Kip poled the raft to the left, keeping the channel. "The people of Nirvana cannot. There is no God, just the State. We are discouraged from studying the heavens and asking the bigger questions. Even if it's science-based."

"And why is that?" Rock asked.

Kip considered the question given all they had discussed. The answer hit him hard. "Because there can't be a higher power than the Citizen Leaders. There would be people that'd follow God's word and not the Elites. They'd lose control of the masses."

Rock twisted around to face him. "You're a quick study, young man."

Chapter 28
Tuesday, January 15, 2075

The first rays of the morning sun streamed through the eastern skies. Kip lay resting on the wooden beams in a semi-slumber, gently rocking with the water. They had traveled downstream, past where the lower fork merged with the main river and through the last vestiges of greenery and the old civilization. The skeletons of a few ghost towns popped up along the shoreline, their dilapidated housing and weed-infested streets telling the story of a bygone era where avarice reigned, and poor decisions followed. Kip didn't know the details of what caused civilization's collapse, only the State-sponsored drivel taught in schools that regaled the story of State heroism in the salvation of humankind. Knowing what he knew now, he'd bet the cause was intentional from the beginning. Create a problem so big that only the government itself can fix it. And do so in such a way as to ensure the new world that rises fits the order those in charge desire.

For his part, Rock was downright stoic, content on standing in a peaceful silence, letting the world glide by. This was fine by Kip. Never in his life had he sat under the open stars watching the beauty of nature at night unfold. Besides the stars and the powerful message they evoked, he witnessed deer, elk, and a close-up view of a mountain lion drinking from the river. There was something special about seeing the lion outside of a zoo. The wild glow in its eyes was inspiring. It brought back memories of Leo and the cage holding him. Blu was right. He was fed and cared for, but that's not what lions have evolved to. They were meant to live wild on the open land, to hunt for their food, to face the uncertainty of survival every day, then wake up and do it again. You could see it in Leo's eyes—they were broken and dying. Living the safe life behind protective walls and not working for his food is not what he was created for.

Kip felt the raft change course. He swiveled his head to see Rock poling them toward the shore.

"What's up?"

"Time to get off the river. Too many eyes in the daylight." He pushed on the pole once more. "We'll find a place to rest for the morning, then start for Nirvana this afternoon." The raft grounded on the shore.

Kip jumped off and pulled the weighty craft a few more inches onto the hard ground so the current wouldn't float it away. After Rock had gathered the remaining food, Kip threw some random driftwood on top, trying to make the raft appear weathered versus recently abandoned. In the end, he thought it was a sellable job.

With Rock leading, they set off to the south across a desertlike, rocky terrain, the sun now fully visible to their left. The crusty red dirt on which they trod bore some small cacti, the random thorny bush, and some miscellaneous hostile weeds. Kip noted that everything had thorns or nettles, a natural defense against would-be predators. The clothes and shoes Maja provided gave adequate protection against the hostile environment. Kip appreciated this. If Rock noticed any discomfort, once again, he did not show it.

Rock kept a hard pace. Kip assumed this was to make good time as well as to limit their exposure to hostile eyes. He wondered what camp or hiding spot his friend was searching for. As sweat streamed down his temple, the morning rest that Rock had mentioned earlier sounded really good.

Rock stopped running and moved to a crouched position behind some oversized red stones. He motioned for Kip to get low, then mouthed the word *house*.

Kip nodded his understanding and moved to one knee to catch his breath. Staying low, Rock held the blaster and crept forward. Kip waited, but raised his head to see the top of a mud house in the distance.

This type of single-room home was the most common structure in the Outer Boundary, where building materials were limited to some wood and lots of dirt. Loners who avoided the city centers many times sought their future by attempting to hunt and farm in this desolate land. These experiments often ended in tragedy. This particular homestead was rundown and appeared uninhabited, but assumptions could be deadly.

With Rock steps ahead, Kip followed in silence. Creeping foot by foot, they moved within an arm's reach of the back of the home. They stood motionless and listened to the sounds. It was there, the sound of a child crying—people. Rock readied his weapon as a big man with unkempt sandy hair stepped around the corner, holding up a rusted hoe. The chubby man wore traditional Nirvana laborer pants with an unbuttoned shirt covering a sweat-stained undershirt that matched his grubby set of dust-covered leather shoes.

The man immediately raised the hoe high in surrender, not wanting to test Rock's gun. "Hold on. Hold on! I mean you no harm," the man said as he tossed the farm tool harmlessly to the ground.

Rock lowered the weapon but kept it charged. "We're just passing through and saw your home. Thought you may have food and water we could buy."

"We do," the farmer said with a shake in his voice. "We have some fire-roasted fish, caught yesterday from the river, and some well water. You're welcome to all you can drink." He nervously took a step to the front of the house and glanced back at Rock's gun. "I'm Das. My family is inside. Let me assure them everything is alright."

He walked away, circling the small home to its front. Rock and Kip followed two steps behind. Kip noted that there was a small area in the large front yard that had been farmed and showed some signs of green growth and a recent harvest.

The man went to the door and started to pull.

"Stop," Rock ordered.

The baby's screaming got louder. With his gun raised, Rock motioned for Das to move away from the door. Das stepped back a few paces.

"What are you doing?" Kip asked.

"Confirming there are no weapons inside," Rock said. He cracked the beaten door, which was no more than old wooden slats nailed on a frame, and peeked inside. His body visibly relaxed by what he saw. He said something about "you're safe" in a low tone to the person inside.

"You leave my wife and baby alone!" the farmer commanded. "They can't harm you."

Rock said nothing but held the door open as a petite woman with dark hair and brown eyes walked out, holding a young child swaddled in a pink blanket. The poor woman appeared distressed. She was shaking, and terror filled her eyes. She cradled the baby to her body, offering the child whatever protection she could provide.

Kip's heart went out to her immediately. "We won't hurt you."

The farmer rushed the woman and snatched the baby from her arms. She shrieked, "No, Morgan!"

He wrapped a single arm around the baby and pinned it against his chest. "You leave now! Leave my family alone."

The young mother made a grab for the child, but Das pushed her away. "I'll protect him," he hissed at her.

Rock raised his rifle and pointed it at the man. "Give the child to the woman."

"You're going to shoot me and my baby?"

The woman cried, "Please don't hurt my Morgan." The baby started to cry.

"Just you," Rock said. "If you want to live, hand the baby to her mother."

The man glared at Rock for a long moment. With his free arm, he reached into his open shirt and withdrew a double-bladed knife. He held it to the child's throat. "Drop your weapon." He tightened his grip on the infant, knife shaking back and forth. "Drop—"

He didn't get the chance to finish. His words were cut short by the hiss of Rock's gun. The blast took half the farmer's head off. He started to fall. Kip shot over and grabbed the screaming child from the dead man's arm, and a second later his lifeless body landed with a thud.

With care, Kip handed the child to her sobbing mother. The petite woman couldn't speak. She hugged her baby as if it were her last day on Earth.

Kip put his arm around her to console her. "I'm sorry about your husband. He didn't give him much choice."

"That's not your husband, is it?" Rock interjected.

She shook her head, trembling.

"What's your name?"

"Lib."

"Lib, is your husband alive?"

Lib shook her head again, this time pointing a finger to the field. "He's dead, his throat cut by him," she said through tears.

"Do you have family nearby? Someone you can stay with and maybe help bury his body?"

Lib nodded this time. "About a thirty-minute walk." She squeezed her child again, burying her face into the child's neck while holding back tears.

"Can we help you get there?" Kip asked.

She nodded again. "If you can walk us to the bridge, I'll be safe from there. And that road will take you to Nirvana. I assume that's where you're going."

"We're headed south of Nirvana, meeting family in the Outer Boundary," Rock lied. "With that said, we're happy to escort you to the bridge."

Kip assumed the lie was to protect the woman in case soldiers came through inquiring. "Lib, do you need to pack anything?" he asked.

"I just have to grab a few things. My family will come back for the rest." She hugged her child, then started toward the house.

Rock stopped her. "The child, Morgan, is a girl?"

Lib nodded. "Yeah, why?"

"No reason," Rock said.

She opened the door and disappeared.

Once alone, Kip asked, "How'd you know?"

Rock gave a small shrug. "His clothes. They're not a farmer's, especially the shoes."

Kip examined the dead man's shoes. Rock was correct. "Those aren't farming shoes. And?"

"And when I opened the door, there was relief in her eyes that it was me, not him."

"But you couldn't be certain of that."

"No, but when the man referred to the baby with a pink blanket as 'him,' I was pretty sure."

Kip listened, more than impressed. "And when were you sure-sure?"

"When he took the child. I could tell he was holding her like a shield. I'm sorry I couldn't tell you more. I was hoping to diffuse the situation without blood."

"Like I said, he didn't give you much choice." Kip hesitated, a troubling feeling in his gut.

"What's wrong?" Rock asked.

"I don't feel any remorse. Not for killing Finna, not for the soldiers who died with the spiders, or at Shonto, and not for this man."

"How about empathy for Fawn and the school children, for Maja? For this young lady and her fatherless child?"

Kip hesitated, taking stock in his emotional state. "Yeah, I guess I do. This is wrong. All of it was wrong."

"Good, that means you have a moral center. You protected the weak against evil. Embrace that, trust it, and nourish it. Use it to identify the wicked and depraved, whether it be this depraved man or Citizen One. Criminals come with many faces and from all walks of life. Unfortunately, the price of freedom is that you are compelled to act and fight the monstrosity of evil for the benefit of others."

Kip peered at the dead man, then back to Rock. He nodded his head. "I understand and will."

"And, like you saw today," Rock continued, "don't hesitate. It could cost an innocent their life." Rock leaned down and grabbed the dead man's foot. "Help me move this body."

Kip grabbed the other foot. They dragged the remains through the dirt and placed it in the field next to the farmer that he had killed. The farmer's body lay sprawled unnaturally in the dirt, a deep knife wound through his neck. He had died quickly.

Rock nodded to Lib's dead husband. "Last lesson for today. What happened when you tried protecting your family in Nirvana?"

"I was punished."

"Out here, you're punished if you don't protect them."

The door swung open and Lib stepped out, her eyes red from crying. She now wore a backpack and carried the child on her hip. In her right hand, she held a brown cloth sack.

The two men stepped away from the bodies to meet her, saving her from reliving the emotional trauma.

She offered the sack to Kip. "We don't have much, but here's some food and a skin of water. It's all I have." She forced a smile. "Thank you both for what you did. You saved our lives."

Chapter 29

The two men hiked through the rugged yet beautiful terrain. They had cut cross-country to avoid the main road and its travelers, believing that a safe gap was in their best interest for the time being. Kip guessed the route was also more direct, thus saving some distance, albeit adding some obstacles. This resulted in a slower but steady pace.

They had escorted Lib and her child through her family's fields and then along a short section of brown land that paralleled the water. Kip volunteered and happily carried Morgan for a good part of the trek. They walked until they came to a narrow section of the river that was defined by its unusual stone falls. Only yards in width, it was three times that in height, with a large pool of water standing behind it. The falls were made by two giant rocks lying side by side to create the dam, but their tops had eroded away over time, leaving a smooth, flat outcrop that poured water like the spout of a pitcher. Both upstream and downstream of the falls were packed dirt trails formed by people portaging their boats and rafts around. Two small rafts were presently moored at the upstream shore.

Downstream of the falls, at the narrowest point of the river, a sturdy wooden bridge traversed the river high above the water. At the near end of the bridge, an old toll collector stood in front of a massive gate, gun on his belt, guarding the crossing. He recognized Lib at once. He left his post, rushing to the mother and her child. Lib burst out in tears, running to meet him, the stress of the day finally breaking through. Kip handed Morgan to the old man, who, after hearing the full story, introduced himself with an iron handshake as Trim, Lib's uncle.

Trim eyed Kip and Rock for a long moment, then said, "You two seem familiar." He extended his hospitality and asked, "Do you need a safe place to stay?" while motioning to the far side of the river.

"No thank you," Rock said. "We're heading south as soon as possible."

Kip wondered whether he recognized them or not, but it was here they said goodbye to Lib and Morgan. Lib gave a hug to both men, holding Rock for a few extra moments.

Trim offered a respectful bow before pointing to a road with broken pavement. "Nirvana is due south that way, a half day's hike. So, you probably want to stay clear of that, lots of soldiers and scrutiny that way. There is, however, a little-used path about a ten-minute walk through that field," he gestured toward the open land. "It'll take you close to Nirvana and it's safe enough." He ended with a wink, then put his arm around Lib to escort her and Morgan over the bridge.

Following Trim's guidance, they hiked most of the day, stopping only for a brief rest and to eat the food and drink the water provided by Lib. Kip appreciated her gesture, and was now convinced that Rock was right—the vast majority of people are good in heart. Unfortunately, it's usually the Dases of the world people hear about.

During the second stop, Rock sipped some water, then handed the skin to Kip. "We haven't spoken about your plan. We should."

Kip gave a loud sigh. "To be honest, I don't really have one except proving you're alive and I'm not a killer. Was hoping to come up with something that would expose that truth." He took a drink and wiped his mouth with the back of his hand. "And, if I can choose the ending, I'd prefer one that ends in a painful death for Citizen One."

Rock smiled at the joke, a rare display of emotion. "You said let's bring the fight to Nirvana. They have a lot of soldiers, technology, and guns. You know attacking them could mean your death?"

"Yes, I've thought about that a lot since my fall off the bridge."

"Does it scare you?"

"I'd be lying if I said no. Fear of the unknown and all." Kip met Rock's eyes. "But after the bridge, something inside has changed. I feel there is something more to our existence than just flesh and bone." He watched the sky. A raptor circled overhead, and the sun was low on the horizon. "Do I sound crazy?"

"I'd think you were crazy if you didn't think that. We're more than just flesh and blood, we are also spirit."

Kip thought of Yahweh again, and a sense a calm flowed through him. "My inner voice is telling me that not only is this the truth, but this is the right path for me, despite the risk." He took another sip of water. "What about you? This could mean your death too."

Rock shrugged. "As I've said, I believe in something more. I have faith our human energy does not die, and I will see my wife and child again in the next life. In fact, I look forward to it."

Kip offered the skin of water to Rock. "Drink. We'll have access to water soon."

Rock took the water and gulped some. "What will we do when we get to Nirvana?" Rock asked.

"We'll go to Pubtown. I have a few friends there who may be able to help, or at least hide us for a few days while we figure something out."

"That's a start," Rock said as he stood. "Let's get going."

* * *

They made good time reaching the outskirts of Pubtown. As they approached the city, the last rays of sunlight streaked through the sky, giving way to the night. It was then that the cross-country path they traveled terminated into the main road that led to the city. While they had avoided the vigilant eyes of the State to that moment, the risk of such an encounter was now high and growing with each step forward. Kip felt it best to evade unwanted attention by entering the city under the cover of darkness. As they mixed into the ambling travelers approaching the city, he realized this plan had failed before it began.

Since his departure a week ago, the city had fortified its outer perimeter with heavy barbed wire. Using the river as one terminal point, it appeared they had encircled the city limits with razor fencing all the way to the cliffs of the Heights, creating a fortress. All travelers in and out of the city were being funneled through a single point on the main road that ran adjacent to the river. The two men slid into the line for the entrance that was at least twenty deep, including the carts being pulled by vendors bringing wares to sell from the country. Kip noted that the line exiting the city was of equal length. The fence was the perfect mechanism for both keeping people in and locking people out.

Kip watched as the line moved. There were three security guards observing the crowd and two more at the bottleneck checking the implants of those who had them. The Outlanders with no implants were forced into a temporary holding pen that was nothing more than a hastily built fenced-in mud pit with no shelter or comforts. The prison-like area held hundreds of asylum seekers, all huddled together for warmth or security. Kip

KP Boudreaux

observed as the pen's single guard holding a wand removed a young, attractive woman from the larger group. She and her family screamed and fought the soldier accosting her, but to no avail. She was removed from the enclosure. Kip suspected the worst, as did the man who continued to rage both verbally and physically against their aggressor until the soldier turned and hit him with the wand. The family rushed to the fallen man's aid, their discontent now silent while the guard led the sobbing woman away.

Concerned about the deteriorating situation, Kip started to walk away from the line when a soldier called out, "Hey, farm-ass! Get back in line!"

Rock touched Kip's arm. "Don't do anything to draw attention to yourself."

"We can't go through here," Kip whispered. "My implant will connect to their system any second. I'm wanted, so it'll flag me, and if they scan it, lots of people will die."

"I know, but if we run, they'll kill us now. There's nowhere to hide," Rock whispered back. "We've always got the element of surprise." He flashed the hidden gun barrel from the laser at Kip.

The line moved forward, as did the two men's fate with the soldiers. In his mind, Kip started rehearsing his answers to the guards. They were five people away when the holding pen erupted. People began screaming as one of the fence posts fell,

298

pulled by a rope and an unseen force. Kip could have sworn he saw a vehicle in the shadows, but that would be an overt assault on State property. This was a dangerous and escalating action, and the State would be mobilizing its forces in response. The only question was how fast.

What was certain is that this single aggression was the trigger to chaos. The caged people started to flee over the downed section of fence. With the sole guard who had been watching the pen gone, the other soldiers ran to the melee of escaping inmates, leaving the front gate unguarded. Seeing the opportunity, people on both sides of the bottleneck also decided it was best to capitalize on the turmoil and get through while they could and try to escape the soldiers.

"Move," Rock ordered.

They rushed through the unguarded gate, and Kip led them into the outer neighborhood of the city. They immediately got off the main road and onto the secondary streets with the rundown houses and businesses of ill repute. With no streetlights in this area, the shadows were deep and ideal for those not wanting to be seen.

They heard sirens blaring in the distance and the buzz of drones overhead. Reinforcements were on their way.

"We need to get off the streets. They'll do a wide sweep of bodies and implants soon to identify who's in the area and who shouldn't be. We're at risk," Kip said.

"This is your party. Where to?" Rock said.

"I only know two places and can't risk going to one of them," Kip answered.

"Sounds like an easy choice."

With Kip leading, they hurried through the narrow streets and back alleys, cutting over to River Street. Kip studied both directions, ensuring they were still alone before taking the corner. Fortunately, this area was around a big bend in the river, thus temporarily safe from the chaos at the gate. There would still be aerial scanning, but not as a priority here, meaning they should have some time to hide.

Kip led Rock down River Street, coming from the opposite direction of his last trip. They stayed deep in the shadows until they arrived at his old house. Kip crept up the stairs, trying not to scare the residents or neighbors. Rock followed, not making a sound. Both men slid past the unlocked front door and into the hallway leading to Trase's apartment, the old floorboards screaming their arrival. Kip knocked on Trase's door.

"Go away or I'll call security!" Trase answered in a gruff tone.

Kip didn't answer, but knocked again, softer this time, then whispered, "Trase."

The door cracked open. Kip saw half of the old woman's face. "I've been expecting you," she said softly, her eye wide with excitement.

She opened the door more to see who else was there, then reached out and pulled Kip in. Rock followed quickly behind. "Hurry, the scanners can't be far off. We need to get you hidden." She paused to study Rock. "Are you . . . the guy from the Games?"

Rock nodded.

"No implant, right?"

"No implant."

"Good, follow me."

She led them to her back room, pulled up a rug, and then the trap door it covered. Kip stepped down an old ladder that was as tall as he was and into a small room that appeared to be lined with metal. He squeezed to the back, allowing space for Rock to sit comfortably. Trase handed down some bread, a jar of water, a candle, and matches.

She started to close the door, then whispered, "I'll be back as soon as they pass. You're safe. They won't see you down there."

She closed the door with a click, and everything went dark.

Chapter 30

Kip drummed his leg with his fingers, then tapped it again, and then again. An ill-defined darkness had washed through him, and the more time ticked away, the more at-risk he felt. He guessed it had been a couple of hours of sitting in Trase's smuggling box with nothing to do but have his mind wander about the events happening outside. The candle had burned halfway down and the bread had been eaten. Now, they just waited in a brooding silence.

Kip's mind churned. Had the scanners come by? And if so, where was Trase? Why didn't she put her head down the stairs and affirm that everything was all right? He had gone to the trapdoor more than a couple of times and tried to open it, but it was locked tight. Could she have betrayed them, locking them in and leading the soldiers here? If so, where were they?

As these thoughts gnawed at him, Rock lay on the ground, eyes closed, his body quiet and still. Kip couldn't say if he was even awake.

Until Rock spoke. "Remember what we talked about in Torg's caves? You're doing the negative energy thing again."

Kip knew he was right. "Sorry, it's just my nature to worry."

"Master your nature. We chose the best option we had in coming here. She'll be back and it'll either be good news or bad news. We'll address it when we see her. Until then, we don't know and shouldn't assume. Worrying never helps."

Kip shifted his weight. Hours of sitting on the hard metal floor had become increasingly uncomfortable. "You're right. I'll tone it down."

He stopped talking and listened intently, hoping every house creak was the sound of footsteps. It was maddening. He needed to change his mindset. "What do you think Trase meant when she said she was expecting me? You heard that, right?"

"I did, and I can't say what she meant besides the simple interpretation. She was expecting you, but that doesn't help any. The 'when' and 'why' are the critical information."

"It's weird. She would have known I was sent to reeducation, and no way she knew we were back."

A muffled slam of a door came from the apartment above, followed by clomping footsteps crossing the creaky wooden floor.

"Guess we'll find out now," Rock said, sitting up.

The trap door opened and light flooded down the stairs. Trase's voice came in a hushed tone, "Come up, it's safe now."

"You first," Rock said with deference.

Kip sprang up the ladder, his time in the square box mercifully over. Rock climbed behind him.

Trase leaned in and whispered, "Sorry for the delay, but it was worth it. We're going to meet some friends who can help. Kip knows them. For now, we need silence and speed." She pulled out a reinforced black knit hat. "This is for you." She handed it to Kip. "Wear the lined side over your implant."

"What is it?"

"A safety precaution. It keeps your implant from connecting into the AST system and blocks any wide-range scanning. If the watchers are out still, they won't know who you are."

Kip slid the cap on.

"Stay close and act like you belong here."

As they exited the house, Kip noted the moon was still high in the evening sky. They navigated their way through a maze of darkened streets and alleys. Given the number of turns, Kip began to think they were trying to lose somebody tailing them. They passed several small groups or individuals huddled in corners or loitering on the street. Kip was surprised at the number of people that were still out given the earlier events. In all cases these strangers kept to themselves. No one tried to engage with them.

They eventually made their way to the alley to find Jun waiting once more, a small light in his hand. They stopped a few feet off the street where Trase stepped in close to Kip. "This is where I say goodbye." She gave a motherly smile, placing her hand on his arm. "Be safe and careful who you trust."

"Thank you for the help," Kip said.

Rock nodded to her.

Jun reached over. "You know the drill." He reached up and pulled down the black cap to cover Kip's eyes. "For everyone's safety, not even a peek. We can't risk some officer scanning your implant later and finding this location."

"What about you?" Rock asked Jun.

"I'm a drunk that lives here, so what I have on my implant is very believable. Also, unlike you, I'm not of interest to Security."

"And me?" Rock asked.

"No implant, no blindfold required." Jun grabbed Kip's arm and started escorting him through the shadows. He turned back to Rock. "They may torture you for the info, but we'll be long gone by then."

Jun navigated with the same care as Kip's last journey down the alley, soon arriving at the meeting spot. "You're here," he said, releasing Kip's arm. "You can take the hat off now."

Kip removed it and placed it on the table where he had previously sat with Ann and Ell. He scanned the room. It hadn't changed, still the small table and four chairs. There was, however, a shiny new electronic device centered on the table. The constant background hum still vibrated through the area.

The door squeaked open, and in walked Ann in her server's apron. Ell came in next, smelling of Ooze and wearing the same dirty clothes in which Kip last saw him.

"The prodigal son returns," Ell said, a hint of derision in his tone.

Ell pulled back a chair for Ann, who was the first to sit. "We're surprised to see you, Kip," she offered in a gentle way, then pointed to the open seats. "And even more so your friend. Must be quite a story."

"It is." Kip pulled out a chair and sat down. Rock did the same. "We didn't know where else to go," Kip said.

"It was dangerous coming here!" Ell shot back. "The two most wanted men on the planet in one of our best hideouts? What could go wrong? Especially—"

Ann put her hand on Ell's arm in a calming way, stopping his rant. "I'm sorry for Ell. He's been a little agitated since earlier today when we heard of your return."

"Earlier today?" Rock said. "We've only been here a few hours."

"We got a message from a mutual friend, Trim," Ann said. "He recognized you and suspected you'd be coming back here. He said to tell you thank you for what you did but didn't elaborate."

"How'd you think you got into the city, luck?" Ell interjected. "We knew you were coming and sent our people to pull down the fence at the right time to distract the guards. You'd both be dead now if it wasn't for us."

Rock studied Ell for a moment. "Thank you for your help." He stood, pushing his chair back. "I can appreciate that our presence is a risk for you. We'll leave and find another way."

Ann raised her hands in a calming gesture. "Please, sit. It's Rock, correct?" She motioned to Jun. "Can you please run and get us four Oozes? Leave them outside the door, then go to your post. We'll grab them when ready."

"Of course." Jun took his leave.

"Alright, is everybody calm?" Ann said. "We have stuff to share that could be helpful to you. And you've got a story we need to hear." She met Rock's eyes. He sat back down, saying nothing. "Okay, as a gesture of good will, I'll go first."

Kip nodded.

"First thing for you, Kip," Ann said, "Tik is back, and not doing well. I thought you'd want to know."

"Who's Tik?" Rock asked.

"My old boss at the zoo and the person who connected us," Kip said. "He went for a black-market kidney replacement. The State denied him a lab-grown one." He paused. "Where is he and what's the issue?"

"He's home trying to rest, and it's either rejection or infection. He's in pain and running a high fever. If it gets much worse, he'll have to be admitted to Nirvana's medical. Which is another issue altogether."

"That's not good," Kip said. "If they heal him, they'll send him to the Seniors Resort for rehab, then probably a stint in reeducation for breaking the law. Is there anything we can do to help him?"

"No, he needs a good doctor and a lot of luck," Ann said. "Next is your partner Sky." She watched Kip for a reaction and got none. "We continued digging and did find something odd. The day of the Changing, she was awarded 400 social score credits and her basic income was upped. Not crazy unusual, but the timing was. It wasn't on her typical evaluation cycle. Meaning, she may be compromised."

"She is compromised," Ell forcefully interjected. "We can't afford to believe in coincidences."

Kip slouched, head hanging just over the old table, a heavy feeling in his chest. He thought of Sky and their time together when the obvious hit him.

"We don't know that she is, but the risk is high." Ann tried to be less harsh.

Kip sat up. "No, I think Ell is right. Even if she's not now, she was."

"Why do you say that?" Ann asked.

"We met randomly at the Games because she was sitting next to me, meaning our social scores were in the same range,"

309

Kip explained. "When we exited the Changing, her social score flashed up. It was almost 400 points greater than mine. She made a bad joke about saving a busload of orphans. I was so out of it that I didn't pick up on it at the time."

"That's consistent with what we saw. But we can't determine why she was given 400 social credits. There may be an innocent explanation," Ann said.

"Nobody gets 400 credits unless they're dirty," Ell said in a matter-of-fact tone, then glanced at Kip, adding, "I'm sorry. I know you like her."

Ell's offering didn't help, Kip felt foolish. He had been betrayed, it was clear to him now.

Ann got up and opened the door. She retrieved the four Oozes sitting outside, placing one in front of each person. "This is about as good a time as any for this. Your body language says you could use a drink."

"Thank you, I can." Kip gulped the Ooze, not caring how retched it was. After Torg's brew, Ooze was easy. As everyone sat, sipping their brew, Kip processed Sky's actions. He couldn't shake his inner voice telling him that their connection was real. Was it possible she had faked everything? Was he clinging to a false hope? And then true clarity hit.

"Then again . . ." Kip started.

"Go on," Rock said.

Kip continued, "There's something I keep coming back to. On the day of Citizen Eight's death, Sky met me at the zoo. It was an unusual visit."

"How so?" Ann asked.

"She said she wanted to tell me something, basically saying she hadn't been honest and wanted to start over."

"She came to confess?" Rock interjected, before sipping his Ooze. His only reaction to the brew was a faint smile.

"Or to lure you there to frame you for the murder of Citizen Eight," Ell said.

Kip spoke to Ell. "Maybe, but not knowingly. She had tears in her eyes, there was no faking that. I'm sure of it."

"Sure enough to bet your life on it?" Ell said. "Because that's what you'll be doing if you see her again."

"Enough," Ann interjected. "We're not going to solve this now." She spoke to Kip. "Ell's right, though. You can't be positive she's not involved. I'd be careful about trusting her." Ann sipped her Ooze. "The last thing I'll share is we think we've been compromised. Hence Ell's warm reaction to your arrival."

"How so?" Kip asked.

"Couple of operations have gone bad, including one yesterday. Our people were arrested," Ell answered.

"Anybody in a critical role?" Rock asked.

"No planners, all ground operatives. But the odd thing is, Nirvana security has been waiting for us each time. Feels like they're getting close," Ann said.

"They knew in advance," Ell said sharply. "Somebody has been tipping them off. It's why we didn't tell anybody you were coming in. As far as our people know, the fence assignment was solely to free those new arrivals."

"Or they have your places bugged," Kip said.

"Possible but improbable," Ann said. "Like here, we have sound protection in our key planning areas. And it seems they're only coming for the people on the ground, not the planners. They'd raid here if they had anything on us."

"That makes sense," Rock said.

"That said," Ann added, "trust no one outside this room until we find the leak." She spoke to Kip, "Now, let's hear your story. How did you escape reeducation?" She then turned to Rock. "And, how are you alive?"

Kip sipped his Ooze. "I don't even know where to start."

Ell laughed out loud. "You're not going to." He flipped a switch on the circular device on the table. It started to project a fuzzy holograph over its top. Ell then grabbed the silver circular device from his pocket and, as he had done before, held it near Kip's head. He pressed a button on the scanner, and Kip's implant images were now shown as a holograph above the device.

"We've made progress since we last saw you," Ell said to Kip. "I can pretty much project these images to any device now."

Rock stared in a disgusted amazement. "Doesn't it bother you to read a man's life like this?"

"One of many things you get used to if you want to survive," Ann answered.

"I'm working on one that will read thoughts even without an implant." Ell's eyes went wide toward Rock, feigning shock.

"Not sure if you're joking or serious, but that's terrifying," Kip said, knowing that the wrong hands would abuse such technology.

Rock scowled, then gulped his Ooze.

Ell rewound Kip's images until he was approaching the zoo bench with Sky waiting for him. After a quick review, they all, including Ell, agreed she seemed sincere. Kip still had a lingering doubt given all that occurred, but would worry about that later. The group then proceeded to fast-forward through Kip's life for the last few days. They'd stop at important moments where Kip or Rock explained the events. They'd then discuss any questions from Ell and Ann before moving on. When the first image of Ben came on the screen, Ell stopped the memory.

"What'd you think of Ben?" Ell asked. "It took a lot of money and corruption to get him on that bus."

"He was awesome, just what I needed to toughen up. I don't think I would've survived without him."

"He's one of our best," Ann said. "And with a little luck, he'll be out tomorrow."

"How's that?" Kip asked. "He was in isolation like me."

Ann sipped her Ooze. "An Officer Tak spoke on his behalf. Said Ben helped in a dangerous situation. He's being released with time served."

"He did help with Bane and Ped," Kip said. "As an aside, you can trust Tak to follow the law. He's not one of the corrupt Security Force."

Ann nodded at Ell, taking note.

As the memories rolled by, they came to the events at Shonto when Kip executed Officer Finna.

"Whoa, stop there," Ann said.

Ell stopped the memory.

Kip shifted in his chair, uncomfortable with the moment displayed on the video. "You had to be there to understand," Kip said.

Ell's eyes were wide. "I didn't think you had that in you."

"I was there; it was a mercy killing. The man was going to die," Rock added, an obvious attempt to help Kip's unease.

"No, not that. If this guy is anything like his brother, he deserved much worse," Ann said while Ell scrolled forward so the gruesome death was no longer visible. "I'm intrigued by the dead guard Finna. What are the chances that one brother is seen by you, Kip, supposedly killing him"—she pointed at Rock—"and then the other brother is assigned to guard you, the only witness to Rock's killing, at Elysian Fields."

"And eventually placed on the capture team," Ell added. "That makes no sense. Those teams are unique. They train separately."

"That man was sent to kill you. And somebody with power had to pull the strings to get him into those highly secure assignments," Rock said.

"Well, he tried with Bane. I got lucky," Kip said.

"This is huge. It's a conspiracy that goes all the way to Citizen One." Ann tapped the table with her fingers. "If we could get this to the public, it would expose the butchers for what they are. The type that blows up a school full of children."

The room was quiet while that insight sunk in.

"Let's keep going," Kip said.

Ell zoomed by the rafting memories, pausing for a minute at the goodbyes with Lib and Trim.

Ell said, "Trim used to live in Nirvana, got out and now scratches a living in the Outer Boundary. Says it's liberating, nobody controlling your life, debiting credits, dictating housing, or deciding who you'll be with."

"And nobody to replay your memories," Rock added, a hint of sarcasm in his voice.

"It's true. Nobody is in your head," Ell agreed.

They rolled through the final moments of Kip's video up until Trase answered the door. Ell shut off the machine.

"We should erase your images. In case they find you."

"Can you do it selectively? Keep my time in reeducation with Ped and Bane and the part with the school being blown up? The rest can go."

Ell started methodically scanning through the video. Every now and again, he'd pause, press a few buttons, then restart. A few minutes later, he was complete.

"That's it. Now what?" Ell asked.

Kip said, "How far away does your implant-reading gadget work?"

Ell shrugged. "I don't know exactly, but quite a way. Although, the farther out you go, the more implant units you have to sort through to get to the right one. I'll have to find and select the unit to scan."

"And can you scan anybody?"

"In theory, yes, but some people, like the Citizen Leaders, are encrypted so I need to hack into theirs. It takes some time, but definitely doable."

"What are you thinking?" Ann asked.

Kip stroked his chin, deep in thought. "I'm thinking we can use their technology on them to awaken the masses. With a little luck, we can find out where Sky's allegiance lies, and maybe even flush out your spy."

Rock raised his Ooze in a toast. "That sounds like the making of a plan I can support."

Chapter 31
Thursday, January 17, 2075

"So, that's it. We're set?" Kip asked while walking, the anticipation bubbling inside. It had been just over a day since they met in Ann's hideaway. Kip had felt captive while waiting for the arrangements to be made and passed the time locked in a safe house with nothing to do but pace. But now, he was going to meet Sky. Well, at least he hoped.

"Should be," Ell answered. "Trase connected with Sky. They're on their way here. I've got Jun with Rock at the River Market waiting for word from us. Bear is guarding Ann at a safe place in Pubtown. And we have a few other key people on watch for soldier movement around the designated locations."

"I hope Ann's not at the place you brought me. That may be compromised now."

"Unless Bear is the leak, she'll be safe." He gave a causal shrug. "We don't know you well enough to bring you to the real safe house. Maybe someday."

Kip checked his shirt and pants, straightening them both. Despite Ell's gift of a pressed Nirvana laborer outfit, he knew he appeared worse for the wear due to the trials of the last week. He hoped Sky could see beyond that to the old him.

"Relax, you look great. Like a sexy Nirvana bricklayer," Ell said, cracking a smile.

"Good, I hope that means I blend in," Kip said. "Was there any word on Sky's reaction?"

"No. Only confirmation that she's coming. But that tells you something in and of itself."

"Yeah, either she wants to see me or hang me," Kip said.

"That's right. It would have been easy to walk away and never see you again."

"I wouldn't really blame her." Kip ran his fingers through his hair. "We were only together a few days, and all of this is beyond crazy."

They stopped for a moment at the massive gates that stood at the entrance to Founders Park. The two ornate wrought-iron doors sat open as a welcoming beacon to all Citizens of Nirvana. Kip knew from school that the park was built as a testimonial to the inspirational people that helped create the State. These were not only the Citizen Leader statesmen and dignitaries but also philosophers and business leaders that shaped the society the Citizens now toiled under.

"It's beyond crazy. It's pretty much insane," Ell said with another laugh. "You still want to go through with this? It's not too late to call it off."

Kip nodded. "I have it from a higher authority that I need to do this, no matter where it leads. The right path is not always the easy one. You can quote me on that."

Ell gave an odd stare, like Kip needed psychological help.

They entered through the gate, strolling down the sidewalk that meandered through the sizeable, manicured grass fields and the occasional hardwood trees. The path wound its way, circling and dissecting the park leading to various monuments to the Founders, reminding the Citizens of their contributions.

Ell sat on a bench situated next to a large marble statue of a Citizen Leader from the year 2055. There was a plaque on the front of its base. "Relax, let's wait and see what happens," he said while crossing his legs.

Kip scanned the area. "Where are we meeting her?"

"There's a bench in that grove of trees. Thought it would give you some cover from drones." Ell yawned and stretched his arms, fitting into the image of a lackadaisical park visitor. "Look like a tourist. Pretend you're reading the plaque."

Kip did as suggested, reading the square white marble engraving, pretending he was interested.

Nirvana holds that all Citizens are equal. And within this foundation of equality, each Citizen also has strengths, and as such these strengths should be optimized by the State, at the discretion of the State, and for the benefit of the State until such time as the Leaders deem the work no longer useful. At which time, the State will dispose of the work. Underlying this edict is the wisdom that a Citizen's talent is in fact a genesis of the State, and without such infrastructure, the Citizen's talents would cease to develop, function, and exist. —Citizen Three

"I wonder if this Citizen Three lady provided the guidance that dictates the State determining your work and future," Kip said.

"Yep, I'm sure she did. She's a Founder after all," Ell said. "You want to hear something really mind bending?"

"Of course." Kip had started to appreciate Ell's talent and wit.

"That's not even the real quote, it was changed. The two words *work* should read *workers*. Citizen Three detested Nirvana's laborers, thought of them as disposable property. And now they pay homage to her as an illustrious Founder. Guess they didn't want the Citizens to know they'd work their whole lives only to be thrown into retirement prisons in the end."

"Tell a lie long enough with frequency and it becomes a fact," Kip said.

"Correct, and the winners write history. Which now gives us false testimony in our outdoor recreational areas," Ell said, a sarcastic tone in his voice.

Kip chuckled, then scanned the park again. Beyond the typical people walking or sitting, there were no police or soldiers on the ground, and even better, no drones in the air. "What do you think?"

"I think we're clear. If she arrives, it's a go."

Kip joined Ell on the bench. Sitting far enough away to appear as individuals and not friends.

Ell checked his watch. "It's a quarter of. You should make your way over. Remember, we'll be around if not visible. If you get a bad feeling, call it off and get out. We'll regroup later at the usual spot."

Kip straightened his clothes again, then moved closer to Ell. "Enough straightening already, she'll be glad to see you," Ell said with frustration. "Now, spin around, don't look back at me, and don't say another word. I'm erasing the last forty-eight hours of your implant. When I say 'look at the bird' I'm done."

Kip turned his back to Ell.

Ell held up the electronic scanner for a few seconds. "Look at the bird," is all Ell said.

Facing the grove of trees, Kip strolled down the sidewalk, like any tourist would do. He observed left then right, slowing his gait to study a flower before moving forward to scan the woods in front of him, acting as casual as possible.

Ahead, he saw a woman sitting on the bench. His heart beat faster, and his pace quickened. He was approaching from behind, so while he could tell she had Sky's build, he couldn't see her face. Until she turned, and there was no doubt. When their eyes met, she sprang off the bench and rushed to him.

She covered the few steps quickly and wrapped her arms around his neck. With tears streaming down her face, she buried it in his chest. "I thought you were dead," she whispered.

He tried pulling away, but she wouldn't let go and started sobbing. He squeezed her tighter, holding her, feeling her body tremble, letting her emotions release. He leaned down and kissed her lips. They held one another in that embrace, feeling that special connection once again, love rekindled. Kip couldn't remember being so happy, so relieved, so connected to another human as he was at that perfect moment.

"I have missed you so much," he said softly, holding her tight.

She finally let go, her eyes meeting his. "Me too. I've got so much to tell you. I promised myself no more lies. You need to know everything, but we need to be quick."

"Agreed. I don't have much time. I just wanted to see you one more time, before—"

"Don't tell me your plans. I don't want to know. You're safer that way," Sky said.

"That day at the zoo, you wanted to tell me something. I've been wracking my brain trying to figure it out."

"Let's start there." She looked down at the ground. "I wasn't honest with you and want to be now. I've never felt this way about someone before, and I want to see where it leads. Just know that if you hear me out and need to walk away, I understand."

Kip gently pulled her chin up and reengaged with her beautiful eyes. "I love you," he said for the first time in his life. He put his arm around her, she snuggled in, and they started walking toward the bench. He knew public displays of affection were unusual for partners and frowned upon by the State. Kip didn't care.

They sat down on the bench, the cold of its hard metal radiating through his pants. Kip faced her, holding her hand with both of his, periodically scanning over her shoulder, viewing the park and its patrons.

"The day at the Games was real," she said hesitantly. "The nights we spent were real. Everything I said and did, I meant and felt with all my heart. You must believe that."

"I do," Kip said.

"That's what made it hard."

"What was hard?" Kip prodded.

"Lying to you." She glanced away. "I was asked, more like blackmailed, to set you up." She rubbed her thumb across his hand. "To lie to you, to report in on you . . ." She paused, trembling, afraid to speak her next words. "And . . . to get you to the zoo."

The words hit like a punch to Kip's gut. "Why?"

325

"I don't know. They wouldn't tell me. They approached me after the Games, with a deal I couldn't say no to. They told me I had to be with you, partner with you, and report in."

"Or what? What would happen? Do they have something on you?"

"Not what, who. They threatened to take Bug away. They implied they'd hurt her, and she would never get back. I didn't know you then, and I didn't know I'd feel this way." She rambled, eyes tearing. "I just thought it'd be a couple of days and then it would be over and Bug would be safe." Kip squeezed her hand. "They paid me 400 credits. I tried to give them to you, to save you from going to Pubtown, but they said no." She started full-on crying again. "I'm so sorry. I didn't know someone would get killed and you'd be blamed. You've got to believe me."

"I do believe you," he said. Bringing her hand to his lips, he kissed it. "You're as much a victim of this as I am." He scanned the area. Ell was still sitting on the bench, watching. "My last question is who? Who was your handler?"

Sky's eyes went to the ground. "I don't know her name. She didn't tell me, and I didn't ask. She said to never tell anyone of our contact."

"Describe her."

"An older woman, gray hair, a gravelly voice, and—"

Kip heard the buzz of the drone before she finished. He stood, still clasping her hand. "They're here. We need to go."

Sky stood. "You run, go . . . out of the city! I'll find you somehow!"

Kip kissed her lips one more time, then walked away. He glanced to the bench Ell had been on. It was empty. Ell had left him.

He started to sprint toward the gate on the far side of the park. Kip was just out of the grove, hitting his stride, when soldiers and Security Force came from three directions. They swarmed around him, fencing him in with blasters raised.

Kip skidded to a stop and put up his hands, showing he had no weapons. They stood around him, guns leveled at all parts of his body. A small group of Elite police came from the woods escorting someone cuffed. Kip's first instinct was that they'd captured Sky, but as they approached, he recognized the aged face of Trase. They had found and arrested her as well.

Sky came walking up, alone. With no attention from any of the Security Force. She hovered just outside their circle.

Trase was escorted in, wrists secured behind her back, and placed in front of Kip. "Fancy meeting you here," she said with a sneer to the guards.

"No!" Sky broke through the soldier's ring, trying to get to Kip. She kneed the guard who stepped to block her, then pushed him away. Two more guards came. She lost control, throwing punches, elbows, and kicks. Anything to get to Kip, she tried.

A policewoman in full gear with a black riot helmet finally restrained her, bear-hugging her from behind, then body-slamming her to the grass. She flipped Sky over, pushing her into the turf, then cuffed her. She jerked Sky to her feet.

"Stop it, he's innocent!" Sky yelled, grass blades sticking in her messed-up hair.

A crowd of park goers began assembling. People started taking pictures with their cameras, whispering, and pointing fingers at Kip.

Kip met Trase's eyes. "Let her go. You know she did nothing wrong, and you don't need her anymore."

Trase said nothing, staring at him for a long moment. With a nod of her head, she broke into a smile, then started fiddling with her cuffs behind her back. They released. She removed the last clip from her left wrist, then hung them on her belt. "So, you figured it out. How?"

"She's the handler," Sky blurted out.

Kip shook his head at Sky, and mouthed, *Don't.* Then he addressed Trase's question. "The moment you said you were expecting us when we showed up at your door."

"I thought I covered that slip well. In the end, it doesn't matter." She stepped to him, removed the cuffs from her belt, and clipped them on his wrists behind his back. "Where's Ell and the others?"

"I don't know and wouldn't tell you if I did."

"No problem. We have people who specialize in . . . incentivizing you to talk."

A hulking soldier in full riot gear grabbed Kip by the arm, pulling him toward an armored truck. He forcibly twisted back to Trase and screamed, "Let her go, or else!"

"Or else what?" Trase shot back, the veins in her temple bulging. "You'll die a little quicker?" A few of the soldiers laughed. Trase said, "Bring the woman as well. Keep them separated."

As they walked to the truck, the now sizeable crowd stopped photographing and started clapping. A few shouts of support came for the police, but Kip noted something else, something odd. A few boos rose from the Citizens and some shouts of "Let him go."

He wasn't alone in this fight.

Chapter 32
Sunday, January 20, 2075

Kip rested in his bunk with little to do but stare at the gray ceiling, awaiting the next visitor. He'd been in prison, isolated in this antiseptic, hardened cell, for what he thought was three days. It was amazing what no access to sunshine or starlight did to one's inner clock. With that said, he had had a stream of visitors who seemed to come between certain hours, most likely daylight hours. From psychologists who probed to psychopaths who tortured him, they all came seeking information. Kip guessed they were all one and the same, both doctor and sadist, working together to break his spirit. Their primary focus was learning more about Rock and the Resistance—who they were, where they were, and how they operate. Fortunately, Kip didn't know much on the subject and his implant had been erased, giving them little information. Well, except for the most damaging items to Nirvana, such as their soldiers blowing up a school full of innocents. This evidence was extremely problematic for those holding him. They even brought in the State's expert on implants to better understand how part of his stored data was gone while the damning images remained.

For Kip's part, he claimed ignorance, pointing to the missing images with Officer Finne at the zoo and suggesting it was a faulty implant. He found the duplicity of his claim pleasing.

Given that they were using the AST system to read his thoughts, Kip stayed mentally positive, focusing on memories of Sky, caring for the animals at the zoo, and his time on the river. There was nothing like freedom, work, and love to keep his prison guardians in check.

He rolled to his side with a grimace. His ribs still hurt from where the last Citizen "interviewer" incentivized him to tell them what they wanted to know. Given the AST system, they would ask a question, Kip would answer, then they would beat him, hoping his thoughts would betray his verbal claims. As far as Kip knew, there were no discrepancies between the two. Their anger toward him and the recurrence of visits seemed to confirm this belief. Although, in their last visit, they attempted to bait him, referring to what they were doing to Sky and how much she seemed to enjoy the attention. He didn't bite, choosing passivity.

Kip rose from his bed, dropping to the floor to do some pushups. The discomfort from his beatings was bearable, and burning some energy felt good. It relaxed his mind and helped to change the negative narrative that he so often went through. As he pumped up and down, Rock's advice came to mind, reminding him that it does no good to worry about things you can't control.

He abruptly stopped when he heard the outer door open. It seemed too early for his daily allotment of Green; must be another doctor to screw with his mind.

His lock clicked, the metal handle twisted, and the door opened. His temple started to throb, the stress of past beatings taking its toll. In walked a familiar soldier, the man who had taken over for Kip at the Punishment, Rage. Both taller and thicker than Kip, he had long black hair, brown skin, and a scar that ran the length of his right cheek. His most distressing characteristic was his dead, black eyes, which bore into Kip with a gleam of recognition before moving to scan the room. Kip's heart pounded even faster under the weight of the what-ifs spinning through his mind. This man was the definition of his worst nightmare.

Kip started to stand, expecting to leave for his next "incentivizing" session, but the soldier reached over and shoved him onto his bed. "Sit." He commanded in a guttural grunt before going over the room again. He was searching for something. Kip could only guess what, maybe he thought a weapon was hidden. The brute bulled in next to him to lift the small pillow off his bed before tossing back the blanket, ensuring nothing was hidden.

He stepped in close and placed a giant hand on Kip's neck, tightening his grip to ensure Kip felt it. "I'm going to say this only once. If I need to come back in this room, it'll be the worst day of your life. Nod if you understand me."

With little to lose, Kip thought about saying "fuck off" but gave a short nod, not wanting to test his luck here and now.

"Good," the man snarled, releasing his grip. He walked back to the door and opened it. In strolled a tall man, dressed in Citizen robes, his hair perfectly coiffed. Citizen One stood for a moment, taking in the whole scene. The brute returned with a single chair and left it in the middle of the cell. "Call out if you need me," he said while staring at Kip. "I don't think you will though."

"Thank you, Rage," Citizen One said. "I don't think I will either. Right JU450625?"

Kip seethed inside but managed to control his emotions outwardly. "No sir," he said. He took a deep breath, remembering what Ben said—they were testing him. He needed his mind right.

"I see you've learned to control your impulses," Citizen One began. "I seem to have underestimated your learning curve." The Citizen Leader gave a nod to the soldier, who left the room, leaving the door cracked open.

"Are you surprised to see me here?"

"As a matter of fact, yes," Kip answered. "I did offer one of your sadists to tell you personally what I knew, but never thought he'd take me seriously."

"I assure you, he did not." Citizen One crossed his legs, getting comfortable. "I'm here of my own volition. To offer you a deal."

"Not interested," Kip shot back.

"At least hear me out. After very publicly returning from the dead, you've created quite a mess for me. Your picture is everywhere, and people are starting to make you into some kind of anti-State hero. And we can't have that. Can we?"

"What do you want?"

"To the point, I like that." He raised his finger and tipped it at Kip. "I want you to fight in a special Games as a soldier of Nirvana. If you win, you'll get a full pardon and I'll reinstate your partnership with Sky. This is a real pardon, no tricks, but you will have to leave Nirvana."

"I'm not a soldier or a trained fighter. I'd be an easy kill."

"The Games aren't for a few days. We'll give you training, good accommodations, and plenty of food to build your strength. It's as fair as I can make it." He leaned forward, arms on his knees. "I saw the video of you fighting in Shonto. You underestimate your own skills."

"You mean where you opened fire on a school full of children?" Kip hissed.

"Like Officer Finna's death, a casualty of war." A smug smile crossed the leader's face. "Besides, the savages picked that fight when they helped you and Rock."

"They offered food, medicine, and shelter to people in need. There is no crime in showing kindness to strangers."

"You're so naïve, like a child, really." He studied Kip's face. "Let me make it easy for you. Shonto and all the other wars in the Wasteland are a means to an end. A common enemy used to keep the Citizens afraid and aligned. You played into my hands showing up there."

"That's crazy."

"You would understand if you walked in my shoes." He paused, fidgeting in his chair. "And you're not answering my question. Will you fight?"

"Still not interested. Lie in the bed you made."

Citizen One's jaw clenched. "So, the carrot doesn't work. I thought not." He locked eyes with Kip. "Let's try the stick," he hissed. "If you don't take my deal, your pretty ex-partner will find herself an accessory to terrorism for helping you. Meaning prison, then reeducation, loss of all credits, not to mention housing in Pubtown. I will make it my mission in life to ensure the only way for her to survive will be to sell her body to the scum that infest that sewer." He leaned back in comfort, putting his hands behind his head.

"Like what you did to me."

"What I did to you will seem like child's play."

"Why? Why do you need me to fight?"

"If you win, you're a hero for the State, and I salvaged you for the masses. If you lose, you lose. Fate has chosen you, and your death wasn't by my hand. The anti-State hero no more."

He touched his head as if he just recalled something. "Oh, and in that tragic event, know that Sky will live and be awarded a lavish lifestyle for your sacrifice. She will become royalty among the Elites."

"You've hurt her enough. Leave her out of this."

He shook his head. "No, I will not. She's been a fantastic, coerced participant. She took a lot of persuading and even more arm twisting, but in the end, ruthlessly effective." The Leader exhaled loudly. "Enough. Your answer is?"

Kip hesitated before answering. "I'll fight. With one condition."

"That depends on what."

"I want the truth."

"I have no secrets. What truth are you seeking?"

"Why the murder and subterfuge with Citizen Eight? And why choose me as your pawn to sacrifice?"

"Ha!" Citizen One forced the laugh. "Your condition is rejected."

"No secrets? I guess we're at an impasse." Kip locked eyes with him. "Then I won't fight. And while I care for Sky, she wouldn't want me to enter the Games anyway. Not for her."

Citizen One peered up, as if studying the ceiling, clearly considering his options. "Okay, you can have the truth. You can't do anything with it. You're stuck here with no one to tell. Even if you did, who would believe you?"

337

"Make it the truth for my own edification," Kip said.

Citizen One leaned in and spoke just above a whisper, as if the shared truth would escape the very walls in which they sat. "There are missing people, lots of them, taken from poverty and used for the more carnal pleasures and necessities of life."

"Meaning sex trafficking and organ harvesting," Kip said.

Citizen One's eyes went wide, surprised by his answer. "Yes, to be blunt. Both are very lucrative and thriving in the black market."

Kip thought of Tik and his present condition. "Well, if you opened the medical state, allowed the non-Elite transplants, people wouldn't go to the black market."

"Cure the rabble who have abused themselves, their bodies, their very lives? What a novel idea." His voice dripped with sarcasm. "More importantly, where's the profit in that? The State pays credits for one and receives credits in the other. Do the math."

"I have. A friend of mine is one of your numbers."

"It's not a perfect world, but close to it," Citizen One said.

"Why kill Citizen Eight?" Kip asked.

"Citizen Eight was investigating the powers behind the black market and was getting close to a revelation. There are certain doors that even I dare not look behind. The Elites enjoy their pleasures and anonymity."

"You killed an innocent man at the zoo, framing Rock in the process to protect your secrets."

"Hardly innocent. That man was a habitual abuser who conveniently looked like your friend, Rock. He was a lost cause, a throwaway that wasted his life. We did him and the State a favor ending his suffering."

"So, no due process, you play God. I got it, all men are equal, some are just more equal than others." Kip had an uneasy feeling he was pressing his luck. But what the hell, he would probably be dead soon anyway. "So then, why me?"

"The easiest of the questions asked." Citizen One leaned forward again, ensuring that Kip watched his face. "First, you embarrassed me and the State with your antics at the Games. That kind of behavior is contagious and must be stamped out publicly. Second, and the reason I find myself having this inane conversation is you're too smart for your own good. You don't follow authority. In short, you can't be controlled." He leaned back again. "You've been on our radar for some time. Oh yes, we watch you and monitor you and even tried to program you with State-friendly messages."

"So, you feed me—the Citizens—State propaganda?" Kip asked.

"Such an ugly word. We like to say educational reinforcement. They're fed directly into your house, phone, or whatever you're engaged with." Citizen One sneered. "In your case, unsuccessfully, I might add."

"Why are you trying to control me? Control us? Why not let the people decide their own fate? You have the Citizens of Nirvana afraid to do or think anything that's not State approved. You have the ultimate power."

Citizen One thought about the question, then answered with confidence. "Because the average Citizen of Nirvana is stupid, weak of spirit, and lazy. And the power those idiots wield when acting in mass is truly frightening, no matter how ridiculous the cause. We tried free will many years ago and consider where it led us: war, pandemic, the brink of annihilation. We've learned to keep people isolated for their own safety. So we, the State, give them food, clean air, and water. We provide them unlimited procreation while maintaining the species. And for entertainment, we give them the Games and recreational drugs. What more could our Citizens want?"

"Not want, need," Kip snapped back. "People require life experiences beyond the carnal. Every person needs to know the love of family and to explore the spiritual. You've taken that all away." He shook his head, his tone more conciliatory. "We should be pushing our boundaries out of the safe zone and feel what it's like to truly be free with no guarantees of success. What you offer is not living. You have your people penned like animals in the zoo, only their cages are invisible. That's not a life, that's passing time until death."

Citizen One bristled, clearly taken aback by his words. "I'm not going to try to convince you. Your opinion means nothing. We provide the people what they need to survive their own weaknesses. We keep them safe. The end."

"No." Kip sat up tall and raised his head confidently. "You enslave them by telling the people what they want to hear and giving them the minimum to keep them lazy and reliant on the State. You do this to keep yourself in power. If you wanted to help, you'd teach them hard work, self-reliance, and independence. But you don't. Your actions speak louder than your corrupt words."

"This is going nowhere," Citizen One said, a scowl on his face. "In fairness, I tried. I thought maybe you were smart enough to see the greater good. I was wrong." He stood, readying his exit. "I've answered your questions, and now you must answer mine. Will you fight in the Games as a soldier of Nirvana?"

Kip swallowed hard. "I will."

"Good. Sky is safe as long as you meet your end of this bargain."

"Who will I fight?"

"That's not a worry for you. We'll find someone suitable."

Chapter 33
Tuesday, January 22, 2075

"Block, block, block, thrust, now . . . attack!" the soldier yelled.

Kip reacted slowly in the moment, slicing down with his sword. The soldier blocked his slash, then butt-ended his helmet. She finished by sweeping his feet. Kip landed with a heavy thump.

The soldier stepped back. She removed her helmet, letting her black hair fall to her shoulders. "What are you doing? We've been practicing for a couple of days and you're still hesitating. You're going to be dead in minutes if you don't attack when you have the advantage."

Kip rose from the ground, raising his helmet's visor, allowing him a full range of vision. "I'm sorry, Pege. I'm just not used to the sword yet. Maybe I shouldn't choose it."

"You let your opponent select their weapon first, then you pick the optimal counter to it, and that may be the sword. Sword versus spear, remember that," she lectured. "Now let's go through it again. This time, attack like you mean it."

Kip slid his visor back down and took the ready stance. Pege attacked, probing with her spear. Kip parried her jab, then evaded the second. When the third jab came, he blocked up and away, then stepped forward in a spin and crushed his hard, plastic sword into her shoulder pad. The force of the strike sent Pege to the ground.

Sitting in the dirt on her butt, Pege raised her visor. "That's it! That's what I'm talking about. Use your advantage with no mercy."

Kip offered her a hand up. She took it. "Did I hurt you?"

"Stop asking that. It's part of drilling." Pege dusted off. "Now the only thing I'm going to suggest is you don't spin. It garners power, but it's slow and you don't need the added power. Quicker for you to just slice down on the arm. It's all about speed and power in combination."

"Like Rock and Trex."

"Exactly like that. Trex was swinging that heavy mace, and Rock was just too fast. Use that same strategy to your advantage. Identify whether you're fighting speed or power and adjust accordingly."

"What happens if I go up against both speed and power?"

"Then use your mind and hope you figure something out before they get to you."

A piercing horn blew. Kip knew that signified the end of the session.

"That's all for today," Pege said. "You've got one more day of training. Make the most of it. Focus on your moves as you lie in bed. Get your mind right."

Kip snapped his head around, "Did you say, 'get your mind right'?"

"Yeah. Why?"

"A guy I met once said the same."

"A guy named Ben, perhaps?" Pege gave a grin. "He served in my platoon. I asked for this assignment." She winked. "Trust in the plan. You'll have help when needed."

"I'll have help?" Kip asked as a soldier walked up.

"JU450625, you have a visitor," the man interrupted.

"A visitor?" Kip handed Pege his sword. "See you tomorrow."

Pege affirmed with a nod. "Keep it short, no distractions."

Kip's mind raced as he followed the soldier out of the dirt training pit and into the armory. He wondered if Citizen One was back to revise, or worse, renege his deal. Maybe it was Sky coming to say goodbye. Although he hadn't seen her, he had been told she was a guest of Citizen One and staying in lavish Uptown accommodations. Kip shook his head and buried his anger. A cell was a cell regardless of the thread count of your sheets.

He didn't have to wait long to find out. The soldier led him down the short hall to the end room. The door opened to sparse furnishings, just an old table and two equally aged chairs.

In the far chair sat Blu, dressed in Kip's favorite outfit and makeup that highlighted her gorgeous eyes.

She stood as he entered, then moved toward him, stopping a step away. She spoke to the guard. "Is it okay if I give him a hug?"

"Yes. He's a soldier of Nirvana, not a prisoner." His misleading answer was curt. "You have five minutes. I'll be right outside," he said to Kip as he exited, closing the door.

Blu stepped in and gave him an uncharacteristic hug. Which lasted way longer than any embrace she had ever given him. "Are you okay?" she whispered.

She let go, and Kip moved from her reach. "I'm fine. How are you?"

"I'm worried . . . worried for you." She motioned to the table. "Should we sit?"

"Sure." Being polite, Kip pulled out her chair, then slid it in under her. Kip went to the open chair. "Thanks for coming to visit. But I must admit, I'm a little surprised."

She reached over and took his hand. "I know I haven't been the best friend or partner to you. But I wanted to see you before the Games to wish you luck." Her eyes started to tear.

"Don't Blu, don't cry. I'm going to be fine."

"I know you are." Blu wiped a falling tear and changed the subject. "I've seen you everywhere. You're on the Holovision all the time. You and that savage are all anyone talks about.

346

Escaping from being kidnapped, surviving the Outer Boundary, not to mention finally overcoming Rock and his tribe. I'm glad they finally caught him. They're saying you're a national hero."

"Wait, hold on." Kip raised a hand. "Caught who?"

"You haven't heard." Blu beamed, happy to deliver the news. "That savage, Rock, was caught last night in the city by the security drones. It wasn't him that was killed at the zoo. Citizen One said it was a terrible mistake by the coroner. He's being sent to reeducation. But they cleared your name and said you were right about not being involved with Citizen Eight's death." She rubbed her finger on his hand. "You're cleared, and now you're fighting as a hero for Nirvana."

Kip took a deep breath. Rock was now in custody and the web of lies had been spun. "That makes for a good story, Blu, but the reality is way less exciting. I'm lucky to be here."

"But you are here. And I wanted to tell you that I knew you had this in you. I always believed in you. And"—she bit her lip, the next statement difficult—"I should have been a better partner. Will you forgive me?"

"Yes, totally. I forgive you. I have nothing but good feelings about our time together." Her smile confirmed Kip's fib had alleviated her conscious. "Speaking of partners, how is your new one? Pinc told me you had an early night."

"I did. He's great." Her eyes betrayed her words. "You were right. I just did what I always do, and he wanted to partner. It was . . . quick. Unlike you." She gave a flirtatious giggle.

"And what does he do?"

"He's very successful with a high social score. An officer of the Security Force." Her eyes went wide with excitement. She removed her hand from his to cover her mouth. "Oh my gosh, it just dawned on me that you may have heard of him. He was at the zoo when Citizen Eight was killed. Security Officer Finne, did you run into him?"

Kip felt flush, a wave of nausea hitting. He leaned on the table, putting his head in his hands.

"Are you okay?" Blu asked.

"Yeah, I'm fine. Probably too much training. Anyway, I don't recall him, but maybe we crossed paths."

"You should get some rest. You'll want to be fresh for the Games." She stood and circled the table to get to him. "I wish we had more time. Like the night we met at our Changing." She ran her finger down his chest.

Kip stood, taking her wandering hand into his, Blu practically purring her approval. "Blu, I want you to be careful. Things aren't always what they appear."

She went to her toes, leaving a lingering kiss on his cheek. "I know, just like you and your newfound fame. People can surprise you. I mean, we were together for three years—who knew? You don't know what's inside them until that moment that fate discloses it." She squeezed his hand. "I'll be in Citizen One's box, rooting for you. Please find me." Releasing his hand, she walked to the door and gave him one final seductive smile before exiting.

Kip sat down again, that bad feeling now gnawing in his gut. Finne partnering with Blu was not by chance.

Chapter 34
Friday, January 25, 2075

Kip jolted awake, eyes popping open, the last vestiges of his nightmare forgotten.

There'll be no more sleep for me today, for that matter, maybe ever. Is today the day I will die? What awaits me after that fateful moment when I cross over from the living to the dead? Will it be painful, or soothing, like the connection with Yahweh? Will she be waiting for me again? His mind raced and his adrenaline surged, the thoughts and worry overwhelming him in the moment. He took a deep breath and exhaled, then another. What would Rock say now? "Don't worry about things you cannot control. It burns energy and saps the strength." Kip would do exactly that, focusing on his present and living the best day he could.

He rolled from bed and washed up, then dressed in his issued soldier uniform. A knock at his door startled him. A second knock came, then the door clicked open and a tall woman in an enhancing dress walked in. She was holding a white uniform on a hanger. Kip guessed it was a uniform, as half of the shirt was missing.

"Good morning," she said with a gleam in her eye. "Big day for you."

"Good morning to you," Kip responded.

"I'm Lana, and responsible for your clothes today." She held up the uniform so Kip could see the entire length. "This beauty is your designer suit of armor for the games. Got to have you strong and sexy." She flipped the edge on the shirt straight.

"Strong and sexy?" Kip repeated incredulously. "You know I'm fighting to the death."

"Oh yes, I meet all the contestants. It's hard for me sometimes, but you know what they say, the show must go on." She held up the outfit, oblivious to the shallowness of her own words. "The Citizens are going to love you in this. I think this is one of the sleekest uniforms yet. Stylish yet functional. The leather is strengthened to give you some protection." She rotated the outfit so Kip could see it all.

The entire ensemble was of the same white leather, which appeared to be tailored to Kip's size. The design was based on a Nirvana soldier uniform, only the shirt was cut, so his abs showed, and it had no sleeves. Hanging on a string were two thin, hardened arm pads with attaching bands to protect his shoulders and biceps.

Lana offered the outfit to Kip. "The Games start at one o'clock. Depending on how the early matches go, you'll be out between two and two-thirty. So, you need to be dressed for photos, say, by one.”

Kip took the outfit and laid it on the bed. “Photos? Why?”

“They say historical significance, documenting the games.” Lana leaned in and whispered, “I think it’s all marketing. Can’t wait to see your action figure.” She leaned back and laughed at her own joke.

Kip shook his head.

“Alright, my job is done here, other deliveries to make.” She started to leave then stopped. “I hope I see you again. I’d love to do your next uniform.” She gave a finger wave goodbye and left, closing the door behind her.

Kip groaned. This was going to be both the longest and possibly the shortest day of his life.

* * *

The door swung closed with a slam. Kip didn’t care, he was emotionally exhausted and still had a fight to the death in front of him. Since Lana’s visit in the morning, Kip had the choreographer visit, a man named Pom, where they went through the pregame theatrics and the Games storyline. Kip didn’t learn much beyond where to stand, when to get his weapon, and that he was a soldier of Nirvana, so to act appropriately during the prefight drama created by the announcer.

After the choreographer, he was mandated to attend, as the special invitee, a brunch that catered to the Elites and their guests. He was even asked to say a few words for the crowd's entertainment that followed with questions. Kip struggled through both, just trying to be the honest and humble person he was. Which was difficult to do when the guests want to know which weapon he'll use and if he'll go for the head.

Kip sat in his chair, with eyes closed and head leaning back, trying to find his inner peace. He attempted to calm his mind, thinking of Yahweh and the harmony she brought. She would see him through this day, he knew it in his heart. Unfortunately, the moment of life and death crept back into his thoughts. It was scarcely an hour away.

"Knock, knock." A voice came from outside the room. The door opened. Citizen One walked in, his hair slicked to perfection once again. The ornate white robes of the Citizen Elite flowed around him. He held out his hand in mock introduction. "You may remember your old partner, Sky."

Sky came in wearing a revealing white outfit made and cut like Kip's. Her thin, strapped top covered her breasts and not much else, exposing her athletic waist and broad shoulders. Her skirt was tight and cut along her upper thigh, highlighting her long muscular legs. She walked in white high heels, with her hair down and makeup that accentuated her beautiful but worried face. Kip couldn't take his eyes off her.

Sky started in toward him, but Citizen One stopped her short, forcefully grabbing her arm. "Let's wait on that until after we talk," Citizen One said.

Kip gave a quick smile to reassure Sky, then addressed Citizen One. "What do you want?" Kip asked, his tone intentionally curt. "Or are you here for mind games?"

"No, no mind games. I brought Sky to see you, and I'm here to ensure what every Citizen wants, an entertaining battle where one contestant dies and the other lives."

"I think I've got that."

"There's more, of course. There's a script you need to follow." Citizen One stepped past Kip casually, like a professor in the middle of his lecture. "Like all good entertainment, the better the story, the better the show."

"And?"

"And we have the best story ever, for you and Sky. You lost your three-year partnership, a commitment destroyed in its infancy by the savage, Rock. But alas, your destiny together was meant to be as you fought through the Outer Boundary and its ruthless killers to reveal the plot against Citizen Eight and bring us back the murderer, Rock." Citizen One orated like he stood before the masses. "And now you have your chance to settle the score with your enemy, once and for all, on behalf of Nirvana and its Citizens."

"That's not the story. Rock was nowhere near the zoo. He was chained to a bed in your hospital, waiting to have his organs harvested."

"He's part of the conspiracy, and it's the story you'll tell the moronic masses that worship you. Or our deal is off." He grabbed Sky by the arm again, pulling her close, smelling her neck. "The things I would do to you." He gently caressed her arm with his free hand. "You'll be the focus of every camera in the place. Nothing like a little sex to sell interest." He turned back to Kip. "Just remember, she'll be in my box, next to me, only a knife blade away."

Sky jerked her arm away, a look of repulsion on her face. Citizen One let her go.

"The deal is on. Leave her alone. You gave me your word." Kip's fingers nervously stroked his cheek. "This means I'm fighting Rock."

"Nirvana's finest versus The Savage from the Wasteland. The last battle for all to see."

"Rock won't do it. He'll die first."

"Well, so be it, and you will have to act. Kill or be killed and she'll be safe. That's our deal." He started for the door. "I should tell you that I promised to bomb a dozen schools in the Wasteland if he doesn't fight." He winked at Kip. "So best of luck to you." He turned to glare at Sky. "You have two minutes to say goodbye and know we're listening."

Once the door closed, Sky rushed to him, wrapping her arms around him. She held him close, kissing his lips like it was the last time she would ever be in his embrace. Kip pulled her in tight, feeling her heartbeat, bonding with her love, and connecting to her soul. He no longer cared if he died today. He finally found what he was desperate for, a connection in life— love. As the wave of emotions peaked, Kip wondered if this was the time Yahweh predicted, the moment he finally knew love and what it meant to be human.

Sky squeezed him tight, resting her head in his chest then whispered, "Don't speak, just listen. You need to fight for us, for Bug, for Ellie . . . fight hard, at least ten minutes." She pulled back and met his eyes. "Ten minutes for Ellie, I promised her," she repeated. "I'm not saying goodbye to you. You've got this." She tapped his heart with her hand, her fingers lingering a moment, then turned and walked away.

Kip said nothing in response, only watched the door slam. *For Ellie?*

Chapter 35

"Okay, that's it. No more pictures!" Pom yelled at the crowd. All cameras went down without hesitation and the room started emptying. It was all so civilized at such an uncivilized event.

Kip took a step away from the departing photographers. He was cut off by Pom, whom he was beginning to hate. "Don't go too far, the last match just ended. Aiko won again by decapitation," he said, a hint of excitement in his voice. "You're on after the prelims."

"What are the prelims?" Kip asked, wondering if he really wanted to know.

"Intro movies for you and Rock." He pointed to the screen on the wall. "You can watch them here. Then announcer introductions, scan of the crowds to highlight a few celebrities, finishing with giving a few random credits out. You know, all the stuff that gets the Citizens amped up."

"So, two men fighting where one decapitates the other isn't enough electricity?"

The man gave an odd stare, as if Kip were crazy. "Umm, no such thing as too much energy."

Kip adjusted his thin shoulder and bicep pads, which had slipped after the pictures. Pom scurried over to tighten the straps, fiddling while Kip lived in his mind. He hated the "uniform." It was just like Nirvana—all style and no substance. The white leather was tight in all the wrong places and stiff, impeding motion. Worse than that, there was no way this outfit would shield him from injury in any battle, much less against a soldier in the Wasteland. But it was sexy, and all those Citizens attracted to men would be captivated. Kip hated everything about the event. With that said, it was time to get his mind right. A battle to the death was moments away.

The announcer interrupted Kip's inner monologue. "Citizens of Nirvana!" he exclaimed into his microphone. Kip watched the nearest screen, which was being broadcast throughout the city. "Welcome to the main event, where an age-old war is revisited, right here, right now, and you, the Citizens of Nirvana, have a front-row seat!" He paused while the crowd roared its appreciation. Even from where he stood in the underground of the arena, Kip had never heard the cheering so loud.

The announcer raised his hand for quiet, and a hush fell over the spectators. "You remember him from his resounding defeat of Trex and watched in horror as his assassin butchered our very own Citizen Eight. You've heard the stories of the kidnapping and the murders of over twenty hardened soldiers.

He's a monster that knows no civilized bounds! He's The Savage from the Wasteland . . . Rock!"

A movie started playing on the screens around the stadium. Kip stepped closer to better see his screen. The video displayed Rock's slaying of Trex, then rolled to an exciting portrayal of the death of Citizen Eight. It then moved to Rock fighting the soldiers in Shonto when he threw the incendiary into their craft, which was depicted as the catalyst that blew up the school. It ended with a montage of images of Rock assaulting and killing soldiers with his bare hands. Kip knew those were deep fake images, a technique long used by the State to evoke strong emotions, in this case a seething hatred of "the savage." The movie ended in a chilling closeup of Rock's contorted face, while the audio established his hatred for all things enlightened, like Nirvana. Rock walked out into the arena, wearing the same outfit as when he fought Trex. He was greeted with a chorus of boos, swearing, middle finger salutes, and thumbs down. Those closest even tried spitting. To say he was reviled with passion was an understatement.

Kip shook his head. Nothing but first-class propaganda that painted his very civilized friend as an evil psychopath. These thoughts stewed in Kip's mind when the Nirvana State anthem started, and the announcer sparked up his microphone again. "Citizens of Nirvana, please join me in welcoming one of our own soldiers into the ring. A man who has just earned the title of

Captain in the Guard for bravery in the battle of Shonto. He has endured false accusations and a hastily dissolved partnership. He's survived a life-threatening kidnapping and a horde of savages in the wilds to return home to you and defend our honor. Here's the protector of the innocent, the defender of the State, not to mention a close friend of Citizen One . . . Captain Kip!"

The crowd went nuts; applause, screams, and whistles filled the air. All in loving admiration of their hometown hero.

A new video rolled, this one of Kip. It started with sweet images of him as a child and scrolled by his teen years through the present, ending with a long pause of a picture of him cheering at the last Games. The montage revealed an all-Nirvana boy who loved the State. The narrator portrayed him as a great Citizen with a conscience who wanted to severely punish Rock but out of the public view. The video showed him running after Citizen Eight's killer, flashed to the corrupt coroner, then finished with him at the hospital helping Officer Tak to the ward. It moved to him fighting with the natives in Shonto and ended with a scene like the agonizing death of Officer Finna—only the image wasn't of Finna but edited to show a fierce, long-haired warrior from Shonto. More fake propaganda.

"Ready to go?" Pom interrupted, touching Kip's arm. "You're just over a minute out."

Kip swiveled back to the video. They were now flashing sexy images of Sky, telling the narrative that he fought his way back to her in hopes of fulfilling his three-year commitment. It ended with a warning to all interested in intimacy with Kip to not get their hopes up; he was a committed man. The final image was of Sky and him in Founders Park, embracing with a sunset behind them. It nauseated him.

The screen then showed a closeup of Sky in Citizen One's box. She appeared beautiful and confident. Citizen One waved and blew kisses to the crowd. The camera zoomed in on her then transitioned to him so he could speak. "Welcome Citizens here at the stadium and those of you who don't have the social score to be here but are watching from home. This is truly a rare edition of the Games!" He stopped for the applause then held his hand high for quiet. "We have a very, very special match, in fact, unprecedented! The Savage from the Wasteland that took out one of Nirvana's favorites, Trex . . ." Boos came raining down. Citizen One held up his hand again until there was silence. "Against one of our finest soldiers, someone who was wrongly persecuted due to a corrupt medical professional, leading to his kidnapping by this half human." He pointed to Rock. "A soldier who literally fought his way back against all odds to fulfill his commitment to the State and his beautiful partner, Sky!" The cameras zoomed in on Sky, taking care to include her tight-fitting outfit. The stadium became pandemonium, with people throwing flowers of love and admiration into the arena while screaming to both Sky and Kip. Citizen One continued. "With no further ado, here's Nirvana's own and my close friend, Captain Kip!"

Pom pushed Kip in the back. "Go, now! And don't forget to wave!"

Kip walked out through a tunnel into the arena that was guarded by a platoon of soldiers. He was followed by a group of performers in outfits that matched his. When they got into the open pit of the stadium, they separated and started a synchronized dance all around him. The crowd ate it up. Everyone was on their feet, clapping and cheering for him and lapping up the mindless theatrics before violence. He waved to the crowd as he shook his head, trying to eliminate the distracting thoughts. *Get your mind right.*

Kip joined Rock in the middle of the ring. Per Pom's earlier instructions, they faced one another. Rock winked at Kip, then threw a right cross at his head. Kip dodged the blow but didn't think he really had to as it appeared to him that Rock had pulled off the punch anyway, intentionally missing. Kip grabbed his friend, wrestling him to the ground. Rock whispered, "Ten minutes."

Why the stagecraft? Kip thought. The message finally hit, triggering in his mind. Kip finally understood.

Two soldiers rushed over and pulled Kip off him. Kip milked it for all it was worth, kicking and screaming at Rock. The crowd roared, both cheering and booing together.

The lead soldier separated the fighters. Even through the helmet and face shield, Kip knew—it was Pege, who had no qualms about using violence against either man. The second soldier pushed Kip back and pointed at him, then stepped in close. "Is your mind right?" he asked.

Kip did a double take, focusing on the soldier's bearded face. It couldn't be . . . "Ben?" he said under his breath. He pretended to push by the soldier who held him up. "What the fuck?" he whispered.

With Ben now standing between the fighters and Pege striding just in front, they walked to Citizen One's box. The two soldiers saluted the leader, then stepped to the side, allowing him to face the two contestants. He barely made eye contact with Rock, focusing almost exclusively on Kip. "Contestants." He spoke so all could hear. "This is a death match, which means the only rule is you kill or be killed. If you choose to not participate, the decision will be made for you." Pege stepped forward and removed her hand blaster from its holster.

Citizen One continued, "I wish you both the grace of Nirvana." He bowed to the two men, then sat in his seat as the crowd started screaming, "Kip! Kip! Kip!"

Kip barely listened, focusing more on Sky seated directly next to Citizen One. If she was worried, she didn't show it. Blu sat next to Sky and was leaning into her, a shallow attempt to get

Kip's attention. Officer Finne, who sat next to Blu, offered only a cruel stare.

The announcer said, "Rock will make the first selection from the Armament Wall." A chorus of boos thundered down. Rock ignored them and methodically stepped to the sheer wall to remove the same type of double-pointed spear that he used to defeat Trex. He stood, feigning jabs, spinning the weapon in his hands as the crowd taunted him. The savage strolled to the middle of the pit, not a care in the world.

The announcer spoke again. "Nirvana's son, Captain Kip, please make your selection."

As Kip started walking to the wall, Pege murmured, "Sword." Trying to play it cool, Kip walked by without a hint of recognition. He hoped she knew how much he appreciated her efforts.

The crowd, however, had different opinions, each person cheering for their own favorite instrument of death. Kip heard calls for mace, sword, axe, trident, hammer, and club, but ignored them all and went directly to the thin, double-edge sword. The tool he had practiced with the most. Scattered applause greeted his decision.

Kip's image flashed on the big screens as he made his way to the center of the pit and confronted Rock. He glared at his friend like he would a mortal enemy, then made one last check on Sky in the box. He could feel it in his chest when Sky tapped her hand on her heart.

A bell clanged and, as it had many times before, a clock on the giant screens started counting down from fifteen. Kip readied his sword. Rock prepared, crouching with his spear pointed forward. In unison, the crowd counted down, "Six, five, four, three, two, one!"

A horn sounded and the word *Fight!* flashed on all the screens.

Rock came out fast, jabbing with his spear. Thrust-block, thrust-block. Kip kept his sword up and the spear tip at bay. *Rock is quick, keep your motions short,* flashed in his head.

Rock made a big thrust, then spun, looping the spear low toward Kip's feet. Kip saw it coming and jumped the dagger point. He responded with a quick counterthrust of his sword, lunging toward Rock. Kip's blade brushed against his forearm. Rock stepped back, resetting the battle. Red oozed down his wrist. *First Blood* flashed on the screens. The crowd frenzied, the chant of "Kip" reaching its crescendo as the two men stared at one another.

Rock reset, moving a slow step toward Kip, his spear readied. With no warning, he rushed, executing a series of thrusting jabs. Kip retreated, throwing wild parries to slow Rock's momentum. His sword clanged on the spear tip, pushing it away, allowing Rock's momentum to carry the spear's point

367

past him. Kip closed, trying to get leverage with his free hand. Rock pushed his left hand forward and up, smacking Kip's face with the middle of the spear's handle. The hardened metal cracked just below his nose. Kip saw stars and tasted the metallic tang of blood as it filled his mouth.

Rock spun and caught Kip flush with an elbow in the head, sending him to the ground. The savage stabbed down, going for the kill. Instinctively, Kip rolled, then rolled again, the spear's point missing him, hitting only dirt. From his defensive ground position, Kip swiped low with his sword. Rock had no choice but to jump back, allowing Kip to rise to a neutral position. The crowd oohed and aahed at each precarious moment.

The fight continued along a similar ebb and flow with the two combatants exchanging the upper hand, then fighting from behind. After all swings up or down, the match cycled back to neutral. It wasn't long before Kip felt exhausted. Even worse, Rock appeared as fresh as ever.

Kip rushed, clearing the spear tip with his sword, then lunged, throwing a punch with his free hand. Rock reacted slowly, and the punch connected with a crack, sending his friend to the ground. Kip stepped on his spear handle with his full weight, forcing its release from Rock's hand, then went for a kick to the head. Rock saw the blow coming and blocked his foot before grabbing his planted leg and pulling. Kip fell like a tree and landed with a crack, his sword slipping from his grip.

Kip rolled in the dirt, dragging himself to his knees and then to his feet. The two men now faced each other, weaponless. Being bigger, Kip felt he had the advantage in hand-to-hand fighting, thus pressed forward, lunging at Rock. The crowd screamed its approval at this more animalistic turn of events.

They exchanged blows, each man giving, then taking the other's best shots from body to face and back. With both men now clearly exhausted, Rock spun and sent a roundhouse kick into the side of Kip's head. The pain was beyond excruciating. Kip could not stop his collapse, hitting the dirt hard. Rock stumbled forward, rolling Kip to his back, and straddling him. He locked his hand around Kip's neck and squeezed.

Rock's eyes bore into him with a crazed hatred, or maybe it was fear. What was certain was in that moment, Kip was no longer sure if this was still a game or real. His adrenaline spiked, and he threw punch after punch, hammering his friend. Rock's grip didn't break. With one last surge, he pushed Rock as far away as he could, and threw a right cross that finally crumpled his friend's grip. Rock tumbled off and rolled to his back. The crowd's calls crescendoed again, urging Kip to get up and finish the savage.

Kip turned, finding Sky in the crowd, his bloodied face once again plastered on the screen. She smiled as only she could and tapped her heart once more. Kip knew what he had to do. He rose to his feet, stumbling to pick Rock's spear off the ground.

He now stood over his friend, who lay gasping for breath. Kip raised the spear high above his head. The crowd cheered for a bloody end, the chant of "Kill him!" rising above the rest of the noise. Kip drove the spear tip down. . . .

Chapter 36

The giant screens around the stadium went blank. Kip couldn't help but look and guessed that all of Nirvana's screens, everywhere in the State, did the same. A skeletal face flashed up, giving an eerie laugh, capturing the attention of every eye in the stadium. The mob had forgotten about the battle for the moment and followed the screens.

The skeleton spoke. "You've been lied to by this man." An image of Citizen One sitting in his box flashed up. He stood and pointed at the main screen, barking orders to stop the show. No one listened, even if they could hear him. The stage was set, and the mob wanted to see the end of the play.

The words *Sex Trafficking* flashed on the screen, followed by the images of the young girls Kip observed in Pubtown waiting for clients, the Nirvana Security Officers standing next to them, directing them. The skeleton's voice spoke as the images ran. "Who uses these services, more importantly, who profits from them, and who is providing the protection?" Once more, Citizen One's face flashed to the screen.

The words *Organ Trafficking* flashed up next. Tik's whiteboard was seen in a visual cut from Kip's old memories. *My kidneys are dying, the government won't grow me a new one in the lab, too expensive and I'm not useful enough to save.* The writing continued, *Yes, so I'm going on a vacation to get a new kidney from the black market. I've got twelve hours before the surgery, and I need a few days of bed rest.*

The image cut to Citizen One talking. The clip again taken from Kip's visual memory implant. "There are missing people, lots of them, taken from poverty and used for the more carnal pleasures and necessities of life."

"Meaning sex trafficking and organ harvesting." Kip's voice was heard but his image not seen. Kip's visual of the prisoner lying in the Elysian Fields hospital flashed up. The clipboard reading *Kidney Infection* blown up so all could read.

"Yes, to be blunt. Both are very lucrative and thriving in the black market," Citizen One answered.

"Well, if you opened the medical state, allowed the non-Elites transplants, people wouldn't go to the black market," Kip's voice said.

"Cure the rabble who have abused themselves, their bodies, their very lives? What a novel idea." The stadium crowd started booing. The movie continued, "More importantly, where's the profit in that? The State pays credits for one and receives credits in the other. Do the math."

"I have. A friend of mine is one of your numbers." Kip's voice again.

"It's not a perfect world, but close to it." Citizen One finished on the screen.

In real time, Citizen One was now frantic in his box, waving his arms, ordering his guards to cut the cameras. But there'd be no ending this show. Nothing could stop what was coming.

The skull returned and the words *Black Market Control and Citizen Eight* were on the screen. The image of Citizen One talking flashed up again. "Citizen Eight was investigating the powers behind the black market and was getting close to a revelation. There are certain doors that even I dare not look behind. The Elites enjoy their pleasures and anonymity."

"You killed an innocent man at the zoo, framing Rock in the process to protect your secrets."

"Hardly innocent. That man was a habitual abuser who conveniently looked like your friend, Rock. He was a lost cause, a throwaway that wasted his life. We did him and the State a favor ending his suffering."

"So, no due process, you play God. I got it, all men are equal, some are just more equal than others." Kip's voice rang clear. The stadium fell silent.

Once more, words shown on the screen. *War in the Wastelands.*

Citizen One was again sitting and talking on the screen. "I saw the video of you fighting in Shonto. You underestimate your own skills."

Kip's voice responded. "You mean where you opened fire on a school full of children?" The video of the battle cruiser shelling the school came on. Gasps and cries of, "Oh no!" erupted from the crowd.

Citizen One flashed back on the screen, talking. "I should tell you that I promised to bomb a dozen more schools in the Wasteland if he doesn't fight. So, best of luck to you." The video flashed to Kip's recorded image, the anger on his face unmistakable.

Citizen One, sitting as he visited Kip, came on the screen again. "Like Officer Finna's death, a causality of war." That smug smile crossing the leader's face. "Besides, the savages picked that fight when they helped you and Rock."

"They offered food, medicine, and shelter to people in need. There is no crime in showing kindness to strangers."

"You're so naïve, like a child, really. Let me make it easy for you. Shonto and all the other wars in the Wasteland are a means to an end. A common enemy used to keep the Citizens afraid and aligned. You played into my hands showing up there." He paused. "And you're not answering my question. Will you fight?"

"Still not interested. Lie in the bed you made."

On the screen, Citizen One glared with his jaw clenched. "So, the carrot doesn't work. I thought not. Let's try the stick. If you don't take my deal, your pretty ex-partner will find herself an accessory to terrorism for helping you. Meaning prison, then reeducation, loss of all credits, not to mention housing in Pubtown. I will make it my mission in life to ensure the only way for her to survive will be to sell her body to the scum that infest that sewer." The live cameras flashed to Sky. She was covering her mouth with her hand.

"Like what you did to me?"

"What I did to you will seem like child's play," the leader responded.

The skull face popped up again, then the words, *Their Contempt for Citizens*. Kip's image came on the screen. "Why are you trying to control me? Control us? Why not let the people decide their own fate? You have the Citizens of Nirvana afraid to do or think anything that's not State approved. You have the ultimate power."

The image switched to Citizen One talking. "Because the average Citizen of Nirvana is stupid, weak of spirit, and lazy. And the power those idiots wield when acting in mass is truly frightening, no matter how ridiculous the cause. We tried free will many years ago and consider where it led us: war, pandemic, the brink of annihilation. We've learned to keep people isolated for their own safety. So we, the State, give them food, clean air,

375

and water. We provide them unlimited procreation while maintaining the species. And for entertainment, we give them the Games and recreational drugs. What more could our Citizens want?"

"Not want, need," Kip snapped back. "People require life experiences beyond the carnal. Every person needs to know the love of family and to explore the spiritual. You've taken that all away." He shook his head on the screen. "We should be pushing our boundaries out of the safe zone and feel what it's like to truly be free with no guarantees of success. What you offer is not living. You have your people penned like animals in the zoo, only their cages are invisible. That's not a life, that's only passing time until death."

The stadium stayed silent. Every person was waiting for the next pin to drop.

Kip reached down and offered Rock his hand. Rock had recovered but still lay on the ground, the spear embedded in the dirt next to his head. He clasped Kip's hand, allowing him to pull him to his feet. They stood exhausted, side by side, as the movie finished. A few people pointed from the stands and started clapping. The majority did not notice. Their eyes were still locked on the screens, waiting for the skull's next message.

The cameras went to Rage, who had stood from his seat and jumped over the wall, leaving Citizen One's side. He landed with an audible thud, his massive frame now in the pit. As he walked toward Kip and Rock, he unbuckled his gun holster, freeing his blaster.

Officer Finne did the same, leaving Blu's side as he hopped the wall. The two men strode together until just out of arm's reach from Kip and Rock. The crowd had stopped following the screens and now watched the four men facing one another. They started to cheer, the chants "Kip" and "Rock" reverberating through the stadium. Finne pulled his gun and held it at his side. Rage stood motionless, staring at Rock. The crowd oohed then started to scream obscenities.

"Remember my brother?" Finne hissed. He raised the weapon.

A blast came from the side. A soldier had fired, his laser hitting Finne's arm. Finne dropped his gun. Ben started sprinting toward them, blaster raised. Kip didn't wait for him. He lunged, throwing a punch that clipped Finne's jaw, sending him down. The crowd went crazy.

Finne rose, seizing Kip's lost sword from the dirt. He rushed at Kip, weapon ready. Kip snatched Rock's spear planted in the ground, its lethal tip pointed at his oncoming assailant.

He wouldn't need it. Ben fired again. This time the blast clipped the back of Finne's head, blowing a piece off. In midstride, Finne collapsed, hitting the ground, dead, the sword falling with him. The crowd roared its approval.

Kip spun to see Rock motionless on the ground, Rage on top of him, driving his fist into his friend's face, then again into his body. He was being beaten to death, one crushing blow at a time.

Reacting on instinct, Kip sprinted to Rock, spear in hand, as Rage swung for the kill. Using his full momentum and holding the spear with both hands, Kip slammed the spear's handle into the back of the giant's head. The crushing impact sent Rage tumbling into the dirt of the pit, away from Rock. Kip watched, hoping for an end, as the giant lay motionless. But Rage stirred. First his arm pushed his torso up, and then he got to a knee. The stadium fell into utter silence.

Taking his time and carrying the utmost confidence, Rage stood to face Kip, shaking his head, clearing the cobwebs from the blow. He gave a devilish grin while stepping toward his attacker. Kip held the double-pointed spear out, maintaining his distance. The weapon didn't dissuade Rage a bit. He came in a rush at his foe, his hand knocking the spear's tip away from his chest. Kip managed to bury it in his bicep. With his free hand, Rage clubbed Kip, lifting him off his feet and sending him sprawling to the ground. Kip had never been hit that hard. A sharp pain and shooting lights flashed through his head as he landed with a dusty thump. With adrenaline surging, he rolled to his knees next to Finne's body. His hand brushed something metal in the dirt.

Rage didn't wait for him to rise. With his arm bleeding, he rushed at Kip again, spear now in his good hand. Kip grabbed his sword from the dirt, raising it just in time to clink the spear's tip away. He raised the sword's blade, allowing Rage's own momentum to impale it through the giant's neck. Kip let the sword handle go as Rage fell to his knees, the vacancy of impending death in his eyes. He wheezed and spit blood before twisting sideways and collapsing to the ground.

Kip picked up the dropped spear and walked to the fallen man. Not caring if he was dead or alive, he raised the weapon high and held it above the brute's head. He turned to Citizen One and screamed, "Kill or be killed, that's what you said, you twisted bastard!" Once more, he powered the spear tip deep into the blood-stained dirt.

Citizen One thundered, "Kill them all!"

The soldiers in the pit responded, rushing toward Kip and the three fallen men. Kip didn't care what they did. He bent down to check his friend and clasped Rock's hand, holding it. He whispered, "Fight. You've got to fight." Rock's swollen eyes creased and blood oozed from his mouth. His lips moved as he attempted to speak, but nothing came.

The platoon of soldiers arrived one by one, Ben and Pege reaching first. They circled the two men, surrounding them with weapons raised. The crowd hushed.

Pege commanded, "Protect."

Each of the soldiers spun to face away from the two contestants, creating a protective circle with Kip and Rock in its center.

Citizen One's anger turned to outrage. He now screamed, "Treason!" and barked orders at anyone who would listen. No one did.

Kip watched helplessly as Citizen One grabbed Sky and pulled his knife, holding it near her throat. She fought back, elbowing his chest, slipping his hold then using her fists and elbows to drive him back. Blu joined the fray, grasping his arm, holding the knife and pinning it. The crowd started to collapse on the leader, their fury rising. Citizen One pushed Sky away, then launched himself over the railing. He ran toward the tunnel Kip had entered through, a mob of Citizens chasing just behind.

The skull popped on the screen one more time, its voice echoing through the stadium. "They hate you, they fear you, so they control you. . . . Don't let them. Fight back!"

The crowd responded, raging against the machine that was the State. Thousands of Citizens rushed from their seats and into the arena. They tore down anything with a State logo. They assaulted any non-soldiers in a State uniform, creating the chaos the skull called for.

The screens around the arena flashed to the four different districts of Nirvana. Mayhem was spreading. Fires burned and explosions erupted. The stadium was a microcosm of the anarchy that sparked across the city.

Citizens everywhere were rioting, except for Uptown, where the Elites now hid, fearing for their lives. Kip watched the monitors as the wall protecting Uptown came down and the mob streamed into that sacred compound.

Chapter 37
Saturday, January 26, 2075

Leo yawned, exposing his massive canines. The morning sun had risen, and his lazy day had begun. Kip, on the other hand, had just been released from a long night of protective custody at the stadium and had finally made his way to the zoo and his friends. He watched the big cat from the observing platform, still amazed by its size and beauty. The animal rose and walked to the cage's gate for his daily food allotment. Jen placed his lab-created meat in its bin and pushed it through. The lion trotted over and started licking the slab. Jen repeated the process for Sinbad, who ambled to his breakfast. Anastasia lay in the distance, unworried where her next meal was coming from. Jen then opened the cage door for a moment to clear some scat from the compound entry. The cats eyed her, but in the end couldn't care less. They had their food, water, and knotted balls for entertainment, thus were satisfied with their situation.

Blu approached Kip on the platform. After her partner had been killed, she was held with Kip and Sky during the peak of the riots, and then released with Sky near dawn. Kip could see she'd been crying; her eyes were bloodshot with bags underneath. She sat down, resting next to Kip, her body touching his, then reached over and took his hand. "The others want to see you. Something is happening." Kip started to stand but Blu held his hand tight, keeping him seated. "Can we talk just for a minute, like the old days?"

Kip caressed her hand. "You okay?"

In an uncharacteristic move, she leaned her head on his shoulder, seeming to enjoy the contact. "I just wanted to say I was wrong about you. I now understand what I didn't see . . . you were fighting their deception and control." She rambled, not expecting a response. "But now I do."

"You weren't alone." Kip brushed the hair from her face. "It was pretty well hidden."

"I just want you to know I'm happy you're free, and I'm sorry for the way I treated you. Life's not about social score."

"Don't relive the past. We're here now." Kip raised her chin with his finger, so their eyes met. "Always remember, I have nothing but good memories."

"I will." Blu watched Leo, who was now lying on the ground. "Maybe you're right. Maybe they should be free."

"I think we're both right. Some lions need a cage and some need to hunt." He smiled at her.

"You're going to leave with Sky, aren't you?"

"Yes, I have to," he said with no hesitation. "But when will depend on what the big happenings are." He stood, helping her up.

She leaned in and kissed him on the lips, holding it for a moment, then slowly breaking it off, blushing from her actions. "I had three years to do that. I can't believe I never tried."

"You'll know when it's right for you, just like I did." Kip squeezed her hand. "Let's go find out what's going on."

* * *

Kip and Blu walked into the old zoo office. It had been transformed into an operations center. A radio broadcast played in the background and sounded like an alternating police scanner and news service. Kip perused the room, seeing Ell, Ann, Pege, Ben, and, surprisingly, Officer Tak. All were busy performing some task, oblivious to their entrance.

Ell was on the phone when he happened to see Kip. "I'll call you right back," he said, ending the call. "Hey, you did it."

"Did what?"

"Survived. We were worried for a bit." Ell walked over and gave Kip a slap on the back. "That was a great plan," he said.

One by one, Tak, Pege, and Ben came over and shook Kip's hand.

"Thank you for what you did," Tak said.

"Thank you for not shooting me in the mines. I wish I could have told you more."

"You told and showed me enough," Tak answered. "On your advice, these guys contacted me and gave me the rest, especially this convict." He smiled, motioning to Ben.

385

"I'm glad I could help," Ben said. "And you can thank her. She got me in, then out of Elysian." He touched Pege's shoulder, who gave an acknowledging nod.

Sky walked in, dressed in her usual clothing. "What plan?" she asked Kip.

Not one to honor himself, Kip answered, "It was nothing," then tried changing the subject. "Any news on Rock?"

"He's in pretty bad shape, but he's going to make it," Ann said. "I was just speaking with the doctor." Her eyes went to the ground, then met Kip's. "Unfortunately, he also said Tik passed last night. I'm sorry."

Sky walked over and put her arm around Kip, then reached with her other hand touching Blu's shoulder. "Sorry you two, I know he was a friend."

Kip shook his head. "He will be missed." The room was quiet for a moment while the news sunk in. Sky broke the silence.

"What plan?" Sky said, pulling Kip tight.

Ell was all too happy to spill. "It was Kip's idea to be taken captive by Citizen One and somehow get him to talk. Then for me to hack into our dear leader's implant and play it for the masses."

Kip shrugged. "It was our plan. We all contributed to it. You're the one who hacked his implant and got into the State's systems."

"Yeah, sorry for the delay on that. Glad you and Rock put on such a good show. It was close. Citizen One's encryption was sophisticated. Took me most of the match to get inside," he explained excitedly. "When your image flashed up at the end of the fight, that was right after I got him."

"It was close, but it all worked out," Ann added. "At least for now."

"That was an incredible plan." Sky squeezed Kip's arm. "The talking skull was brilliant. Nobody could turn away."

"There's going to be a lot more released. I uploaded all of it," Ell said. "There's at least thirty days, including the 'erased' material. We got names, images, and crimes. Things are about to get hot for Citizen One."

"Any word on him?" Blu asked.

"None, literally radio silence. I've been monitoring the police chatter," Pege answered. "But the State announced they'll have an official message issued shortly and will be running it for the next few days."

"What about Trase, Bear, and Jun?" Kip asked.

"Bear and Jun were clean, no evidence of duplicity. The opposite for Trase. Seems Citizen One had a growing network, trying to infiltrate those who opposed him. Trase was a key part of that. What happens to her officially depends on the State. Unofficially, she's missing." Ann used finger quotes as she said "missing."

"And what about you two and your platoon?" Sky asked Pege and Ben.

"Depends on the State's next move. I can't speak for the group but will stay and fight for the people if it comes to that," Pege answered. "The good guys will need help."

"Same," Ben said. "Hopefully the State stays away from the people in the Wastelands too."

"How about things in the city? Are the riots still going?" Kip asked.

"I don't think so. Seems to have calmed around six this morning. Emergency calls have dropped off," Ann said. "Most of the later ones were looting in the Uptown anyway."

"People got tired and headed home. Just some hardcore free spirits out there now," Pege said.

"Hey, hey, the State message is starting." Ell hit a button on the computer, the holograph projected and the volume raised. Everyone in the room closed ranks to see and hear. "Attention, attention, attention," replayed. The image's voice narrating was soothing.

"Citizens of Nirvana, we request your attention for an urgent message. Repeat, an urgent message. During the most entertaining of Games yesterday, our State systems were hijacked illegally, revealing classified information Statewide, leading to an unauthorized demonstration across the State of Nirvana. This message is in response to our investigation into those actions.

"We find compelling evidence of an illegal conspiracy to traffic minors and murder in the theft of human organs. This conspiracy appeared to be led by Citizen One. An appointment of a Citizen-Level Special Council will be made in the next few weeks to examine the facts and hold all those involved in the conspiracy accountable under Nirvana Law.

"We find compelling evidence that the wars fought in the Wastelands have been based on fabricated evidence and happily announce an immediate cease-fire while a thorough review of the conflict is made.

"For accountability, we regretfully report that Citizen One has been killed trying to escape capture. We find the individuals known as Rock and JU450625 were illegally detained and forced into the Games. They are granted full pardons with all Citizen benefits restored and are invited to leave the State of Nirvana as soon as possible. For all those who participated in the illegal demonstrations and/or soldiers who fought to expose the conspiracy, we grant full pardons starting at eight o'clock this morning. Anybody arrested after that time will be prosecuted to the fullest extent of State law.

"For rewards, as a token of our generosity and display of the State's commitment to our beloved Citizens, we grant each individual thirty bank credits and thirty points on their social score. Every Citizen will receive one extra helping of Green per week for one month, one additional HAP, and may attend a new

Changing scheduled for one month from today. You, of course, may keep your same partner.

"Lastly and most importantly, we recognize that all Citizens may not appreciate the benefits of Citizenship to the State of Nirvana. These people are invited to leave by twelve o'clock, three days from now. Busing arrangements out of the State will be made. There will be a zero-tolerance policy for animosity toward the State effective then. The AST system will be fully utilized to root out offenders."

The message started to replay. "Attention, attention . . ." Ell turned off the hologram.

Kip slammed his fist on the table. "They killed Citizen One. And everything he knows went with him."

"Did you expect any different?" Tak asked. "The Elites won't let anything out. He said it himself, there are doors that even he dares not look behind."

"Not everything." Ell held up a portable storage drive. "Don't forget his implant. If they don't play nice, we won't either."

"They pacify the people's anger with a few credits, some food, sex, and drugs." Ben laughed derisively. "So typical."

"And sadly, that's all it really takes," Sky added.

Chapter 38
Tuesday, January 29, 2075

Kip sat in Tik's chair, reflecting on the Games and the events that followed. In the last three days, the city had quieted, the people now standing in an uneasy truce with their leaders. The social changes had been identified and commitments had been made; now it was time for execution. Only time would tell if real change would come.

Kip inspected Tik's tidy desk and thought of the man and the events he put into motion that led them all to this moment. Who would've thought that the Citizen with the highest regard for rule-following was a hidden catalyst to an uprising that could change everything? Blu was right, people can surprise you. Tik will be remembered.

He took one last scan of the area. Kip would miss his job at the zoo, as infuriating as it was at times. In the end, he would remember it all with fondness, but it was now time for him to be free.

He exited the office and saw Tom busy at the table, thumbing through his picture book of animals. He waved while walking past. "Bye Tom, enjoy the bears."

"Bye Kip, grizzly bears are the best." He gave a thumbs-up before going back to his pages.

Kip walked out of the building for the last time. He exited into the sunshine, making his way to the lions' cage. Leo and Sinbad were sunning themselves, seeming to enjoy the warmth of the day. Anastasia rolled in the dust. All seemingly content in life.

"Wait up," Rock called.

Kip spun to see his friend limping toward him, his face still badly bruised, a sling on his arm and a gimp in his step. "Mind if I hitch a ride to the caravan?"

"Of course not. It's the least I could do after the beating I gave you in the Games." Kip laughed.

"I went easy on you," Rock chided back. "We'll see what happens next time."

"There won't be a next time." Kip placed his hand on Rock's good shoulder. "I'm not coming back."

"That's what I said after the first Games." Rock chuckled. "Yet here I stand." He started a slow walk. "Come on, let's go home."

* * *

A line of beaten-up buses filled the open lot in Pubtown. A small group of people milled about, waiting for the group departure. Kip scanned the crowd. Not seeing Sky, he checked his watch. 11:45 a.m.

"Is Sky coming?" Ann asked.

"She said she was," Kip answered. "She had to take care of something but didn't say what, although she did sound a little uncertain." He glanced at the road leading to the lot. Nothing was moving on it. "How about you?"

"I'm staying for now. I received amnesty, so I will be here to hold the Leaders accountable," Ann said. "But if things go south, don't think I won't be finding you."

Rock limped over. "Fifteen minutes to departure. I thought there'd be more people leaving."

"I'm not surprised," Kip said. "The Citizens have been caged too long and want security above all else. Freedom is risk, it's danger, it means change to the status quo, which requires work. They'll gladly trade some personal intrusions for comfort and ease of living." He rolled his eyes. "What's worse is they know it'll lead to complete subjectification in the end, like an animal in the zoo. But it's the easy path."

"Agreed. They know it, but it's a problem they'll worry about later," Ann said. "Comfort sets in and entitlement grows with every generation." Ann gave an inquisitive look. "I wonder what the Elites' endgame is. A structured society that exists, but for what purpose? We're not needed for continuing the species. The labs take care of that."

"A classed society where the Elites make the decisions, and the others are used to service them in whatever mode they

393

desire," Rock said. "It's been like that forever. Nothing has changed."

There was a long silence. Kip found the thought disturbing. "It's odd," he finally said. "Despite all that's happened, I've never felt so happy, so relieved."

"Love will do that to you," Rock answered. "You wake up anticipating what the day will bring regardless of what the tasks are in front of you."

"Definitely, it's love of a good partner," Ann said. "I can see it in your face as you watch for her now."

"That's what's wrong with this place. Love is missing," Rock continued. "The Elites destroyed it on purpose, replacing it with lust. In the end, you can't. Humans need love. It's the spiritual connection that fulfills your soul, nurturing you from birth until death. It makes you strong and willing to sacrifice for others." He met Kip's eyes. "You feel how it's impacted you with Sky. In the village, you've witnessed how it moves the human family, and you've felt its power with Yahweh."

"Why did the Elites destroy it?" Ann asked.

"The Elites fear love more than anything," Rock said, "because it means they lose control over you. Something more powerful motivates you than self-interest and preservation."

Kip considered his words. "I suspect you're right. Another reason I need to leave. There's no going back." Kip glanced to the road again, seeing a bus pull up. He watched as the door opened and a few Citizens deboarded. Last out was Sky. She stood on the steps and waved, then reached back to take the hand of a young girl. They each carried a single backpack and nothing else. Hand in hand, they walked to Kip.

Sky smiled as she approached. She leaned in and kissed Kip. She squatted to be eye level with the child. "Bug, I want you to meet Mr. Kip. We're going to be leaving with him."

Kip did the same, going down to one knee. "Hi Bug, are you ready for an adventure?"

* * *

The group of five hiked down into the valley. The river, now a constant companion, burbled on their left in what was a slow section. Kip led the group at a leisurely pace with Bug sitting on his shoulders, riding with a graceful ease. Sky trailed next in line, followed by two women and a man, freedom seekers from Nirvana. The group had separated the day before from Rock and the others as he led a larger group to his village. The goodbye to his friend was difficult, but Kip knew in his heart it was "until next time" and not a final farewell.

They rounded a wooded hillside, the path cutting through a stand of dense pine. Kip could smell the smoke from a nearby fire. They were getting close. Continuing for a few more minutes, the first houses of Shonto came into sight. There were children playing in front of the burned-out schoolhouse. The carcass of the Nirvana battlecraft still lay on the road's edge. The heavy scars of the two attacks were a long way from healing.

The children stopped playing when they saw the strangers approach. One child ran down the dirt road and into Maja's house. The same child exited the door soon thereafter, Maja and Moot in tow. As they approached, other villagers came out of their houses to see their new visitors.

Kip put Bug down. She was warily eyeing the children in front of the schoolhouse. Kip said, "It's okay, you can go play." She raced to join the children in their games.

Maja arrived first and gave Kip a smothering hug. Moot wrapped his hand around Kip's, almost breaking it with his shake.

As introductions flowed, Fawn approached with a skip in her step, coming from the caves at the back of the destroyed school. She beamed a huge smile when embracing Kip, then did the same to Sky. "I never thought I'd see you again," she said to him.

"I feared the same about you and the children," Kip said.

"Thanks to you, we made it into the caves before this." She pointed to the building's remains. "And now you're here to stay?" she asked.

"If you'll have us," Sky said.

Maja made a sweeping motion toward the town. "Welcome home to Shonto."

Acknowledgments

Thank you for reading *The State of Nirvana: Awakenings*. I hope you enjoyed reading this book as much as I have enjoyed writing it. Thank you to my editor, Katherine Bartis, and to beta readers Greg Boudreaux, Jane Boudreaux, Amanda Sullivan, Kelly Jo Pardue (author), and Christina Hiller for their review and editorial contributions. Special thanks to my parents, my brothers, and my children for the unwavering support. A super-special thank you to Veronica, to whom I am forever grateful for taking the path less traveled.

www.ingramcontent.com/pod-product-compliance
Lightning Source LLC
Chambersburg PA
CBHW050024030726

47506CB00001B/111